"The neighbors will be watching," she murmured.

"In that case…" Grayson bent down and swept his arms around her. He lifted her in his arms and strode toward the front door. But, oh, the price of it. Using techniques a trauma therapist had taught him, he blanked his mind completely. And then bit by bit, he let in the details of this one moment. The cool air. The autumn smell of burned leaves. The weight and softness of the woman in his arms. A hint of roses as she shifted slightly. The way his breathing deepened in response to her.

Laughing, she reached down to open the door for him. He added the sultry delight in her laughter to his inventory of sensations.

Carefully, carefully he reached past this moment to the next safest thing: his job. This was a cover. They had to establish themselves as a couple. Being absolutely certain to let no emotion creep into him, he paused in the doorway and leaned his head down to kiss her.

Dear Reader,

As you may have noticed this month, Harlequin Romantic Suspense has a brand-new look that's a fresh take on our beautiful covers. We are delighted at this transformation and hope you enjoy it, too.

There's more! Along with new covers, the stories are longer—more action, more excitement, more romance. Follow your beloved characters on their passion-filled adventures. Be sure to look for our newly packaged and longer Harlequin Romantic Suspense stories wherever you buy books.

Check out this month's adrenaline-charged reads:

COWBOY WITH A CAUSE by Carla Cassidy

A WIDOW'S GUILTY SECRET by Marie Ferrarella

DEADLY SIGHT by Cindy Dees

GUARDING THE PRINCESS by Loreth Anne White

Happy reading!

Patience Bloom

Senior Editor

CINDY DEES

Deadly Sight

HARLEQUIN®

entertain, enrich, inspire™

Recycling programs
for this product may
not exist in your area.

ISBN-13: 978-0-373-27807-7

DEADLY SIGHT

Printed in U.S.A.

Books by Cindy Dees

CINDY DEES

started flying airplanes while sitting in her dad's lap at the age of three and got a pilot's license before she got a driver's license. At age fifteen, she dropped out of high school and left the horse farm in Michigan, where she grew up, to attend the University of Michigan. After earning a degree in Russian and East European studies, she joined the U.S. Air Force and became the youngest female pilot in its history. She flew supersonic jets, VIP airlift and the C-5 Galaxy, the world's largest airplane. During her military career, she traveled to forty countries on five continents, was detained by the KGB and East German secret police, got shot at, flew in the first Gulf War and amassed a lifetime's worth of war stories.

Her hobbies include medieval reenacting, professional Middle Eastern dancing and Japanese gardening.

This RITA® Award-winning author's first book was published in 2002 and since then she has published more than twenty-five bestselling and award-winning novels. She loves to hear from readers and can be contacted at www.cindydees.com.

Chapter 1

Grayson Pierce looked at his watch impatiently. The plane was late. Either that or his Rolex had suddenly lost its orderly Swiss mind. How he was supposed to help with this very, very off-book investigation, he had no idea. But his old fraternity brother from Stanford, Jeff Winston, had asked for help, and that was enough for him.

The way he heard it, Jeff had been doing the U.S. government massive favors left, right and center, and Uncle Sam owed Jeff one back. Gray frowned. What kind of debt merited pulling a senior field agent like him out of deep cover on no notice and sending him to West Virginia, of all places? What crisis of national security significance could be afoot in this bucolic setting?

Finally. The whine of a jet became audible in the distance. Gray picked out the white speck, which rapidly grew larger, descending on final approach into the Elkins-Randolph County Regional Airport. Jeff was sending some guy named Sam Jessup here to help with whatever was brewing around a local cult leader named Proctor.

The thrust reversers of a sleek Learjet bearing the Winston Enterprises logo screamed as the plane came to a stop at the far end of the runway, did a one-eighty, and taxied toward him. He was parked in a vintage 1972 Ford Bronco outside the gold, two-story box of a terminal, such as it was. Chicago O'Hare, this airport was not. He pulled up beside the low jet and hopped out as the hatch popped open. A pilot wearing a crisp uniform trotted down the steps.

A pair of high-heeled, black leather boots with chrome ankle chains and stiletto heels that looked like lethal weapons appeared on the top steps. Slim calves came into view. The shapely legs turned out to be a mile long and sheathed in leather that looked painted on. A black leather jacket with slashes of red leather under the arms emerged from the shadows. Good Lord, the jacket was unzipped down to…well, that was an impressive flash of cleavage. What did the woman have on under the jacket to cause that gravity-defying display? An urge to tug the zipper down and find out made his fingers itch.

A swirl of flaming red hair swished over her shoulder. It was the color of strawberries and oranges if they got together and made a baby. A slender, porcelain-pale neck came into view, and then lush lips painted the most improbable shade of scarlet he'd seen in a long time.

The asymmetric triangles of her black sunglasses wrapped around her head like something straight out of a science-fiction movie. He'd lay odds she had body piercings in places he did *not* want to know about, too.

Who the hell was she? Surely Jessup didn't bring his sex-kitten girlfriend on whatever mission this was. Maybe she was some sort of contact who would take him to Jessup. Gray frowned as no one else was forthcoming from the jet. The goth chick was looking at him expectantly, so he stepped forward and held out his hand. "Welcome to West Virginia. I'm Grayson Pierce."

She took his hand in the firm grip most American women used, and which still startled him. "Sammie Jo Jessup. Nice to meet you."

"Sammie Jo—" *Oh, dear God. No.* "As in Sam Jessup?"

The woman's lips curved into a dazzling smile that almost, but not quite, redeemed her extreme attire. "Let me guess. Jeff didn't tell you I'm a woman. He thinks that's hilarious to spring on people."

"Right. Hilarious," he replied dryly.

"So let's blow this popsicle stand," she declared, "and you can brief me in. Call me Sam if you like."

He didn't like. The name made her sound like a man. And despite her…avant-garde…fashion choices, she was anything but masculine under all that leather and chrome.

He slung her black duffel bag in the back of the Bronco, and with a word of thanks to the pilot, she climbed in next to him. Oddly, she smelled like roses. The old-fashioned kind with undertones of Earl Grey tea and cinnamon. A dim memory of his grandmother's formal rose garden flashed to mind. Acres of manicured green lawns and white-linen tablecloths covered with Royal Albert china rolled through his mind's eye unbidden. Bemused, he guided the Bronco out of the airport and onto an asphalt road that wound up into the Blue Ridge Mountains.

Although they weren't blue at all. Fall was just starting to paint the rolling hillsides in splashes of gold and crimson, oranges and maroons that were rapidly overtaking the carpet of green.

"Wow. Pretty," Sammie Jo commented at random.

He glanced over at her and was startled that she appeared to be studying him and not the scenery. It was hard to tell behind those dark sunglasses of hers. Had she just called *him* pretty? He chose to pretend she'd been referring to the scenery. "I'm told it's spectacular when the colors peak around here."

"Mmm. So why am I here?"

Direct, this woman. "I have no idea. Jeff Winston called me and said he needed my help figuring out what some local nut job is up to. Guy named Proctor. I assumed you would know what's going on since you work for Jeff."

"Nope. He didn't tell me anything more than that. But Jeff never does anything randomly. He clearly wants you and me to have a look around the local area. Turn over a few rocks and see what we find."

"That seems damned random of him."

"Agreed." She nodded. "There's clearly something going on. He must want us to take an unbiased look at it."

Frustration rattled through him. "Look. I have other responsibilities to get back to, and I don't have time for chasing shadows and vague rumors."

An eyebrow climbed above the upper rim of one tilting triangle of her sunglasses. "Like I *do* have time for games?" she demanded.

"Hey. He's your boss. Take it up with Winston."

They fell into silence and drove for some miles before he felt the least bit inclined to be civil again. Dammit, Jeff was his fraternity brother and had been a loyal friend through some rough times. He owed the guy at least a shot at making this investigation, or whatever it was, work.

Gray sighed and said, "Jeff rented us a motel room in a burg called Mapletop. It's smack-dab in the middle of the National Radio Quiet Zone. Are you familiar with that?"

"Tell me about it."

"It's an area encompassing 13,000 square miles and straddling the Virginia-West Virginia border. It was set aside in the 1950s to surround the world's largest radio telescope, which is an incredibly sensitive instrument. Inside the Zone, only very limited radio emissions are allowed. There are no cell phones, no Wi-Fi and only a handful of low-power radio stations. All electronic emissions generated in this area have to be approved so they don't interfere with the telescopes."

She nodded as if she already knew all that.

"We'll enter the NRQZ in a few miles, and your wireless devices will lose signal shortly thereafter. If you have any last-minute phone calls to make, email to check, or texts to send, now's the time to do it."

"No one to call," she said grimly.

His finely honed intuition sensed a story, but he didn't pry. She wasn't here to overshare her personal life with him, and he didn't want to know, anyway. He had a job to do—assuming he could figure out what the damned job was.

What had Jeff been thinking to send this woman, who was as clueless as him, out here? It wasn't like she was going to blend in with the locals in the least. This region was about country music, log cabins and out-door sports. Sammie Jo Jessup looked like a character from a science-fiction movie.

As they turned into the parking lot of the motel, his alien-wannabe companion broke the silence. "You still haven't told me why you're here," she prodded. "Who are you?"

"I'm an old buddy of Jeff's who owes the bastard a favor," he retorted. "Why he chose to collect it like this is beyond me."

He assumed she was looking at him. Her sunglasses were pointed at him, at least. "What kind of work do you do?" she asked.

Caution kicked in and he said carefully, "I work with computers."

"Hmm. Why would Jeff bring you here, then, where you're useless?"

He knew all too well the feeling of being useless. It had ripped out his soul, burned every last bit of the humanity out of him and left him the hull of a man he was today. But to be told he was useless by this imper-tinent female didn't sit well with him.

Irritation flared in his gut. An errant urge to tell her the truth rose in the back of his throat. But the pain rose, too, and he wasn't prepared to face the fire today. He pushed down the grief, pushed down the memories, pushed down any feeling at all.

He guided the Bronco into a parking spot in front of the two-bedroom motel bungalow Jeff had arranged for them. Gray's manners were too deeply ingrained to ignore no matter how irritating this woman might be, so he went around the SUV to open her door for her. But of course, she'd already barged out of the car and stood beside it looking around.

"What?" she demanded as he frowned at her.

"I would've opened your door for you."

She snorted. "I can get my own doors."

"I'm sure you can. But that doesn't mean I still shouldn't open them for you."

"Are you some kind of throwback to the olden days?"

He allowed himself a little smile. Wait till she got a load of how people lived in this region. The whole place was one giant throwback. "Something like that."

He fetched her bag and headed for Home Sweet Home. The mint-green cinder-block structure had the metal roof so common in this region. Either that, or someone had gone to a hell of a lot of trouble to paint rust stains on the thing. Metal apparently helped shield the minor electrical emissions of small household appliances from the nearby telescopes.

He hurried his steps to reach the door first and opened it for her with a flourish. He couldn't actually see if she rolled her eyes at him, but he sensed that she did. He smirked at her back in satisfaction as he followed her inside.

"Wow. This is…rustic," she declared.

He snorted. "This is as modern as it gets this far inside the NRQZ."

His gaze strayed to her delicious tush, cupped in that naughty black leather as she closed the vinyl-lined curtains over both living-room windows. She headed for the kitchenette's tiny window, and he enjoyed the view as she bent over the rim of the sink to yank the curtains closed over the small, high window there. The cabin's interior went dim. But oddly, she didn't remove her sunglasses. Hangover from partying too hard the night before? Or maybe something more mundane like a migraine?

"Better," she announced. She turned back toward him but stopped abruptly as she caught sight of the pictures spread out across the counter. He'd forgotten those were there. She stared at the surveillance photographs closely. "Who's this guy?"

"His name is Luke Zimmer. Jeff sent me those and the kid's dossier yesterday morning."

"He's cute. You stalking him?"

She was clearly trying to get a rise out of him, therefore he refused to take the bait. He answered blandly, "Jeff hired young Luke a few months back to come here and have a look around. Kid has a history of some rather extreme political views and has been known to act upon them from time to time."

"What constitutes extreme in your world? Which side of the political spectrum do you fall on?"

It went contrary to every bit of his training and years of field experience to tell a complete stranger any details of his personal life. He was all about living the cover story. He never revealed the real man inside, for down that path lay self-destruction. "Not pertinent to the investigation at hand," he replied stiffly.

"Are you always this uptight?" she asked curiously.

"Uptight? Why…I… Not at all," he spluttered. Lord, this woman threw him off balance.

She strolled right up to him in a sexy catwalk, invading his personal space. Ahh. Come-ons by hot chicks— now those he had down pat. His world righted itself and, as he regained his equilibrium, his right eyebrow went up in sardonic amusement. She had another think coming if she thought she was going to intimidate him. One nicely shaped, albeit black, fingernail ran down the front of his shirt. Damned if his pecs didn't tense at her touch, though, in spite of his best effort not to react.

"You don't look like the jeans-and-flannel-shirt type, Sparky," she purred. "And those hiking boots look brand-spanking-new. They're a dead giveaway that you're a city slicker."

"Like you're one to talk," he retorted. "You'll fit in around here about like an alien from outer space."

She sat down on the couch and crossed one long leg over the other in a blatantly sexy display. "But I'm not trying to fit in. I don't even know why I'm here."

"Neither do I," he snapped. "Jeff Winston asked for my help and, for some reason that completely escapes me, saw fit to send me *you*."

He packed all the derision he could muster into that last word. Man, this woman got under his skin. Nobody ever got this big a rise out of him this fast. And that was bad. For him, feelings were dangerous things. Lethal even. If he felt too much he might lose control, and then he might let go of his will to live. He hadn't fought to hang on this long only to let go now.

He commented more reasonably, "I have no idea whatsoever what I'm supposed to do with you."

"I could make a few suggestions." Her lips curved into a sinful smile. "You look like you could stand to learn a thing or two from me."

An unwilling grin tugged at the corners of his mouth. He was confident enough in his skills in *that* department that he definitely didn't need to rise to that jab. But she was tempting.

"Tell me about you," he said in as businesslike a tone as he could manage.

"I work for Winston Enterprises. I'm an operations controller and analyst in the Winston Operations Center. Are you familiar with it?"

He nodded. He'd visited the high-tech, information-gathering hub once and been stunned. Most governments didn't have anything better. Winston Enterprises, which was a sprawling international conglomerate of dozens of companies, practically had its own private intelligence agency.

"I've worked with Jeff for five years," she continued. "Two years ago, I volunteered for the HIVE Project. Are you familiar with that?"

"Nope. Never heard of it."

"That explains a lot," she replied cryptically.

"What is it?"

"Hang on a sec," she muttered as she fished in her jacket pocket and emerged with a cell phone. "I've got to talk to Jeff."

"Your phone won't work. No cell phone towers inside the NRQZ. And if you turn it on, the radio emissions police may show up and bust you."

She swore colorfully as she stuffed the device back in her pocket. "Have you got a string and some tin cans for me to make a call with?"

"Landline's over there on the wall. They bury the phone cables so they don't screw with the telescopes."

She marched over to the ancient rotary phone and glared at it. "How...quaint." She dialed number by slowly rotating number.

"Hi, it's Sam. Is the boss around?" There was a brief pause. "Hey, Jeff. What am I authorized to tell your buddy Grayson about HIVE?" She listened for a moment, and if he wasn't mistaken, surprise crossed her face. But he couldn't be sure. He really wished she'd take those shades off. It was unsettling not being able to read her expressions at all. Was this HIVE thing the reason he'd been dragged into the middle of nowhere and thrust into the company of this annoying woman?

She hung up the receiver. "Apparently, Jeff trusts you a freaking lot because I'm green-lighted to tell you all."

An intimate undertone slid into his voice. "Are you, now?"

She rolled her eyes. "About HIVE. Tell all about HIVE." She was cute when she was discomfited. Speaking hastily to cover her obvious discomfort, she said, "So. Does the local antitechnology monitoring mean this shack isn't under any kind of electronic surveillance?"

"As far as I can tell. The locals would pick up the transmission from a bug or a parabolic microphone in a heartbeat. A few years back, not far from here, a heating pad in a doghouse had a short circuit in it too small for the dog to feel, but it still caused interference with the telescope."

"Cool." She sank down on the sofa facing him and studied her fingernails as if she'd rather avoid the conversation to come.

"So, what's HIVE?" he prompted.

"Human Improvement Via Engineering. The name's actually a joke. The project's head scientist hates the moniker. Real name's Code X."

"Very spooky," he murmured. *Human improvement? What on earth did that mean?* A buzz of consternation vibrated in his gut at the possibilities. He asked much more blandly than he felt, "What kind of engineering?"

"Give the city slicker points for asking the right question."

She stretched a languid arm across the back of the sofa and drummed a complicated rhythm with her fingers on it. More delaying body language. She really didn't want to talk about this HIVE thing. He was intrigued at the aggressive overall body posture. It made her look like some sort of predatory animal at rest, although which kind, he couldn't quite put his finger on.

She continued, "A team of scientists who work for Jeff have been experimenting with a combination of stem-cell therapies and genetic engineering to enhance certain characteristics in test subjects."

"What kinds of characteristics?" he asked.

"When's the last time you saw Jeff? Like in the flesh?"

He was thrown by the abrupt shift of topic. "About two years ago. What does that have to do with anything?"

"Let's just say he has changed a bit since you last saw him."

"What the hell does that mean?" he demanded, alarmed. "You're using *human* test subjects? Has Jeff done this experimenting on *himself?*"

She grinned. "Let's just say he's put on a little, umm, muscle mass. The guy can pick up a Jeep and throw it if he wants to. Literally."

Gray's mind went blank. He couldn't believe the implications of what she was saying. His old friend had used far-out, experimental science to make a...a... superhero of himself? "Has he become some sort of freak?"

The woman flinched at the word. "Yeah," she said grimly. "A freak."

He asked cautiously, "And are you also one of these test subjects?" She didn't look like she could pick up a Jeep, let alone throw it.

"Yes," she answered flatly. "I'm a freak, too."

"You throw Jeeps?"

"No. My special abilities are somewhat different than Jeff's."

"Indeed? Do tell."

That was definitely a wince tightening her facial features. What in the *hell* was going on with her?

Chapter 2

Sam warily eyed the dark-haired man lounging in the chair across from her. She had to admit, he was a hunk. Although that wasn't exactly the right word for him. He looked...patrician. Not a word she used frequently, or that frankly ever came to mind. But it fit him. His features were classically handsome. Heck, flat-out well-bred.

"Do people actually call you Grayson?" she asked abruptly.

He looked irritated at the change of topic. Must be the intensely focused type. In her experience, such men made great lovers if they could get over their other hang-ups. But this guy seemed wired pretty tight. Probably would be as boring as they came in bed.

"My friends call me Gray. Why?"

She snorted. "The name suits you."

A flash of heat flared in his gray-green gaze. Hmm.

Maybe not so boring in bed, after all. Were he not Jeff's friend, she might be tempted to find out for sure.

"What's your super-ability, then?" he demanded.

She never just up and told people about herself like this. But Jeff had been clear. She was to brief in Grayson Pierce fully on Code X. And orders were orders. Taking a deep breath, she removed her sunglasses.

He stared like everyone did at her eyes. No human had eyes that color. At least no normal human did. She knew good and well that she looked like an alien with her eyes uncovered like this.

He mumbled, "Okay, so your eyes are a unique shade of…of gold. And it's very striking, by the way. Surely that's not why Jeff sent you here."

Striking. What a polite word for *weird.* Her eyes were brilliant, freaking yellow. She responded drily, "I imagine he sent me here because I can read a newspaper from a hundred feet away."

"That's it! An eagle," he exclaimed.

"Excuse me?" That was not the usual reaction she got from people when they saw her real eye color or first heard about her eyesight. Usually they called her a damned liar and demanded a demonstration.

"You reminded me of a predator earlier, but I couldn't figure out which kind. It's a bird of prey. A powerful one like an eagle."

"My eyesight is better than an eagle's," she responded, more than a little flummoxed. "They rely on spotting movement, whereas my superior human brain can better process and analyze acuity-based input." She broke off before she could descend into even greater geekdom. She wasn't about to give this guy the slightest advantage over her if she could avoid it.

"Seriously?" he blurted.

"Seriously."

His face lit up. "Surveillance. I'll bet that's why Jeff sent you here."

"Could be. My eyes don't require any electronic enhancements to do their thing."

"If you were to look at a person, how far away could you be and still make a positive facial ID?"

She shrugged. "A mile or so, day or night."

"Huh?"

"I see as well at night as during the day."

"You're kidding."

"Call Jeff if you don't believe me."

"I think I'd rather see a demonstration in person."

There it was. The skepticism and mistrust. This was more like it. She was back on familiar territory with this man who, up till now, had put her so off her stride. She shrugged casually. "Sure. When it gets dark."

"Why not now?"

She glanced at the heavily covered windows. "Sun's out. Small drawback of my eyesight—I have about ten times as many rods in my eyes as you do. Cones see color, but rods are light receptors. And that means I'm a wee bit sensitive to bright light."

"After dark, then. It's a date."

Surely he'd meant those words innocently. But their double meaning sent a ripple of something she'd rather not name through her body. He really was gorgeous in a mysterious, brooding way. He was far too clean-cut for her usual taste, though. She went for wild guys. Losers with no ambition or, more important, no sense of self-preservation.

Gemma Jones said Sam had a death wish but pushed it onto her lovers rather than face it in herself. Whatever the heck *that* meant. Sam had had enough of well-meaning but clueless counselors after she'd landed on the streets in her teens and periodically got dragged into shelters by various do-gooders.

She stood up, acutely aware of Gray's sharp gaze on her. For a moment, she almost regretted her choice of leather, then thought better of it. Let the guy look. It wasn't like he was ever going to get a taste of any Sam candy. With a toss of her head, she announced, "I'm going to go catch a few hours' sleep. I do my best work at night." And she darned well meant that double entendre.

She *lived* nights, truth be told. But she wasn't about to share any more of her personal life than she had to with this man who already knew enough about her to make her feel naked. And frankly, the sensation was unsettling. Grayson Pierce was far too attractive for his own good. She needed to get away from him for a little while. Get her feet back under her.

She had yet to hear about the guy whose pictures were spread all over the kitchen counter and why Jeff had asked her and Gray to check him out, but that would have to wait until she could think clearly. Until she'd achieved a little emotional distance from the disturbing man staring intently at her.

"The second bedroom's pretty small," he offered, "but it's clean and reasonably comfortable."

It sounded like he'd had to go to some effort to achieve both. "Thanks," she muttered. She relished the view of his muscular physique as he showed her down a short hallway and into the room. Streaks of sunshine leaked between the slatted blinds, and she slammed the sunglasses back over her eyes as icepicks of pain stabbed her eyeballs.

"Sorry," he said quickly. "I've got an errand to run, but I should be back by the time you wake up."

As he backed out of the room, she quickly dug in her duffel for eye drops and her good blindfold. She never spent this much time in daylight, and for good reason. She'd forgotten how bad direct sunlight hurt. She put in the anesthetizing eye drops and sighed with relief as they numbed her burning eyeballs. She popped a pain pill for her smashing headache, pulled a velvet blindfold over her eyes and fell asleep to visions of a tall, enigmatic stranger who was far too sexy for his own good and not her type at all.

She woke to the sounds of quiet swearing from the living room. Based on the rosy light that made her squint as she peeled up a corner of her blindfold, it looked to be near sunset. But just to be safe, she donned her sunglasses before taking off her blindfold all the way.

The swearing led her to Gray, who was seated on the living-room floor with nylon cord tangled all around him. And yet, he *still* managed to look…noble.

"Making your own fishing net there, Sparky?" she teased.

"Putting together a new curtain rod for your room. But these instructions stink. They're really, really badly translated into English."

"And I need a new curtain rod why?"

"I got you some blackout shades, but you need something to hang them on."

The thoughtfulness of the gesture pierced her defenses almost painfully. People didn't do nice things for Sammie Jo Jessup. Ever. She knelt down beside him and said softly, "That's incredibly sweet of you. Thank you."

He looked up in surprise and their gazes met. She rocked back on her heels, startled at what she saw there. It was like looking into the depths of…nothing. It wasn't that he was a psychopath. She'd looked into the eyes of guys like that a time or two. After all, punks and jerks were her specialty.

Rather, it was as if everything Gray was had been stripped away from him. As if he was completely, utterly lost. He wasn't caught in the abyss. He *was* the abyss.

Shaken, she offered lamely, "You don't have to bother with a curtain rod." She looked into his eyes again, and this time saw only a wall of gray-green. Had she been hallucinating there for a minute? She mumbled, "If you have a roll of duct tape, just tape the curtain to the wall. Minimizes leakage of light."

"But it won't be very attractive."

She shrugged. "I'm more about functionality than beauty."

"That's too bad," he remarked as he climbed to his feet. "Life's too short not to enjoy its beauty."

The words made sense, but they felt recited. Like he'd heard them before and was parroting them back with no conviction or real understanding. What in the heck was going on with him? Is this why Jeff had sent her out here? To rescue his buddy?

Gray fetched a roll of duct tape from a drawer in the kitchen and she followed him to her bedroom. Bemused, she held the fabric in place as he neatly taped the curtains to the wall. Their shoulders brushed as he taped his way across the top of the window frame, and a strange little shiver of pleasure washed over her.

That was weird. She'd just dumped the latest loser, Ricky "The Rocket" Rossini, and was still deep in her mandatory, man-hating, post-breakup phase. There weren't supposed to be any shivers, thank you very much.

Gray cleared his throat as he stepped back from her hastily. "I got weather stripping for around your door frame, too. It's the self-adhesive kind and shouldn't take long to install."

Stunned, she stood there in the middle of the tiny room and stared at the open doorway through which he'd disappeared. When he came back, holding two rolls of narrow foam stripping, she demanded, "Why are you going to all this trouble for me? You barely know me."

He stared at her and looked downright confused. "Because it's the polite thing to do?"

She scoffed. "What's your angle? What do you want from me?"

He drew himself up to his full height, clearly not missing her implication. "I don't want anything from you," he snapped. "Not in that way. If you can help me figure out what Luke Zimmer and this Proctor guy are up to so we can both go back to our regularly scheduled lives, that would be fantastic. But that's it."

He didn't give off a gay vibe. Was it possible he was straight and actually wasn't interested in her? Truly? Every guy wanted to do her. It was just a fact of life she'd learned to live with. But this one…didn't?

She wasn't quite sure how she felt about that. She supposed she ought to be vastly relieved, particularly since they were going to be working together. But somehow, she wasn't. *Man-hating phase, darn it.* She would be relieved he wasn't panting after her, and that's all there was to it.

"I'm glad we've got that clear," she declared. Yup. Relieved. That was her. Except something buried deep in her gut felt…restless…at the notion.

"Hungry?" he asked casually.

"Uhh, sure." Dang, a man who could cook was smexy—smart *and* sexy!

"What's your pleasure, ma'am?"

Her gaze snapped up to his, startled.

"For supper," he clarified dryly.

Darn it. So much for relieved. "I prefer vegan. But I'll take simple vegetarian."

He snorted. "You *are* going to stick out like a sore thumb around here. This is the land of hardcore carnivores."

"I'll be fine with a salad for now if you've got the stuff. I'll go shopping later and lay in my own food supply."

"Grocery closes at nine," he commented from deep within the refrigerator. He emerged with an armload of salad fixings.

Great. How was she supposed to live her night-owl existence in a town that rolled up its sidewalks and went to bed about when she was waking up? And she wouldn't even have satellite TV or streaming, Wi-Fi internet to keep her company in the wee hours. This place was going to suck.

She hopped off the stool. "If you've got a knife, I'll start chopping. But you're going to have to move those pictures so I can fix my breakfast."

"Would you like an omelet to go with that salad?"

"You know how to make omelets?"

He shrugged. "Sure. They're not that hard."

Hah. She had literally ruined a pot while boiling water before. The crash of the Hindenburg came to mind when she thought about her one and only try at omelet preparation. As she recalled, a fire extinguisher had been necessary before it was all said and done.

"What kind of salad dressing do you like?" he asked.

"Anything sharp and tangy."

"Should've known."

"What's that supposed to mean?" she demanded.

"In my experience, women's food preferences match their personalities."

"I'm *sharp?*" Hey, she'd been on her best behavior for him.

"As in clever and intelligent, yes," he replied smoothly.

"Nice save," she retorted skeptically. She wasn't about to tell him what a sucker she was for a high-quality, smooth milk chocolate to see where he went with *that*. Instead, she said, "Tell me about you."

He went still. Completely, head-to-toe, not-moving-a-muscle still. *That* was weird. He formed words, but they sounded torn from deep inside him. "Not much to tell."

If only she had her laptop and a wireless connection! She'd know everything there was to know about this mysterious man in two minutes. What had happened in his life to make him so brittle and closed? She said lightly, "You know everything about me. Don't you think I deserve a little reciprocation, here?"

"I do *not* know everything about you," he declared.

He was trying to divert her away from the subject of his life. Interesting. She had to find access to the internet, somehow, and get the scoop on this guy. "Name one thing you desperately want to know about me," she declared.

"What did you have on under that leather jacket this afternoon?" he shot back at her.

Her jaw dropped momentarily before she managed to control it. That was way out of left field. Revealing, too. The man found her attractive, after all, huh? That restless feeling in her tummy felt a little better. "Tell you what. I'll wear the same thing tomorrow, and you can find out for yourself…if you've got the courage to try."

He whirled and had his hands on the counter on either side of her so fast she barely saw him move. Trapped between his arms and more titillated than she cared to admit, she stared up at him defiantly.

He spoke quietly, his voice a dangerous caress. "Be very careful about teasing me, little girl. You may get back more than you bargained for."

Little girl? She hadn't been one of those since she was about six and her mom's latest boyfriend made a punching bag out of her for the first time. She ought to be offended. Tell Gray to go to hell. But he actually did make her feel young and rather foolish with that extreme self-control of his.

"That sounds like a challenge," she responded belatedly. It was a lame comeback, but all she could manage with his large, muscular frame only inches from her own. Darned if her breathing wasn't going all wonky, too.

He pushed away from the counter and she let out a careful breath. He turned around and something metal flashed in his hand. *Knife.* Her own hands flashed up defensively and her foot lashed out and connected with his shin. Hard.

"Ouch!" He leaped back from her. "What'd you do that for?"

"The knife… Saw it coming… Didn't stop to think…" She trailed off into silence, too embarrassed to continue.

He was studying her far too intently for her comfort. "Are you a trained martial artist?" he finally asked.

"I've had some self-defense training." Although her reaction had a lot more to do with a long string of jerkwad boyfriends—her mom's and hers—than any self-defense training. But she wasn't about to tell Mr. Perfect that. He'd probably never had a bad breakup in his entire life. But then, he probably never dated nut-balls, either. His women were no doubt as perfect and well-bred as he was.

He laid the knife down carefully on the counter in front of her. "If you'd like to chop up the tomatoes and cucumber, I'll wash the lettuce."

Crap. She berated herself silently for making a fool of herself over a stupid knife and vented her irritation onto the hapless veggies, which she minced nearly into pulp.

The omelet turned out to be as irritatingly perfect as its maker, all fluffy and light and neatly folded. It didn't help her bad mood that Gray was quiet through the meal, alternately staring at his food and glancing up thoughtfully at her. She'd inadvertently revealed far too much of herself to him, and clearly he wasn't hesitating to draw all kinds of no doubt accurate and damning inferences about her.

Too jumpy to stand those thoughtful looks any longer, she leaped up and cleared the table. While she washed and dried the dishes by hand—apparently dish-washers were off-limits in this wacky place—he gathered the pictures he'd piled together earlier and spread them out across the table.

She dried her hands and approached them.

"Sit beside me," he ordered absently.

Startled, she sank into the chair he'd pulled up beside his. It brought their ankles, knees, hips, elbows and shoulders into a proximity that threatened to destroy her concentration. Really, she ought to just jump the guy's bones and get him out of her system so she could work with him. Otherwise, the next few days could be seriously miserable.

Gray filled her in efficiently. "Luke Zimmer's upbringing was pretty normal. Middle class, Midwest, average home, average income. He ran with a neo-Nazi gang in high school, however, in—" he shuffled through the printed pages "—a suburb of Chicago. But his current political leanings are more antisocial than that."

"What's more antisocial than neo-Nazis?" she blurted. She'd hung out with a skinhead or two, and they'd been way too violent for her taste.

Gray continued, "Zimmer moved into this area several months ago, apparently at Jeff's request."

"Given that Jeff mentioned a cult leader to both of us, I'm assuming Luke got sent here to infiltrate Proctor's group on behalf of Winston Enterprises?"

A flicker of something suspiciously like respect passed through Gray's opaque gaze. "That's a good guess. Although why Proctor's a threat to an international conglomerate with no business dealings anywhere near here is a mystery to me."

"Maybe Luke's profile can give us a clue into what kind of a person Proctor is, or at least what the orientation of his cult's stated beliefs is."

The respect thing flickered again in Gray's gaze as he replied, "My main impression of Zimmer is that he's severely paranoid. I did a little reconnaissance on him yesterday, but without electronic equipment, I couldn't get even remotely close to him. Although I don't know if his paranoia predates his relationship with Proctor or is possibly a result of it."

"Enter the girl with eagle eyes."

He smiled a little at her. "If you can point your eagle eyes at this guy and learn more about him, that could be enormously useful."

"Does Luke have a job?" she asked.

"Not that I'm aware of."

"How's he paying his way, then?" she asked. Even losers had to eat and buy drugs.

"I'm working a little too off-book to just stroll into the local bank and ask."

"I could hack into the bank's computers—" she broke off "—but nobody uses computers around here, do they?"

"A few folks actually have them. They have to use hard-wired, buried cable lines, though, and there are no Wi-Fi networks."

She shrugged. "It probably doesn't matter, anyway. Guys like Luke work in cash. Leaves less of a trail for the cops to follow. What else do you know about him?"

"He's twenty-seven years old. Computer science major at Cal Tech. Didn't graduate, though. Busted a couple of times for pot possession by campus cops. Thirty days in jail and a fine the last time. Nothing remarkable about his family. Two brothers—one older, one younger. He got decent grades in high school, ran about a 2.5 GPA in college. Nothing else shows up on him in the system."

She doubted she could dig up more than that if she had a computer and internet access at her disposal. He didn't sound like the kind of guy whose life would leave much of an electronic trail. "Anyone interviewed the family?" she asked.

"I don't have those kinds of resources at my disposal."

She frowned. What the heck did that mean? "What can I do to help your investigation?"

"Anything you can see and learn is more than I have to go on now."

"And who do you work for, exactly?"

He leaned back in his chair. Crossed his arms. Pressed his lips into a thin white line. He even spoke tightly. "At the moment, Jeff Winston."

He might have dodged her question, but all that body language spoke volumes. He had secrets to keep. "You do realize I have the equivalent of military top-secret clearances or better," she commented.

He didn't seem impressed. And he didn't open his mouth. There were not too many employers in the United States who demanded complete and total silence from their employees. She considered him thoughtfully. He didn't look like a mercenary for a private security firm. He was too clean-cut for that. Too by-the-book. Government, then.

"Okay, Sparky. I'm going to assume you work for some spooky, secret government agency until you say otherwise. Which begs the question of why you don't just have your peeps poke around a little and hand you a complete list of names of every known associate of one Luke Zimmer. Order up a little surveillance detail on his cronies, and you'd know what ole Luke's up to in under a week. I don't see why Jeff thought you would need my help at all."

"It's not that simple. Given our total lack of ability to use electronics in this area, the manpower required to mount the sort of surveillance op that you're proposing would be prohibitive. Not to mention, people in this region routinely live completely off the grid. They're nearly impossible to track by any other means than direct visual surveillance. For all I know this kid's using a fake ID and isn't going by the name Luke Zimmer at all."

She nodded. "Fake identities are pretty easy to get."

"You say that like you have one," he replied, amused.

She had several, in point of fact. More than a little of her youth had been misspent. But she wasn't about to admit that to him. "It's dark enough to go outside and do parlor tricks with Sammie's eyesight. If you'll grab something with writing on it, I'll start jogging down the road."

"I have a better idea. Let's put your eyes to work for real," he suggested.

"What do you have in mind?"

"How about you put on some walking shoes and I'll show you?"

He definitely came from the government-intelligence community. Those guys always answered a question with a question. Curious, she went to her room and grabbed her neon yellow running shoes. When she came back, Gray was just finishing packing a rucksack.

"Let me guess," she said dryly. "You were a Boy Scout and you're taking along a few items in case we get stranded in the woods. With angry bears. In a blizzard. On the side of a cliff. And we need to put on Thanksgiving dinner for a dozen guests."

He grinned. "I'm not *that* anal."

"Had me fooled," she grumbled under her breath.

"I'm trained to anticipate contingencies and plan for them."

Oh, yeah. *So* a spy. When he headed for the passenger side of the Bronco, she rolled her eyes. "Really, Gray. I can get my own doors."

"Really, Sammie Jo. Aren't you confident enough to let a man get them for you?"

The quip hurt. She was sure he didn't intend it, though. How could he know how inadequate she felt around polished, sophisticated people like him? To distract herself, she asked, "How old is this vehicle?"

"It's a 1972. The first onboard car computers were put out in 1975, so all the cars permanently in the NRQZ have to be '74s or earlier."

"This place is like some kind of bizarre time warp."

He nodded. "Just think about how bizarre it's going to seem in another twenty years. Tourists will come here to see the living history exhibit it's rapidly becoming."

"Where are we going?"

"Luke lives in the next valley over. Little town called Spruce Hollow. It's known for being a bit cultish."

That lifted her eyebrow. "Define *cultish*."

"I wish I could. But I've only been here one day. As best I can tell, the folks there are particularly intent on eliminating all electronics from their lives. Real back-to-the-good-old-days fanatics. And apparently they're pretty suspicious of outsiders. I thought it might be prudent not to just barge in and start asking questions."

"Good call. I've done cultish before, and you have to be very careful in your approach. Best bet is to find a way to get them to invite you in."

He looked over at her sharply. "Define having done cultish."

She winced. It simply was not in her nature to be secretive. Yet again, her big mouth had given her away. "Let's just say my choice in boys wasn't always stellar. A few of them were gang types."

"What kinds of gangs?"

"Bikers. Skinheads. Drug dealers." She omitted the coming apocalypse bunch her mother had dragged her into the middle of. She nearly hadn't gotten away from that particular cult alive.

To his credit, Gray didn't show any outward signs of horror. He asked casually enough, "Do you still go for guys like that?"

The question stopped her cold. Did she? Until this afternoon, she might have said yes. But Grayson Pierce was a revelation. She'd had no idea that decent men actually existed. She'd always thought they were a figment of television producers' imaginations. She settled for mumbling, "I don't go for men at all at the moment. I'm a committed single person."

He made a sound that was probably supposed to pass for a laugh, but somehow failed. "Me, too."

"Why's that?" she queried. "You must have women falling all over you."

"Work," he answered from between gritted teeth. If she didn't know better, she'd say he'd gone a little pale. *What on earth?*

She waited for more, but he didn't add anything to that one-word response. She prodded, "Most men work and yet manage to have relationships. What's the problem with your work?"

"Long hours. Lots of travel."

"And then there's the whole undercover thing," she added sympathetically. "And the killing."

His hands clenched the steering wheel abruptly, and in the glow of the dashboard, he looked a ghastly shade of gray. He gave no other outward sign of tension, but it was enough. Her eagle eyes didn't miss much. She spoke quietly, "Your secret is safe with me."

"I have no secrets," he ground out.

"Sure you do. You're afraid of women. That's why you avoid us."

That made him actually jerk the steering wheel. The Bronco briefly swerved, and he righted its course angrily. "I am *not* afraid of women!"

So. There was passion beneath that calm, cool, collected exterior. Somehow, his outburst made him seem more human. More approachable. And a little color had returned to his face. Satisfied that he had himself back in hand, she sat back.

"What about you?" he asked. "Why the whole leather and chains bit? The scarlet lipstick and black nails thing shouts of insecurity and need for attention."

He had no idea the nerve he'd just hit. She turned her head to look out the window. And there was no way she would let him see the tears in her eyes. She presented herself to the world as tough and savvy, and she wasn't about to let down that facade.

The interior of the Bronco went silent. She fixedly studied the mountains outside the window. Although they were not all that tall, the terrain was rugged. Steep outcroppings of rock interrupted the carpet of green trees. Here and there she spotted movement. An owl circling in the dark overhead, a coyote slinking across an open field. The night was alive, and she sank into it, becoming a part of it.

"Do eagles hunt at night?" Gray asked without warning.

"They can. Although their prey mostly is active during the day, so they do the bulk of their hunting in daylight."

"We're coming into Spruce Hollow. Luke's place is on the other side of town."

She counted buildings—gas station, small grocery store, car wash, video store. Wow. She hadn't seen one of those in a while. And of course, a church. Several dozen modest homes clustered around the businesses. Soft lights came from a few windows, and she frowned, not placing the dim glows. Those weren't electric. Kerosene lamps, maybe? Wow. These folks did take going off the grid seriously.

"Don't blink or you'll miss the whole town," she joked.

"Hence my confusion over why Jeff Winston saw fit to pull us both and send us here."

"I get it now," she replied quietly. "It is strange, isn't it?"

"Luke's cabin is up that turnoff. I figure we need to head on down the road a bit and hike back."

She looked at the dirt track winding up a mountain into a heavy stand of spruce trees. She'd read before she came here that scientists had planted spruce trees inside the NRQZ in the 1950s because they believed the needles were the right length to absorb radio interference.

"Could we at least park uphill from his place so it's a downhill hike?" she asked.

"You'd still have to hike back to the car."

"I'll wait at the cabin and you can bring the car to pick me up. After all, you're *such* a gentleman."

He murmured as he pulled the car off the narrow road and into the woods. "I'm not always a gentleman."

Her head whipped around and she stared at him in the dark. That sounded like a come-on. Surely this man was not throwing pick-up lines at her. Not after he'd so strongly signaled his complete disinterest in her earlier. His features might be easy to see, but they were not easy to read. His face was completely devoid of hints as to what he'd meant by that comment. Expressionlessness aside, the innuendo behind that comment had not been her imagination. There was definitely something going on between the two of them. A spark. Or at least friction. But what kind of friction, she had no clue.

Gray hefted the rucksack and started off through the woods. He swore quietly as a tree branch snagged his shirt.

"How 'bout you let the lady who can see in the dark go first, Sparky? You just show me which direction we need to head, and I'll take point."

He frowned but said nothing.

"What? You don't like the idea of the girl going first?"

"Actually, I don't."

"Keep in mind I'll be able to see the bad guys *way* before they can see me."

"I still haven't had my demonstration of how well you can see."

She glanced around in the trees, seeing every stick, every leaf. "Follow me." She led him unerringly around the trees, calling out logs and low spots quietly over her shoulder. They topped the ridge that rose behind Zimmer's house in a few minutes. She paused at the edge of a clearing and looked out over the town.

"Want me to start reading license plates in the driveways down there?" she murmured. "You can write them down and check them when we head back through Spruce Hollow."

"What do you see over toward Luke's place?"

She looked where he pointed and made out a darkened cabin through the trees. "No movement through the windows. Dirty dishes in the sink, though. I see muddy footprints on the porch, leading to the door and away from it."

Gray stared at her. "You see footprints?"

"Shall we move in close so the blind, normal guy can verify it?"

"No. I'll take your word for it."

She studied the cabin for a moment. "If we move off to our right a bit, I ought to be able to see if anyone's in bed. The curtains are open in the bedroom."

"By all means," Gray muttered. "All I see is a dark blob where the cabin is."

She moved off confidently through the trees. It took her a minute to find a vantage point through the forest to see the cabin again, but she spotted it and reported, "No one's in bed. Looks like Luke's not home."

Gray murmured, "He's got a big dog. Any sign of him?"

"Nope. There's no movement at all, and I can't imagine any dog leaving the food on the kitchen table undisturbed like that. Luke took Fido with him. Want to move in closer?"

"Sure."

"Too bad we can't plant a few bugs while we're inside."

"I didn't say we'd go inside!" he exclaimed under his breath.

"What's the point of getting close if we don't?" she retorted. "And I saw that eye roll, mister." She grinned at the startled chagrin that crossed his features. It was good to be able to see in the dark.

She led the way down the hill to the cabin, approaching it using tree cover all the way. Gray touched her arm as they drew near and whispered, "We should check the garage. Make sure his truck's gone."

"I see recent tracks in the dirt. It's gone."

"Ohh-kay, then."

"C'mon. The rain barrel on the porch has been moved recently—the ring of dust at its base is disturbed. I bet that's where the spare key is hidden." Sure enough, she was right. In short order, she let them into the cabin while Gray muttered his misgivings under his breath. She paused in the doorway and scanned the room.

"What are you doing?" Gray asked. "We know he's not home."

"Checking for booby traps, Mr. Impatient."

Gray subsided behind her.

"All clear."

He pulled out a flashlight and she slammed her hand over it fast before he could flip it on. "No lights. My eyes are fully dilated right now and you'd injure my retinas. You'll have to make do in the dark as best you can. Downside of hanging out with me."

He nodded his understanding and stowed the light. "What do you see, then?"

She frowned. "Actually, I see what could be signs of a struggle. That chair's at an odd angle from the table. The hand towel lying on the floor was probably pulled off the stove handle and wasn't hung back up. Fork's lying halfway across the table from the unfinished plate of food."

"Those footprints on the back porch. Could those be an intruder coming and going?" Gray asked grimly.

"Find me a pair of Luke's shoes and I'll compare the size to the prints on the porch."

"Good idea." He left and was back in a minute with a ratty pair of combat boots.

They opened the back door and she stared down at the gray floorboards. "The prints are substantially larger than these boots," she announced. "Luke had a visitor recently." She headed down the porch steps to examine the marks more closely. "Oh, wow."

"What?" Gray was instantly at her back, the heat of his big body close enough for her to feel.

"Drag marks. Two thick, parallel lines. Something heavy was pulled out of there."

"Like a body dragging its heels?"

"Yup."

He had a pistol in hand and jumped in front of her so fast she barely saw him move. "Cover your eyes, Sammie Jo. I'm turning on my flashlight."

She slapped a hand over her face.

"Okay. The light's off. I need you to come over here," he announced.

He was crouching a few yards away from her. She joined him and immediately saw what he was looking at. "Do you think that's blood?" she asked in a hushed voice.

He touched a dark, wet cluster of dead leaves and smelled his fingertips. "It's blood, all right. Can you pick up anything from here? A trail?"

She walked around slowly, staring at the ground. "There are too many disturbed leaves and sticks. But I'm not seeing any more blood. Maybe someone bled here and then was carried away from this spot?"

"Could be," he allowed.

She walked in ever wider circles, seeking some clue

as to what had happened here. "I only see a few drops of blood near that first bit you found. I'd say someone was punched there. Maybe knocked out. I can't discern a spatter pattern, and there's not enough blood for a knife wound or gunshot."

"Makes sense." Gray went back into the house to conduct a more thorough search while she continued looking around outside. They'd been at it for maybe ten minutes when she heard something in the woods. And it sounded like it was headed this way.

"Gray," she called out low. "Bring that gun of yours out here."

He was by her side in an instant, shoving her behind him. She peered over his shoulder impatiently. She spotted the movement and let out a relieved breath. "It's a dog."

"I don't see anything."

"That's why I'm here, Smarty Pants."

A big yellow Labrador retriever bounded out of the brush a few moments later.

"That's Luke's dog," Gray said. "Take cover. Zimmer may be close behind." He took her arm, but she stood her ground, staring in horror at the dog.

"Uhh, I don't think so," she said thickly. She turned away, retching.

Gray flashed his light at the dog and swore, confirming what she'd seen. The dog's muzzle and front legs were matted with blood, and he was carrying what looked like a severed human hand in his mouth.

"Here, boy." He whistled to the dog, who bounced over to them eagerly. Gray grabbed the dog's collar. "Can you get me a piece of rope or something to leash him?"

She stumbled back to the house and came back with

an electric extension cord. Gray had disengaged the hand from the animal's mouth. It looked badly mauled, and it looked male. "Luke's?" she choked out.

He shrugged. "Let's see if we can get Fido to lead us back to the rest of this guy." He showed the dog the hand and said urgently, "Go get him, boy."

The dog took off, straining against the makeshift leash. They raced along behind the dog who took off like an arrow through the woods.

The spruce forest had little undergrowth apart from dead, needleless branches that tried to scratch the heck out of her as she barged through them. Were it not for her excellent vision, they'd have succeeded.

The dog whined and Sam strained to see ahead. "There. I see something," she panted to Gray.

He dragged the dog to a walk, and they approached cautiously.

"No movement," she reported quietly. She eased forward, taking the lead whether Gray liked it or not. Her vision was simply so much better than his that she had to go first. There. Something roughly human in size and shape lay on a limestone outcrop. She slowed abruptly and Gray slammed into her nearly knocking her off her feet.

"Ooomph," she grunted as his arms went around her to steady her. Oh, boy. He was as strong as she'd imagined.

"Sorry," he muttered in her ear.

"About a hundred yards ahead," she breathed.

"What direction?"

Usually, when she went out in the field, the men she was with had night-vision equipment. She'd forgotten he was as blind as a kitten out here. She stepped around behind him, turned his shoulders slightly to the left and gave him a little push.

He walked forward cautiously, his arms out in front of him. He looked like a zombie, and an urge to laugh might have claimed her if she wasn't scared to death of whatever was ahead.

They walked for maybe a minute, and then Gray made a sound in his throat. "It's a body. Looks like animals have been at it. You don't have to look if you don't want to."

But that was kind of the whole point of her being out here, wasn't it? She took a deep breath and stepped out from behind him.

Chapter 3

Gray stared in dismay at what had once been a human being but was now an eviscerated mess. Fido whined eagerly, obviously sensing a tasty snack. He tied the dog's makeshift leash to a tree and approached the gory remains cautiously. The guy's face was intact enough for him to murmur, "That's Zimmer."

It could not be good for their investigation that Jeff's undercover cult infiltrator was lying in pieces on the ground. What in the *hell* was going on around here? What had poor Luke stumbled into the middle of? What were he and Sam in the middle of?

"Uhh, Gray," Sammie Jo replied, "you might want to take a closer look at the body with a light. I'll cover my eyes for a second."

Her tone of voice warned him that he wasn't going to like what he saw. He flashed the light down at Luke's head, which was just about the only intact part of him, and reeled back, shocked. The guy's bloody mouth was frozen in a silent scream of terror and agony.

"His wounds don't look like the tearing a snacking predator might cause." Sam swallowed thickly and continued, "The edges are clean. Smooth."

"Like a knife cut?" he asked, startled.

"Exactly."

"I need to photograph this. If you need to move away while I use the camera flash, feel free."

She stumbled away in the dark while he got to work snapping pictures from every angle. His hands shook as he wielded the camera. This grisly scene was all too much like another one, years ago—

Violently, he forced the memory from his mind. This was work. He'd seen plenty of blood and guts before. He could do this, dammit. Besides, how would he explain himself to Sammie Jo if he freaked out and ran screaming?

Clenching his jaw with all his strength, he lifted a flap of skin to examine it. Sammie Jo was right. A blade—a sharp one—had made that cut. Luke had been sliced open from rib to rib and hip to hip, then the two horizontal cuts joined with a vertical slash. He'd been laid open like a book. A methodical killer, then. Possible torture. Not a fight or self-defense.

It looked like a lot of the poor guy's intestines and other organs were missing. Unless Fido or some other critter had eaten them, it would mean Zimmer had been gutted elsewhere. As Gray photographed the ground around the corpse, nowhere near enough blood was present to go along with the crime. Definitely killed elsewhere and dumped here.

The violence of the murder staggered him. Who felt such rage toward Luke Zimmer? Or worse, who would send such a vicious message to others with this killing? Who could the target of such a message be? Zimmer's boss, maybe? Gray's alarm ratcheted up another notch. What in the *hell* had he and Sammie Jo walked into? *Who* was Proctor?

He continued snapping pictures grimly. There were rope burns around Luke's wrists. He'd fought for his life against those ropes, for the skin was raw and bloody. Gray reached down gingerly to test the rigidity of the corpse's clawed hand and arm, and it gave way slightly under pressure.

It took about three hours for rigor mortis to set in and about three days for it to wear off. Luke didn't stink enough to have been dead for three days, which meant his murder—for what else could this be—had been recent, within four or five hours, probably. And that meant he must have been killed relatively near here, too.

He heard movement nearby and whipped out his pistol.

Sammie Jo's voice floated out of the dark. "It's just me. But keep that out."

It was eerie how she could see in this gloom. And why did she want him to keep his weapon drawn? He searched the woods urgently, but saw only darkness and more darkness. She materialized out of nowhere, and even though he knew she was there, she still startled him.

"I've got a blood trail," she murmured. "Is it possible he wasn't killed here?"

"It's probable. Lead on."

"Should we call the police and let them do the tracking?"

"Not until we have a chance to gather data for ourselves," he replied. "Once they get involved, we'll be shut out of the investigation."

She moved off confidently at an oblique angle to the ridgeline. They'd been walking for several minutes when she asked, "Why on earth would the killer kill someone in an isolated spot and then move the body to another isolated spot to dump it? Why not just leave it where he killed the guy?"

"That's an excellent question. Maybe the end of this blood trail will tell us."

No sooner had he said those words than she came to an abrupt halt. His night vision was adapted enough by now for him to stop before he plowed into her, but he didn't see what she was peering at.

"Road ahead," she breathed.

"I'll go first," he bit out. He moved past her and crept forward slowly. Sure enough, a dirt road materialized, although he had to walk a lot farther to find it than he'd expected. He eased up to its margin and checked both directions. Deserted. "Do you see tire tracks?" he asked her.

"Pass me your camera. The tires look new," she commented as she pointed the camera, closed her eyes, and snapped a few pictures.

"See anything else?" he asked her.

"Looks like a vehicle parked here. There's a big cluster of footprints like someone pulled something bulky out of the vehicle here. Then the tracks lead into the woods. I think I see the return set of prints, but they're hard to distinguish."

"Amazing."

"Do you recognize this road?" she asked.

"No, and I've studied the maps of the area exhaustively."

"Google Earth will show it—" she broke off, swearing colorfully. "The guys at Winston Ops will have to mail us a hard copy, won't they?"

He chuckled at her frustration. He'd banged his head against the technology wall out here a few times, too. "You catch on fast, grasshopper."

"I've seen all I can, here. Now what?"

"Now we hike back to the Bronco, drive to town and call the police," he answered. The cops were no doubt going to want a statement from them. "We need to come up with a reason for visiting Luke's place that'll hold up to a police investigation."

Sammie answered gaily, "Well, obviously I went to college with him and have come to town to visit the NRQZ at his suggestion. You're too old to pass for his pal, but I'm not."

"I'm thirty-five," he retorted indignantly.

"Like I said. Ancient."

"How old are you?" he challenged.

"Twenty-eight, Grandpa."

He'd bet she wouldn't call him that if he made love to her— He broke off the thought, appalled. Where had that come from?

"I guess folks will believe you and I are a couple," she commented doubtfully.

He made a worried sound back at her. "I dunno. That's a bit of a stretch. It's not like you're really my type." He didn't need supervision to see the hurt that flashed across her face. "Just kidding," he added hastily.

Huh. Who'd have thought swaggering, leather-clad Sammie Jo had a vulnerable underbelly? Intrigued, he climbed into the Bronco without protesting her opening her own door.

"Okay. So you're Luke's friend and I'm your…"

"Fiancé," she filled in promptly.

The wave of pain that slammed into him was so bad it took his breath away. He'd tried over the years to avoid the pain, to ignore it. But he'd learned the only way to survive it was to go straight into the fire, to experience the hellish agony of it head-on. He took a deep breath and let it wash over him. A person would think that, after five years, it wouldn't hurt so bad. Granted, the waves didn't slam into him as often now, nor bury him so deep. But they still hurt just as much.

When the worst of it had passed, he glanced over at his companion. She wanted to pose as his fiancée and not just a girlfriend, huh? Interesting. It suggested a level of intimacy that would take their cover story to a whole different place. He ought to be game to go there. He *ought* to be all for it, in fact. Those curves of hers practically begged to be touched.

Then the larger problem hit him. "How on earth are we going to explain your—" He broke off.

"Reptilian eyes?" she supplied wryly.

"They don't look reptilian," he retorted indignantly. "Insectoid, maybe, but not reptilian."

Thankfully, he'd judged her correctly. She laughed at the remark. "Seriously," he continued. "We can't waltz into the police station with your eyes exposed. And at this time of night, they'll think you're stoned if you wear sunglasses the whole time."

That made her giggle. She had a great laugh. "I've got it covered, Sparky. I wear brown contact lenses in public."

"All right, then. You're not an alien, and we're getting married. Have we set a date?"

"I doubt the police will ask, but no. We're trying to

figure out where to live first," she answered thought-fully. "Are we considering moving to the NRQZ?"

He liked that idea. It would give them an excuse to poke around the local area openly. "Can you pull off a back-to-nature hippie persona?" he asked her.

"I can be anything you want me to be, big guy," she answered flippantly.

For some reason, the comment set his teeth on edge. "How about you just be yourself with me? I don't need or want pretense from my women."

She looked shocked and fell silent as he guided the car to the Spruce Hollow gas station and its no-kidding, working pay phone. He mentally kicked himself for making that "my women" comment. No sense in lead-ing the poor girl on.

He dialed the number of the police placarded on the side of the pay phone and reported Luke's death. He was not surprised when he was ordered to stay right where he was and wait for a deputy to come meet them.

The remainder of the night went predictably. He and Sammie Jo described arriving at the cabin to find their "friend" gone and his dog bloody. They gave detailed instructions to the sheriff as to where to find Luke's body. They followed a deputy back to the sheriff's of-fice in the Bronco and were ordered to come inside and make statements.

Fido had arrived at the police station to be held as evidence until a forensic pathologist from Charleston could come down and collect the dog to examine. He could be seen jumping around inside playing with a deputy, already on his way to being spoiled rotten. As Gray stared at the well-lit building, he glanced over at Sammie Jo in concern. She was in the middle of putting contact lenses in her eyes. "Are you going to be okay in there? It's pretty bright."

"Artificial light isn't as bad as sunlight. I'll survive. Gemma had these contacts specially made for me. They act like miniature sunglasses. I just can't wear them for more than a few hours at a time."

When they stepped inside, he rather missed the odd, but uniquely Sammie Jo, gold color of her eyes. In spite of the lenses, she squinted heavily and looked like she was in pain as they were seated at desks, pads of paper and pens shoved in front of them, and told to write down their statements.

He had a hard time concentrating on his because a deputy spent the whole damned time hitting on Sammie Jo. She rebuffed him steadily, but the guy just wouldn't catch a clue. By the time Gray laid down his pen, his fist ached to punch something.

When Sammie Jo finished her statement, Gray stood up immediately and moved to her side. "C'mon, sweetheart. It's been a long night. Let's get back to our place and get some sleep." Glaring at the deputy, he placed a possessive arm across her shoulder and pulled her to his side.

She was tall enough that her curves fit against him nicely. Her body was lithe and vibrant against his, softer than he'd expected, and a surge of possessiveness flashed through him. Stunned, he walked her to the Bronco and deposited her in the passenger seat in silence.

As he climbed in and started the car, she asked, "Are you okay?"

"Dim-witted bastard," he muttered. "Couldn't he see you were with me?"

As she popped out the lenses and stored them in

their little plastic case, she commented, "Why, Grayson Pierce. Are you jealous of Barney?"

"Who?"

"Barney Fife. From *The Andy Griffith Show.*"

"Not familiar with it."

"Good grief, man. You've lived a freakishly sheltered life! We must rectify this flaw in your upbringing!"

He doubted his grandmother would agree that his upbringing was flawed. At least not until his American mother divorced his British father and hauled herself and her son back to the States to live. He'd gone straight into high school and hadn't had time or inclination for American television. He'd had enough trouble making the transition to this culture without trying to master that aspect of it.

"Did you get any good pictures of the body?" she asked.

"You tell me. You're the one with supersight." He passed her the digital camera and she peered at the pictures closely.

"God almighty, this is nasty," she muttered. "Somebody really had it in for this guy. I'd love to blow these up on a high-definition computer monitor and have a look at them."

"At a glance, the wounds strike me as too surgical to have been inflicted in uncontrolled rage. I think the killer wanted to send someone a message."

She looked up at him sharply. "It would be a heck of message. Who would the killer send it to?"

"That's what we have to find out."

"Hey, I'm a desk jockey. I don't do the whole dangerous, chase-after-psychopathic-murderers thing."

He glanced over at her in surprise. "With your eyesight? I'd think Winston Enterprises would put you out in the field nonstop."

"Doc Jones has been keeping me close to home for testing, and that's fine with me. I'm a big ole chicken when it comes to scary stuff."

Somehow he doubted that. She'd been fearless trekking through the woods earlier. He commented dryly, "Welcome to the big leagues, kid."

"And what league is that, exactly? You're a spy, right? Who for? Please tell me you have tons of field experience and aren't in over your head here."

"Sorry. I can neither confirm nor—"

"Oh, stop," she interrupted. "If we're going to be working together, you might as well tell me. Besides, if my life's in danger, I have a right to know who I'm depending on to keep me alive."

Depending on. The words staggered him. No. *No!* She mustn't! Panic ripped through him. He failed the people who depended on him! He couldn't be responsible for more violence, more death…

He realized he was about to rip the steering wheel out of its column and forcibly relaxed his fingers. He couldn't work with her if she was expecting to depend on him. She had to get out of here. Far, far away from him. He'd call Jeff when they got back to the motel and tell him to pull her off this op.

How he managed to guide the Bronco the rest of the way back to their motel, he wasn't quite sure. It all passed in a haze of terror. He parked the vehicle and turned off the ignition. "You need to leave. Now. I'll call Jeff and have him send a jet for you in the morning."

"I don't bail out on people because the going gets tough, Gray."

"This isn't about abandoning me. It's about your safety. I won't risk your life—"

"Really. Stop. I realize you're some sort of mega-protective, do-the-right-thing type, but get over it. I'm not leaving."

He closed his mouth on his next protest because it threatened to become a scream of agony. She didn't understand. He couldn't be responsible for her. Not for anybody ever again. He fought his way back to a modicum of sanity by focusing on Sammie Jo. He replayed her protest in his mind. A faint note of desperation in her voice had caught his attention. Something that said no matter how dangerous it got here, she'd rather face this than face whatever waited for her back home.

On a hunch he asked, "What are you running from?"

That stopped her cold in the act of pushing her car door open for herself. "I beg your pardon?"

He took advantage of her distraction to go around and open it for her. He took only a single step back, which forced her to slide past him at a distance of about two inches. When they were chest to chest, he repeated, "Who are you running from, Sammie Jo?"

She hesitated for an instant and then moved past him to the bungalow. As he turned on the lights, she slid a pair of sunglasses over her eyes. He stared at her featureless gaze expectantly.

"Dang, you're good," she commented neutrally.

"Well?"

"I just broke up with a ginormous jerk, and I happen to find a change of scenery refreshing at the moment."

"Is he violent?"

"Possibly."

"Psychotic?"

"Definitely."

His heart was pounding far too hard. She needed protection, and he couldn't possibly do it. She mustn't depend on him. "Anything else I should know about you?" he asked tautly.

"Hey, you're the one with all the secrets, not me," she declared.

And that was how he planned to keep it. There were some things he would never speak of. Ever.

"Now what?" she asked, startling him.

"I don't understand."

"Our only lead on what this Proctor guy's up to is dead. How do you want to proceed with investigating his cult or whatever it is?"

"After I put you on a plane in the morning, I plan to drive up into the mountains and find that road again. Then I'll follow it and see where it leads."

"Why wait till morning? I see great at night. I'll be your eyes."

And apparently, she was bright-eyed and bushytailed at nearly 3:00 a.m. Far be it from him to admit that he was beat and would rather sleep. He picked up the car keys resolutely. "Let's go, then."

Finding the dirt road wasn't hard. His sense of direction was unerring and he went right to it. But it got weird when Sammie Jo announced from the passenger seat that she'd spotted the tire tracks leaving the dropoff point. All he saw was gravel stretching away into the dark in the headlights.

"Slow down," she ordered, leaning forward in her seat. "Okay. Go straight ahead through the intersection."

They followed the tracks for maybe a mile. Then they ran into a paved road and the tracks turned right. But the dust had worn off the tires in a few hundred yards, and Sammie Jo shook her head in disgust. "Lost the tracks. Drat. That vehicle could have gone anywhere from here."

"Let's head back to the motel and get some rest. We can talk to the sheriff tomorrow and see what he's come up with."

"You think he'll work with you?" she asked doubtfully. "He seemed the type to resent outsiders, and he wasn't exactly friendly to us. Now, Deputy Barney seemed all kinds of eager to work with me. I could probably pump him for some—"

"No." She looked far too pleased at his knee-jerk response. He scowled. "Have you got any better ideas?"

"Well, yeah," she answered. "We have to stop being outsiders."

"Come again?"

"Let's move into the area. Settle down."

"What are you talking about?" He was lost, and he considered himself to be a reasonably bright fellow.

"Think about it. We've already established ourselves as a couple. I mentioned to the sheriff that we're thinking about moving off the grid and into this area. So let's rent a little place. Meet the neighbors. They'll be a lot more likely to talk to us than if we're tourists passing through."

The idea of setting up house sent figurative butcher knives slashing through his body. It was a cover, dammit. Just a cover. An act. Lord knew he'd become a hell of an actor over the past few years. He could put on this fake skin and live in it for a while if he had to.

"Where do you suggest we move to?" he asked.

"Spruce Hollow, of course."

"It's a bold gambit."

She grinned over at him. "Are you in?"

"Your middle name is trouble, isn't it?" he grumbled.

"With a capital *T.* Just leave it to me. I'll set up the rest of our cover tomorrow. All I need you to do is get some of the kind of clothes you normally wear."

"That I normally… What are you talking about?"

"You look like a pig dressed up as a showgirl."

"Excuse me?" he exclaimed.

"Well, you don't look like an actual pig. You're quite a hottie, in point of fact. But you look totally uncomfortable in those jeans and that ridiculous flannel shirt. If you're going to blend in, you have to look like yourself."

He frowned. "I'd have to make a trip to a real city to shop."

"You do that and I'll take care of the rest. By the time you get back, I'll have all the arrangements made."

He stared at her in shock. *Steamroller, thy name is Sammie Jo.*

He got back to the motel room after his road trip to Charleston at about noon and found a note on the kitchen table.

G.—I took the liberty of packing your stuff—nice silk boxer shorts, BTW. Check out of the motel and meet me at this address. And for God's sake, wear some uptight rich-guy clothes.
—S.

She'd checked out his underwear? Vixen. He'd have to return the favor sometime. He noticed belatedly that the sticky note was pasted to a hand-drawn map. What had she gone and done?

Bemused, he followed her instructions to Spruce

Hollow's one and only side street and pulled up in front of a one-story brick ranch house that looked straight out of the 1950s. Oh, God. He couldn't do this.

The house was low and rectangular, nothing like the neat, craftsman-style home that flashed into his head with blinding clarity. A home with blood everywhere. Death. And that horrible, primal scream that wouldn't stop.

Chapter 4

He'd done some hard things in his life, seen and survived horrors that would have broken a lesser man—at least that was what the shrinks told him. But turning the Bronco into that little ranch house's driveway, parking it and climbing out like he wasn't screaming in terror inside his head was one of the hardest things he'd ever done.

Two women emerged from the house as he stood by the SUV fighting every warning his body could shout at him to turn and run until he couldn't take another step. The yard was overgrown and full of weeds, but a neat carpet of green swam in his mind's eye. Paint peeled from these shutters, and a rusty rain gutter dangled from the front porch. That other house had been fully restored to pristine perfection.

He forced his mind to a place of calm. No emotion. It had been a long time since he'd had to set a date for himself, but he did so, now. One month from today. If the pain had not subsided by then, he gave himself permission to contemplate ending his life on that day. And with the mental exercise came a modicum of peace. It had been the only way he'd survived those first few years. Making bargains with himself that, if it all became too much for him by some set date, he could check out of life's mortal coil.

He eyed the ranch house critically as he climbed out of the SUV. The roof looked sound and the brick siding looked solid, but that was about the best he could say for the place.

One of the women on the long front porch wore a business suit that screamed Realtor. The other one looked like June Cleaver, complete with pastel-flowered dress, full skirt and a demure little belt cinching in a tiny waist. Her coloring was creamy and soft, her eyes dark, her hair in a French twist…. Good God. Her *red* hair.

He barely recognized Sammie Jo. She looked sweet. Domestic. Gentle, even. Gone was the leather, the loud makeup, the in-your-face swagger. The change staggered him. He climbed out of the Bronco in minor shock.

"Honey, you're here!" Sammie Jo cried. "Isn't it cute? We'll have so much fun fixing it up. Oh, our first place together," she gushed.

Oh, God. *One month.* He could keep up this horrible charade for one month. Jeff Winston deserved that long from him in return for all Jeff had done for him in his darkest days. Gray put one foot in front of him. Then his other foot. One step at a time. One second at a time. *Just keep going. Keep moving.*

Sammie Jo rushed up to him excitedly. "I knew you'd

love it, so I went ahead and started the paperwork. We've only rented it for six months. If you hate it, you won't have to live here that long." She smiled up winningly at him.

"How could I say no to you?" he managed to choke out.

She threw her arms around his neck and kissed him soundly on the mouth. He was so stunned he just stood there and let her.

"Well, don't you two make the most darling couple?" the Realtor cooed from behind Sammie Jo.

Couple? A tiny voice wailed in the back of his mind, *Nooooooo.* One. Month.

He shook hands and murmured appropriate inanities as Sammie Jo introduced him to the Realtor. In a fugue state that made him feel more robot than man, he followed the women inside and duly signed a lease.

He roused enough from his state of horror to register faint surprise at Sammie Jo's signature. Samantha Jessup. Samantha, huh? Suddenly, the idea of calling her Sam didn't seem so wrong. As a derivative of Samantha, it wasn't nearly as masculine and awkward as he'd thought it was. Thankfully, as soon as she dropped a hint about him officially carrying her over the threshold now that it was theirs, the Realtor laughed and took her leave.

"Are you okay?" Sammie Jo mumbled in concern as soon as the Realtor's car door slammed shut.

"What have you done—" he started as they stood on the porch and watched the woman's car pull out of the driveway.

"Inside, sweetheart," she murmured, *sotto voce.* "The neighbors will be watching."

"In that case…" He bent down and swept his arms

around her. He lifted her in his arms and strode toward the front door. But Lord, the price of it. Using techniques a trauma therapist had taught him, he blanked his mind completely. And then, bit by bit, he let in the details of this one moment. The cool air. The autumn smell of burned leaves. The weight and softness of the woman in his arms. A hint of roses as she shifted slightly. The way his breathing deepened in response to her.

Laughing, she reached down to open the door for him. He added the sultry delight in her laughter to his inventory of sensations.

Carefully, carefully he reached past this moment to the next safest thing: his job. This was a cover. They had to establish themselves as a couple. Being absolutely certain to let no emotion creep into him, he paused in the doorway and leaned his head down to kiss her.

What he hadn't counted on was her kissing him back. On her mouth opening in surprise beneath his, on her tasting like chantilly cream, all sweet and fluffy with a hint of vanilla. Her arms went around his neck, and she moaned in her throat. She went soft and warm in his arms, cuddling up against him like a purring kitten. Gone was the predator, replaced by this entirely foreign—and entirely *female*—female.

She casually smashed through every barrier he'd erected for himself, ripping away the fog he'd wrapped himself in like a protective blanket. All that was left was something raw and unnamable, both needy and violent. It scared the living hell out of him.

But the job demanded it, right? It was all part of their cover. It was okay. He let go of the fear and allowed in the sensations bombarding him from every direction. He tested her lips with the tip of his tongue and they were as tasty and alluring as the rest of her. She kissed him back eagerly, almost as if she'd been thinking about it for a while and wondering what it would be like.

And then the heat really amped up between them. What changed, he wasn't sure. But one second they were kissing, and the next, they were *kissing*. She was pulling his head down to hers, he was plundering her mouth with lips and tongue, she was devouring him back, and raging need to get her naked roared through him.

He stepped all the way inside the house and kicked the door shut. Not breaking the incendiary kiss, he let her body slide down to the floor slowly, registering every feminine curve that pressed wantonly against him. It had been so long. So very long…

"You're making me think naughty thoughts," she gasped.

"That's how you like it, isn't it?" he murmured back. "Naughty."

Her lips curved in a smile so smoking hot he was vaguely surprised his hair didn't catch on fire. "I guess you'll just have to find out for yourself."

And with that, she stepped back from him. She spun into the room off the left of the tiny foyer. Her full skirt twirled around her and she looked like a fresh, young girl. Where had the edgy, tough goth chick disappeared to? He fought to form a coherent thought and came up with, "What's with the retro virgin look?"

She laughed gaily. "I gather from the enthusiastic welcome home that you like the look?"

He shrugged. "The neighbors were watching." He wished the words back as soon as he saw her face fall in disappointment. But then she rushed to the corner, yanking at the edge of a horrible gold shag carpet that looked nearly original to the house.

"Check out the hardwood beneath this hideous stuff. Once we pull up the carpet and buff the floor, it'll be gorgeous."

"I'm not doing home improvement projects on our hideout!"

"But that's our cover. We're setting up our first home together. If folks see us doing yard work and painting and replacing carpet, they'll know we're moving in for good. They'll open up to us."

"How long are we supposed to spend playing house and hoping it leads to some information?"

"As long as it takes," she answered blithely.

"You're mad."

She threw him a disingenuously innocent look. "Why, I'm not mad at all. I'm thrilled. Let's make a list and head out to the home-improvement store right now. Shelly—she's the Realtor—told me where it is."

"Seriously, Sam. This is nuts."

"Seriously, Gray. It'll work. Trust me."

"I hardly know you! How am I supposed to be your fiancé full-time and in public, no less?"

She laughed. "That kiss you laid on me was a bit more than a hello-it's-nice-to-meet-you peck. Just go with that."

"What the hell does that kiss have to do with anything?" He would have added that the kiss had just been an act for the nosy neighbors, but he didn't want to make that hurt look pass across her face again. And besides, it would have been a lie.

Damn. *It would have been a lie*. He'd kissed her because he'd been looking for an excuse to do so. The notion staggered him. He hadn't kissed a woman in five years. And it felt disloyal of him to do it now.

"C'mon. I've already got a shopping list started."

She dragged him around the house, for all the world acting like an enthusiastic bride with no sense of how much work she was proposing to take on with the various projects she had in mind. They'd be busy for weeks renovating this stupid house at the rate she was going. He didn't even want to contemplate what it was going to cost him emotionally to get through this. *It was a job. Just a job.* And somehow he suspected he'd be repeating that to himself more times than he cared to count in the days to come.

"How about we start a little smaller and see how things go?" he finally wedged in between bursts of ideas from her.

"Party pooper," she announced.

"Who's paying for all of this, anyway?"

"Jeff Winston. He gave me an expense account."

"Yes, but let's not bankrupt the guy."

She laughed. "In the first place, we could renovate the state of West Virginia and not bankrupt Jeff. And in the second, if we do a great job on the place, our lease includes an option to buy. Jeff can buy it and sell it for a profit."

"Not in this housing market," he snorted.

"You're too practical for your own good," she declared. "You need to loosen up."

He'd heard that before. But for the past few years, he hadn't cared. From her, though, it stung a little.

As they pulled into the parking lot of a home-improvement store a little while later, though, he had to admit her enthusiasm was contagious.

She exclaimed, "This place is so cool! It's a time warp, I'm tellin' ya."

He gazed around the parking lot, populated entirely with vintage cars. Frankly, he found it a little creepy. "Come on, June," he grumbled.

"Who?"

"June Cleaver." He wasn't completely ignorant when it came to American TV.

She flashed him one of those heart-stopping smiles of hers. "Ahh, if only you knew what I'm capable of in the dark. You'd never call me that."

His heart actually skipped a beat. Her sunglasses today were oversize things with white plastic frames and rhinestones that made him think of Marilyn Monroe. He'd give anything to be able to see past those dark lenses to her eyes right now. Was she just teasing him, or was there an edge of truth to her words? Did he detect a hint of an offer in that flirtatious comment? Did he dare contemplate taking her up on it?

She looped her arm in his as he headed for the store. She murmured offhandedly, "That chaste little peck you laid on me back at the house doesn't even constitute a warm-up kiss in my world."

Mentally, his jaw dropped. He swore under his breath at the places his thoughts raced off to and refused to come back from. And that was why she probably got away with buying hundreds of dollars' worth more of paint and light fixtures and curtain rods than they needed. She even managed to cram a half dozen scrawny rosebushes in the back of the Bronco.

As he pulled out of the parking lot, he grumbled, "You took blatant advantage of my distraction to bankrupt Jeff."

"My mother always told me, 'Honey, if you've got it, use it.'"

He rolled his eyes. "I don't like your mother."

Her voice dropped into a grim, tense register he'd never heard out of her before. "Neither do I."

He peered over at her, but she was staring straight ahead and those damned shades gave away nothing. "What's wrong with her?" he ventured to ask.

"I would have to know where she is to be able to answer that fully."

Whoa. "Did she leave you?"

"No." A sigh. "I left her. But by the time I grew up enough to go back and find her, she was gone. Moved away, I guess."

"And with all of Winston Enterprise's resources you haven't been able to locate her?" he blurted, surprised.

"Didn't look."

Instinct told him to let the subject drop. She'd run away from home, huh? How young? It certainly explained her harder edges. So who was the soft, sweet Sammie Jo who'd spent the past few hours with him... and who was suddenly and completely absent?

Although the house was nominally furnished, they still spent much of the afternoon assembling simple furniture and establishing that Sam didn't know a flathead from a Phillips screwdriver. She could clean with a vengeance, however, and the little house fairly sparkled before she slowed down enough to help him tape up black-out shades in a bedroom for her. For his part, he stayed busy and did his best not to think at all. Not to remember. Another first house. Another life.

Sam called him from the living room. She'd unpacked the NRQZ-approved, flat-screen TV he'd carried in for her, but she needed help hooking it to the house's cable system. The phone, electricity and cable were already turned on, so they got a picture right away. She was in transports of ecstasy.

"TV junkie much?" he asked as she nearly bowled him over with a hug of thanks.

Another woman's laughter echoed in his head. Another woman's arms around him. He must not remember!

Sam was speaking. "…have no idea. How else am I supposed to spend my nights?"

His arms tightened involuntarily around her. "I can think of a few ways."

She swatted his arm before he released her and headed for the kitchen. He'd discovered a while back that kitchens were great places to work off a case of panic. Lots of fussy little jobs to do with his hands and attention to detail to distract him. Tomorrow he'd have to go grocery shopping. He already had supplies for a simple spaghetti alfredo in deference to Sam's vegetarian preferences, and he set about whipping it up.

They ate a late lunch on tray tables in the living room, which felt cave-like with the windows draped in thick curtains. She'd taken out her contacts, and her eyes glowed an unearthly shade that was more than a little unsettling. He was fascinated, though, by how Sam continuously cycled through no less than four television shows. "You're going to wear that remote out," he commented.

"Get your own if you're worried about it," she shot back.

The tough, mouthy version of Sammie Jo was back, apparently. Which one was the real person and which one the act? It was hard to tell. He had to give her credit for distracting him, though. He'd made it all the way through the meal without one flashback. *Small steps, buddy. Small steps.*

"So how do we go about gathering all this supposed intel the neighbors possess?" he asked.

"Can you bake?" she asked obliquely.

"What does that have to do with anything?"

"Well, all I can bake are brownies out of a box. That'll do in a pinch, but if you can do anything better like some muffins or bread, that would be helpful."

"You want me to bake my way to mission success?" he challenged incredulously.

"Exactly. The neighbors will bring food to welcome us to the neighborhood and give them an excuse to scope us out. We'll reciprocate, of course. Enter your baked goods. Then I'll draw them out and get them gossiping. And that's when I'll get the dirt on Proctor and whatever else is going on around here. By tomorrow, news of Luke's murder will be all over the county if it isn't already. Everyone will be talking about him, too."

"And when will this food exchange commence?"

"I give it another hour."

She wasn't far wrong. It was actually more like an hour and a half, but he was still impressed. When the doorbell rang, Sam raced for the bathroom to put in her contacts while he answered it. The first neighbor to arrive, casserole dish in hand, was a retired school teacher who lived next door, Maddie Mercer. She struck him as the type to peer out of her windows at all hours of the day and night at the slightest noise or movement. He was worried about the quantity and quality of her prying. Miss Maddie could be a problem going forward. She did, however, make the best homemade macaroni and cheese he'd ever tasted.

As more neighbors commenced dropping in, he lost

track of their names, addresses and connections to one another. And he was usually pretty good at that sort of thing. But Sam made it look effortless, and by early evening seemed to have the genealogies of most of this portion of West Virginia unraveled.

She picked unenthusiastically at a green bean casserole someone had brought over, but he had no qualms about digging into the surprisingly tasty food. At the moment, he was working his way through a plate of some succulent barbecued meat dish.

"What is this I'm eating?" he asked her.

"Don't ask. If it tastes good, just go with it. In this part of the country, it could be anything from pork to possum."

The meat abruptly lost its savor, and he went back to Miss Maddie's macaroni and cheese, which even Sam had declared "fantabulous."

She waited until he had a mouthful of cheesy goodness to say without warning, "So. I assume you know about the *other* radio antenna array in the NRQZ. The classified one the NSA runs that pretends it's a Naval Communications and Signal station."

He choked but managed not to kill himself swallowing. "I can neither confirm nor deny any knowledge of any classified sites in this area."

"You seriously claim not to know that the NSA has a gigantic antenna array at the navy's Shady Grove station?"

"I don't confirm or deny anything," he retorted.

"Ahh. I know that game. That's a yes. If you could deny it, you would. Or you'd lie. Why didn't you? Afraid I could read you and recognize a fib?"

Damn, that woman was quick. Only way to fight

fire was with fire. He shot back at her, "How old were you when you ran away from home?"

"Fifteen," she blurted, looking startled.

Lord, that was young. And naive. So easy to get in awful trouble at that age. His heart ached a little for the scared, angry kid she must have been. "Why'd you go?"

"The usual reasons. I was pissed off at the world, sure I could get it right on my own and sick of the crap at home."

"What kind of crap?"

"The usual kind that makes kids run away." She got up and carried their paper plates to the trash can in the kitchen. "I did the dishes, honey," she called out to him in a saccharine voice.

Hmm. Abuse? Alcohol? Drugs? Arguments? All of the above? Abruptly, he felt incredibly lucky to have had the upbringing he had. He might not have had a dad, but his mom had been a great single parent. He'd have to give her a call when he finished this mission and tell her so.

Last night hadn't included much sleep, not to mention all the shopping and chores today. He called it a night early, and went into his room to face a strange bed. He still struggled with them. After seeing his own bed soaked and dripping with blood—

He slammed the door shut on that memory as hard and fast as he could. That particular chamber of horrors could swallow him in clinical depression for days.

He fell asleep surprisingly fast, but woke up abruptly in the middle of the night. His watch said it was nearly 2:00 a.m. Blue light flickered underneath his door. Sam must still be up and watching TV. He pulled on a T-shirt over his sweatpants and went out to check on her. She was wrapped practically to her nose in a fuzzy blanket and staring blankly at a bad comedy movie. Her eyes glowed like cinders nestled deep in the shadows of her face. But oddly, he felt like he was getting used to the sight of her surreal eyes. He doubted she was seeing a thing on the television.

"Hey," he said quietly. "Everything okay?"

She glanced up as if startled out of deep thoughts. "Yeah. Fine."

He sat down beside her. "You don't look fine."

"I'm good," she insisted.

He wasn't buying that for a minute. "Tell me about it. How did your logic go? If we're going to be partners and it's going to put my life in danger, I have a right to know."

"Nothing in my past is going to endanger you."

Thinking about her past, huh? "They're just memories. They don't have the power to hurt you unless you let them." Her gaze snapped to him as he continued, "All that exists is right now. The past is gone and the future has yet to happen. People get too wrapped up in regretting the one and fearing the other."

"My, that's philosophical of you, Mr. Pierce."

"Just keeping it real. Whatever's bugging you isn't here right now. It's a calm night, you have your cable TV back, and you look warm and cozy. Enjoy the moment."

She ventured a small smile at him. In the light of the television, her eyes glowed a surreal shade of yellow that was a little unnerving. "The company's not half-bad, either," she murmured.

Their gazes met. She leaned toward him and he met her halfway. But he merely gave her a gentle kiss on the cheek. He made a policy of never taking advantage of a woman's emotional weakness to hit on her. "Want some hot chocolate?" he asked. "I hear it's a surefire cure for all that ails a girl."

"Who taught you so much about women?"

"My mother."

"You're a mama's boy?" she asked in surprise.

"It was just the two of us when I was a kid. We were close."

"Do you talk to her often?"

The wistful undertone in Sam's voice took on new significance for him. "We talk as often as I can come up for air. She'd like you. She approves of spunky women."

His mother had approved of another young woman a long time ago. The pain started to come, but he shoved it back ruthlessly, focusing instead on the woman seated next to him.

Hunger flashed across Sam's face. It must be terrible not having any parents. He was a grown man and didn't exactly need his mother to tell him how to live, but it was still powerful to know someone out there loved him with a mother's fierceness. It had saved his life more than once in the past five years.

He made two cups of hot chocolate and carried them back to the living room. They sipped in companionable silence.

"Why didn't you lay a big, wet kiss on me just now?" Sam asked without warning.

"Because it wouldn't be sporting to take advantage of you in that way."

"*Sporting?* Are you English or something? That's not the first time you've said something that sounded like the British Broadcasting Corporation."

"Or something," he answered evasively.

"If you don't start telling me about yourself, I'm calling Jeff tomorrow and getting all the dirt on you."

He groaned. "I quake in my boots at the stories he could tell you. We were fraternity brothers in college."

She grinned knowingly. "Several of the Code X guys are old frat brothers of his. You all must have been really close."

"We were. Who else is in Code X from the old gang?"

"Aiden McKay and Trenton Hollings."

"Which are they? Jeep tossers or eagle eyes?"

"Neither. The researchers are working on different gene sets for each one of us. Aiden swims like a fish and can hold his breath forever, and Trent is *fast*. His quick twitch reflexes are off the charts. I hear Jeff's recruiting someone else as we speak. I think Doc Jones has some mental modifications in mind for the next test subject."

"Who's Doc Jones, exactly?"

"Gemma Jones. She's one of the leading geneticists in the world. Brilliant woman, if a bit of a geek."

"Mental modifications like how?"

"Are you volunteering for the treatment?" she asked.

He reared back, shocked. He would never change himself into a—

A sniff interrupted his train of thought. "Don't want to be a *freak* like me, huh? Why am I not surprised?" She surged up out of her blanket and stormed into her bedroom. The door closed with an ominously soft click.

What in the hell had he done? He never called her a freak! He might have thought it, but a guy couldn't be convicted of just thinking a word. Except she must have seen it in his eyes...he sighed...and he ought to be man enough to admit it.

He went to her door and knocked gently. "Sammie Jo? Can we talk?"

Nothing.

"Sam? Please. I'm sorry."

Still nothing.

"I'm an ass."

Still nothing. *Damn.*

"You're not a freak."

The door cracked open. Her teary gaze looked like molten gold. A quicksilver tear trembled on her cheek. She looked supernatural—stunning and beautiful.

"I truly am sorry. Your special abilities take a little getting used to. Please bear with me while I adjust."

"Now I know what the guys were talking about." He must have looked confused, because she clarified, "Jeff and Aiden were comparing notes about how it sucked when their girlfriends thought they were completely bizzaro."

"You're not bizzaro," he declared. "Just your clothes are," he teased gently.

"Hey! I dressed conservative to come to Hickville."

He made a face. "I'd hate to see your idea of far-out attire."

"That can be arranged," she threatened. A smile broke through and lit her face.

Without the wild makeup her skin was like satin, and its creamy contrast to her hair was striking. "Is that your natural hair color?" he asked.

"Actually, yes."

"Impressive."

"It's just genetics," she commented dryly.

He leaned against the door frame as she opened the door fully. Her pajama pants were baby-blue flannel with cute cartoon sheep sprinkled over them like fluffy marshmallows. The thin white tank T-shirt she wore stood in starkly sexy contrast, announcing in no uncertain terms that she was all woman and nicely endowed. She obviously hadn't needed much help under that leather jacket to create that impressive cleavage. *Must concentrate. Build rapport.* And avoid sexual thoughts since she also appeared to be some kind of mind reader.

"Have your eyes always been that color?" he asked curiously.

"No. They used to be light brown. The changes to my DNA changed both the inside and outside of my eyeballs."

"Did it hurt?"

"No. The treatment was just a series of shots, and the changes were gradual. I've been in the program long enough now that Gemma thinks my modifications are permanent. We've stopped the shots to see if the changes remain."

"And if they don't?"

"I'll go back to taking the shots."

Wow. She didn't hesitate for a moment when she said that. "So you wouldn't consider letting your eyesight return to normal?"

She shook her head. "Once you've experienced life this way, you don't want to go back."

"How's that?"

"I see everything so much more clearly than I used to. It would be like getting used to 3D, HD television and then going back to a 1960s vintage black-and-white TV."

That actually made sense. "What about health side effects?"

"I'll deal with them if and when they manifest. So far, the only real downside is the whole business of sunlight. It has forced me to live more like a vampire than most folks. It took a little getting used to. That and learning to remember other people can't see what I can."

That gave him pause. What did she see when she looked at him? "I'd be afraid of going blind or something terrible later on," he commented.

She shrugged. "There are no guarantees in life, are there? I could be hit by a car tomorrow, and then it wouldn't matter what happens to my vision down the road. Weren't you the one who was just telling me to live in the moment and not fear the future?"

He scowled at having his words turned back on him like that. "Fine. You may be right. But still. I'd worry about the consequences of doing something so drastic to myself."

"It's not like I got a tattoo," she declared indignantly. "Now *that's* something permanent and regrettable down the road."

He laughed. "You're telling me the original wild child doesn't have a tat or two tucked away somewhere on her person?"

She rolled her eyes. "I may dress goth, but I like the skin I came in just the way it is. I never went for tramp stamps."

Frankly, that surprised him. He was careful to keep his expression neutral, however, and not reveal his thoughts. She certainly was an odd mixture of contrasts. Tough and demure, biker chick and church lady, occasionally sensible and often completely impulsive. She didn't hesitate to change her eyesight radically, but she wouldn't dream of marking her skin.

Reflectively, he murmured, "Which version of you is the real one?"

She tilted her head to stare at him. "Who says they're not all me? I don't have to be just one kind of person, do I? Surely you're not always the same guy. In your work as a spy, I'll bet you put on all kinds of personas—different jobs, lifestyles, income and educational levels. You just can't pull off checkered-flannel shirts. But I could see you as a surfing bum or Wall Street banker about equally well."

"I do like to surf."

"See? Behind that ramrod-stiff demeanor, you're a multidimensional guy, after all."

He wasn't ramrod-stiff, thank you very much; he was organized. Logical. Rational. All qualities that had saved his life before and would no doubt do so again.

He must have frowned because she reached up and smoothed her fingertips across his brow. "Live dangerously," she murmured. "Embrace a little variety."

"I'm not *that* big a stick in the mud."

Sammie grinned. "You just keep telling yourself that."

He stepped forward until they stood chest to chest. There was one way to win this argument fast. It would certainly be living dangerously to kiss her into oblivion. Or rather, let her kiss him there. He started the journey gently by bending his head to hers. Exhaling lightly against her temple. Tilting her chin up with a fingertip. Just a light touch of lips to lips. A promise. A hint of more.

He wasn't sure how fragile she was feeling and he let her call the shots, let her lean in against him, let her kiss her way across his neck and toy with the short hair at the back of his neck. But at some point he wanted more. He slipped a hand under the warm weight of her hair and lifted her face to fit his mouth more closely against hers to taste her warmth and softness. He could sip at her all night like this. She was better than a fine wine on his tongue, more savory and complex. The bite of her personality lent just enough zing to keep her from becoming predictable. Oh, yes. She was a woman to be tasted time after time.

She drew a sharp breath and rose on tiptoe, grabbing the back of his head without warning and imploding in his arms. "I'm not supposed to want another man yet," she mumbled against his lips.

"Why not?"

"Two weeks mandatory man-hating, otherwise I risk a rebound relationship. I'm only one week post-breakup."

"Live dangerously, Sam. Embrace variety."

"Smart aleck. Shut up and kiss me."

That he could do. And shockingly, he *wanted* to do it. He didn't stop to think or to question it. He merely stepped into her room, turning her until she pressed back against the wall. Her right leg crept up and wrapped around his hips. It was entirely natural to catch her waist, and as he supported her weight more fully, her left leg joined the right. She didn't weigh much, not that he cared. He didn't need to be able to lift a Jeep to hold her tight as she sucked his tonsils out of his throat.

She kissed with as much gusto as she did everything, her exuberance for life flowing over him like a dancing and healing stream. How long had it been since he'd felt anything like *that?* It soothed him and washed his soul clean, and for the first time in years, he could really breathe. He tore his mouth away from hers to drag in a big, full breath. And another. Who'd have guessed the simple act of breathing could feel so good? Or furthermore, that kissing this woman would make it so?

He stared down at her, amazed.

"What?" she demanded. "Have I grown feathers or something?"

"Good Lord, no. They didn't actually use eagle DNA on you, did they?"

She laughed. "No. It was all my own DNA and stem cells they manipulated."

Relieved, he let out his breath. And even that felt good.

"I think I'm going to be able to sleep now," she murmured. "I guess I'm going to have to get on a more normal schedule if we're going to be social with the neighbors."

"Hey, it was your idea to set up house," he replied.

"When will I quit opening my big mouth and getting into trouble?" she groused.

"I don't know about that. I rather liked it when you opened your mouth."

Her eyes twinkled merrily. "You have no idea, big guy. No idea at all."

And maybe the images her comment conjured were why he stumbled as he let her push him backward out of her room. He stood in front of her closed door and stared at it for a long time. What had just happened to him? For a moment there, he'd almost felt...normal.

Except he of all people was anything but normal. He was Humpty Dumpty. Irrecoverably, irretrievably broken, and nothing and nobody was going to put him back together again.

Chapter 5

It felt weird to wake up before noon, but Sammie Jo dutifully dragged herself out of bed and dressed in simple jeans and a sweatshirt. Of course the sweatshirt had a skull and crossbones on it, but it was the best she could do at approaching normal. In a fit of rebellion against suburbia, she chose her steampunk sunglasses, round lenses with leather flaps at the sides that nicely sealed out secondary sunlight.

Gray was nowhere to be found in the house. She stepped out onto the front porch and was shocked to see him on his knees, efficiently planting her rosebushes. Oh, God. He looked *so* hot. Who knew he'd wear gardening so well? He was carefully forming mounds of dirt in the holes, spreading the roots out symmetrically, and packing enriched planting soil around them.

"Where'd you learn how to plant roses properly?" she asked.

He looked up, a smudge of dirt endearingly tipping his nose. "My granny was a big rose gardener."

"Can I help?"

"Sure. Grab a shovel and dig the next hole."

She started digging, the rich smell of warm earth rising around her. It was strangely soothing.

"Nice shades," he commented.

"Thanks. Personal faves of mine."

"Your eyes doing okay?"

She smiled at his concern. "Fine. These are super dark and the leather flaps—" She broke off as a trio of police cars rounded the corner fast, lights flashing, but sirens silenced. The vehicles raced past, drove up the hill at the back of the neighborhood and stopped in front of the last house, parking in a defensive formation.

"What's that about?" she asked under her breath.

"Don't know."

They planted another rosebush as a half dozen sheriff's deputies surged out of their cars and clustered at the front door of a red brick ranch that looked like every other house in this neighborhood.

On cue, Maddie Mercer stepped out on her front porch in a housedress and slippers to watch the show.

"Back in a sec," Sammie Jo murmured. She strolled over to join the woman, wiping dirt off her hands onto her jeans as she went. "Hey, Miss Maddie. Any idea what's going on?"

The older woman gave her an arch look. "Word has it a young man was found dead."

"Right there in that house?" Sammie Jo asked in mock horror.

"Oh, no. He was found back up in the hollers a ways. Probably a fight over a moonshine still. This is a dry county, you know."

Sammie Jo acted appropriately scandalized. "Then why are the police at that house?"

"Dead guy must've been mixed up with that Proctor gang," Miss Maddie replied knowingly.

"Proctor gang?" Gray asked as he materialized at her side. Sam slipped an arm around his waist and was delighted that he didn't go board stiff at the contact.

She leaned into his warmth and strength as Miss Maddie drew a deep breath to impart clearly treasured gossip. "Wendall Proctor is the leader of a group of hippies and weirdos hereabouts. They're all hepped up about going off the grid. Most of them are looking to live all back-to-nature and organic. That Proctor guy has turned his property into practically a cult compound full of 'em. Women and kids are up there, too. But—" she leaned forward and her voice dropped to a juicy whisper "—I hear there's some wackos among 'em. You know, the kind who think there's government conspiracies all around, and someone's trying to kill them."

Gray nodded toward the police cars. "It looks like no good has already come of it."

Miss Maddie snorted in agreement. "Four of Proctor's boys rented that house a few months back. Mighty suspicious if you ask me. Men coming and going from that place and at all hours of the day and night. No surprise they're mixed up in that young fella's death."

As the woman fell silent, Sammie Jo fanned the gossip flames. "Do you suppose the police will arrest someone?"

"Oughtta arrest 'em all. Throw 'em clean out of the Zone. Damn outsiders."

Gray piped up in his most charming voice, "I hope you won't consider us outsiders for long, Miss Maddie. You make the best macaroni and cheese I've ever tasted, and I'd be mighty sad not to get any more of it."

The woman simpered under his warm regard, and behind her shades, Sammie Jo rolled her eyes.

"Police have been in there a long time if they're just picking someone up," Miss Maddie announced. Her voice dropped in volume. "I'll bet they've got a search warrant."

"You think?" Sammie Jo murmured back. "Maybe I should go for a jog up that way and see if they're tossing the place."

"Oh, my child, I wouldn't go near there. What if it turns into a shoot-out?"

"I'll run away. And I'm really fast."

Gray interrupted. "Miss Maddie has a point, sweetie. I'd hate to see you get hurt."

Sweetie? Grayson Pierce had called her sweetie! How was it one stupid little word that he didn't even mean could knock her completely off balance like that? Of course, it wasn't the word that did it. It was the man saying it who messed her up so bad. Being around him was like hanging out with Prince Charming. And just like a fairy tale, he was too perfect to be real.

She didn't know what his flaw was or where the chinks in the armor might be, but he had to have some. He *had* to. Otherwise, her entire conception of the world was wrong. She'd known for a long time that life was not fair. That happiness was not guaranteed, nor even likely, at the end of the day. A person was born; their life sucked; they died. That's how it went. If she happened to grab a few moments of transitory pleasure along the way, then she was luckier than most.

But this man challenged all of that. If men like him were real, then she had spent her entire adult life failing to search for a man like him. And what a waste would that have been? Had she been completely, totally wrong about everything?

"Honey? Are you okay?"

Honey? Her heart pitter-pattered until she mentally shook herself. "Yes. Of course. I was just thinking about that poor man. The one who died. Do they know who he was?"

Miss Maddie supplied, "Zimmer's the name. Not from around here. Hooked up with Proctor as soon as he got here. Must have known someone on the inside. Way I hear it, Wendall's pretty cautious about outsiders."

"Now why's that, I wonder?" Sammie Jo speculated. "Do you suppose he's got something to hide?"

"Why else would he have all those big fences and guys with guns patrolling his place?" Miss Maddie replied.

Sammie Jo ventured a glance at Gray, who nodded at her infinitesimally. In a hushed voice, she asked Miss Maddie, "Do you suppose it's something illegal?"

"Most folks around here think it's moonshine or marijuana. But I think it's something bigger."

"Why do you say that?" Sammie Jo prompted.

"People been bootleggin' and smokin' weed in these parts forever. And there's never been a need for guns and electric fences before. I think Proctor's going to pull one of those fruit punch massacres."

Alarmed, Sammie Jo blurted, "A what?"

"He's gonna put rat poison or something in fruit punch and make 'em all drink it. The women and kids and everyone."

It wasn't much of a stretch to act suitably shocked. "That's terrible!"

Miss Maddie wagged a warning finger at them. "You

mark my words. No good's coming out of that place or that Proctor guy."

The conversation devolved into meaningless gossip about other neighbors in the area, and Sammie Jo mostly tuned out. She made an appropriate noise of sympathy or shock to keep Miss Maddie happy, but her mind raced elsewhere.

A cult, huh? Why would Jeff Winston care about a bunch of hippies and conspiracy theorists tucked away in the backwoods of West Virginia? There had to be more to this Proctor guy than met the eye. One thing she knew for sure. It was time to have a conversation with her boss.

They went back to the roses and planted the last bush in silence. When they retreated into the house, Sammie Jo turned to Gray immediately. "I need to make a phone call."

"To Jeff?"

"Exactly. Do you suppose the phone line here in the house is secure?"

"I doubt anyone would have tapped the phone on a vacant house, and I checked the box on the telephone pole in the backyard early this morning. It's clean for now."

Cautious man. Of course, just because the phone was safe today didn't mean it would be safe tomorrow. She nodded and headed toward the kitchen.

Gray called from down the hall, "I'm going to jump in the shower. Tell Jeff I'll call him when I get out. I've got a couple of questions about other stuff for him."

Her mental antenna shot up and wiggled warningly. What other stuff? Was he going to pump Jeff for information about her? She shook off the paranoia. Jeff and Gray had known each other forever. For all she knew, they had other business dealings together. It wasn't like Jeff Winston told her everything about his family's vast corporate empire.

She, however, was not above snooping about her partner. The sound of running water came out of the bathroom and she dialed the Winston Ops Center's main line quickly. She recognized the Slavic accent of the duty controller.

"Hey, Novak, it's Sam. Is Jeff about?"

In a moment, her boss's deep voice came on the line. "How's it going, Sam? You and Gray getting along?"

Memory of the searing kisses they'd shared flashed through her mind, and she stammered, "Yeah. Sure. Great guy. So why in heck did you send the two of us out here?"

"Have you found anything?" he asked cautiously.

"Plenty. Your guy, Luke Zimmer, is dead. He was gutted and dumped in the woods behind his place."

"Zimmer was murdered?" Jeff exclaimed.

"Brutally."

Jeff swore roundly.

"Talk to me, boss."

"I sent Zimmer out there to infiltrate a group of folks who ostensibly want to live completely off the grid."

"Wendall Proctor's group?" she asked.

"Exactly. I wanted you two to contact Luke. Give him support and relay information to me from him. That way there'd be no direct connection between him and me."

She made the logical leap immediately. "You were worried Proctor would figure out you and Luke were in cahoots, and you needed a middleman to act as a go-between?"

"Right."

"What was Luke supposed to find out about the Proctor gang for you?"

"What the hell they're up to. I have reason to believe they're far more than an antigovernment separatist group."

"The way I hear it, there's a commune of folks living at his place who want to live technology- and chemical-free."

"Proctor's using them for cover," Jeff replied impatiently. "They're not the heart of his organization."

"Who is?"

"That's what Luke was supposed to find out."

"Since he's dead, I guess that means Gray and I are going to have to make a run at this Proctor guy directly."

"No!"

"What other choice do we have, Jeff?"

"I'll figure out something. But it's too dangerous. I'd lay odds Proctor's behind Zimmer's murder."

That was a bet she wouldn't take. She frowned. Contrary to popular belief, she didn't actually have a death wish. And she was no great fan of serious danger, either. However, she and Gray were already here. "The two of us are in place. We already have a cover story, and we're inserting ourselves into the local community. How long is it going to take you to find another appropriate mole who's also a competent operator, build him or her a cover and move that person into the area without arousing suspicion?"

"You've figured out Gray's competent, eh?"

"It's hard to miss, Jeff. But speaking of which, is everything okay with him?"

"Why do you ask?"

"Now and then I get a flash of…something from

him. Pain. Or maybe grief. It's pretty dark, whatever it is."

Jeff's reply was sharp and immediate. "Leave it alone, Sam. Don't ask and don't pry."

Taken aback by how vehement her boss had gone on her all of a sudden, she replied placatingly, "Okay, okay. I'll leave it alone." Sheesh. She couldn't remember the last time she'd heard Jeff get that tight that fast. She changed the subject. "Gray said he'd call you when he gets out of the shower. You gonna be around for a few more minutes to take his call?"

"Jenn and I are on our way to go parasailing, but I'll have Novak forward his call to my cell phone."

"'Kay. Have fun and don't kill Jennifer. We all like her more than you."

Jeff laughed. "Me, too." His voice took on a serious note. "I promise I'll keep her safe."

Sammie Jo thought she heard a woman's warm, contralto laughter in the background as the phone disconnected. Jeff had been a different man since he met his fiancée, Jennifer Blackfoot, earlier this year.

She felt Gray's humid body heat behind her before she heard him. She turned, startled to realize he'd gotten right up behind her without her hearing a thing. *And he had no shirt on.* Hubba, hubba, that guy had a nice chest. And not an ounce of fat around his waist. Check out those rippling rows of cut abs! "Dang, you're quiet."

"I'm a superspy, remember?"

"Right." A worrisome thought occurred to her. "How much of my talk with Jeff did you hear?"

"I caught something about not killing his fiancée."

She hoped she didn't look too relieved as she passed him the phone. Given how intensely Jeff had reacted to her question about Gray, she didn't think she wanted to see Gray's reaction to the notion of her prying into his deeply mysterious past.

She set about tossing a salad and shamelessly eavesdropping while Gray dialed Jeff.

"Hey, bro," Gray announced. He listened in silence for a few moments, then, "Oh, yeah. It was definitely murder. Sam was able to see where he was attacked in his kitchen and dragged out of his house. The guy's body was gutted with surgical precision. Now that the guy we were supposed to help is dead, what do you want us to do?"

A long silence ensued while Jeff no doubt repeated what he'd already told her.

Then Gray surprised her by asking, "Sam, could you go into my bedroom, find all the paper files I had on Luke Zimmer, and bring them in here? I'd like to look at them."

"Sure." Liar, liar, pants on fire. He wanted to get her out of the room so he could talk to Jeff about her. She strode out of the kitchen but stopped just out of sight in the hall.

Gray said quietly in response to some question by Jeff, "Absolutely. Sam's been a godsend. But what's her story? She ran away from home at fifteen? How rough did things get for her?"

The silence that followed was maddening. She'd never talked with Jeff directly about her early years, but she assumed he knew most of the sordid details. He had an entire team of researchers every bit as good as her, and they could dig up just about anything on anyone with the resources they had in Winston's Operations Center.

"Interesting. Thanks."

What in the heck had Gray found "interesting?"

Damn, she felt at a terrible disadvantage all of a sudden. He apparently knew everything about her, now, and she knew nothing about him, except there was something terrible and painful in Gray's past that Jeff knew about and had warned her off in the strongest possible terms.

Didn't Jeff know telling her to leave it alone was practically an invitation to dig? She was a woman, after all, and had the curiosity of a cat. Damn him! And not a computer in sight for her to do a quick search on Gray. Double damn. She would have to come up with some excuse to go out alone for a while. Even if it meant driving to Charleston to get access to the internet, she *was* going to find out what secrets kept putting that horrible haunted look in Gray's eyes.

It sounded like the two men were winding up. She sprinted on her toes to Gray's room and snatched up the Zimmer pictures and notes. Being sure to make plenty of noise, she entered the kitchen in time to hear Gray say goodbye.

He served up two big bowls of salad and sat down across the kitchen table from her. "Are you thinking the same thing I am? That Proctor's bunch killed Luke?"

She nodded. "No doubt. Looks like the sheriff thinks so, too, or he wouldn't be searching a place rented by Proctor's guys."

Gray said quietly, "Are you also thinking that you and I should take over where Luke left off?"

"Yeah, but whatever Luke was poking into got him killed. I'm not sure I want to take up exactly where he left off." She could do without dying.

Gray frowned. "Two newcomers showing up on the heels of another newcomer's death is going to raise all kinds of red flags for Proctor if he's even half as paranoid as Miss Maddie says he is."

"We'll have to throw Proctor off the scent, then."

"How do you propose we do that?"

She turned over several ideas but discarded them all as too obvious. "Logically, we should make a point of meeting some people in the cult. Get to know them. Gradually earn their trust and get them to invite us in." Gray nodded. She continued, "Which is why that's the one thing we mustn't do."

Gray blinked. "Come again?"

"Best way to throw the enemy off is to do what he doesn't anticipate, right?"

"Sometimes," Gray allowed cautiously.

"So what's the one thing Proctor will least expect? If it's wild enough, he'll have to believe it's true."

Gray leaned back, staring at her speculatively. He commented offhandedly, "I suppose we could always march up to his front gate and announce that I'm a government agent and want into his cult."

"Exactly!" she exclaimed enthusiastically.

"I was kidding, Sam. That would be insane."

"And that's why he'd believe it."

"We'd be shot where we stood!"

She leaned forward eagerly. "Not necessarily. What if you said something along the lines of you don't like what the government's doing to its own citizens. You're concerned that Americans' constitutional rights to privacy are being trampled on."

"It sounds like the sort of message that would resonate with Proctor. Small problem, though. I'm not a government agent." He raised a hand as she opened her mouth to protest. "I'm out here purely as a favor to Jeff, and I don't have any official sanction from my employer, government or otherwise, to be here."

"So you're not officially a spy?" she asked in disappointment.

"Sorry. Not officially."

She perked up. "But you are one in your regular life, yes?"

"Sam," he warned.

"You have *got* to loosen up. I just think it's cool, that's all."

He made an exasperated sound.

"Can you pull some strings? Get someone credible to vouch that you are a government agent? Jeff can probably arrange that if you can't."

"I can arrange that myself, thank you," he replied wryly.

"There you have it. We convince Wendall Proctor that you're a spy and you want to help him bring down the government from the inside."

He shook his head. "It'll never work."

"Do you have a better idea?"

"Yes. We use your eyes to stand off at a distance and watch Wendall and company. See if we can figure out what they're up to."

"My way's better," she declared.

"My way's safer."

They glared at each other, at an impasse.

Gray sighed. "How about this? We try it my way first, and if it doesn't work, then we do it your way."

It would cost them a few days, but that might not be a bad thing. A little more separation from Luke's murder before they showed up on Proctor's doorstep might reduce the suspicion aimed at them. Or not.

They spent the rest of the morning tearing up carpet. It was hard enough work that Gray was mostly able to ignore the disturbing parallels of it to his previous life. He and Sam wrestled the heavy rolls of dusty carpet and truly foul padding out to the front curb together.

"Good riddance," he declared. And he did have to admit the oak flooring beneath the carpet was pretty decent. "I'll rent a buffer tomorrow and start sanding the floors. It's going to be a giant mess."

"Maybe I should run some errands, then, and be out of the house." She tried to sound casual, but her pulse leaped at the idea of getting her hands on a computer.

"We'll need a high-quality polyurethane stain and sealer if we're going to do the floors right."

She laughed at his seriousness over the job. "Do you like dark oak or light?"

"Dark. It gives more of a feeling of age. Importance. Which do you prefer?"

"Why, Grayson Pierce. Who'd have guessed you think about such things? I had no idea you're an interior decorator at heart."

He swatted her playfully on the behind as she walked past him into the house. She squealed and scooted out of his reach. "Hey, while we're redoing the floors, how do you feel about painting the walls? I can't stand that shade of beige."

He grinned. "I didn't know beige came in shades. Who's the decorator at heart now?"

"It's my superior eyesight. I see nuances in color that you normal people don't."

He laughed. "I bow to your supersight, madam. Paint the walls whatever color you want."

"*Any* color?"

"No black. And nothing with the words 'neon' or 'glow-in-the-dark' in its name."

"Stick in the mud."

"Yup. That's me."

And there it was again. That awful haunted look at the back of his gaze that shouted of unspeakable suffering. The only place she'd seen such pain before was in old photographs of Holocaust survivors. What in the *hell* had happened to him?

In anticipation of Sam needing to go different directions from him, Gray drove her to the nearest vintage car rental place to lease her a car for the next several months. He sincerely hoped they were done with their investigation long before then, but right now, they were all about the appearance of settling into the area.

No surprise, she squealed with delight at a late-'60s vintage, red Volkswagen Beetle and just had to have it.

"I'm calling it the Ladybug," she announced as he handed her the keys.

Knowing her, she would be painting black polka dots on it and mounting twin antennas on the windshield before long. "Do you name all your cars?" he asked curiously.

"Absolutely. It makes them feel loved. They run better that way."

"They're machines," he scoffed.

"You watch. If you don't show your Bronco some love and name it, it'll turn on you," she warned.

"Hippie."

"Pig."

He blinked, and then laughed. "You're going to fit in great around here. I bet you eat granola and can make your own yogurt, too."

"Yes to both," she answered indignantly.

"I'll see you back at the house in a few hours?" he asked in good humor.

"Deal. Love ya, babe."

His entire body went hot and cold. Sick to his stomach, he froze as she stood on tiptoe and laid a kiss on him that surely wasn't legal in public. The woman practically had carnal knowledge of his lungs. As she sashayed around to the driver's door of her Bug and swung her mile-long legs into the car, he caught sight of the car salesman gawking. Jealousy flared in his gut. *His* woman—

Not his woman. He stumbled to his own vehicle and climbed in. He rested his head on the steering wheel and concentrated on slowing his breathing to something resembling human. They were just words. She didn't mean them. Didn't know what they meant to him. It wasn't her fault.

"Oh, God," he groaned. A tear spilled onto his hands, hot and painful. What was he doing? He was being disloyal. Unfaithful. Traitorous.

He had to get his head in the game. Finish this damned mission as fast as possible and get away from Sammie Jo Jessup before she tore him to pieces. To that end, he guided his Bronco toward the Shady Grove Naval Signals Intelligence facility. Somewhere along the way, he achieved a state of numb emptiness. That was good. He had lots of practice functioning in that particular vacuum.

An armed guard waved him to a stop as he approached a heavily fortified gate and accompanying guard shack. "Can I help you, sir?"

He handed over an ID badge he dug out of his wallet. The guard stepped into the shack and ran it through a magnetic scanner. "Welcome to Shady Grove, Agent Pierce."

Chapter 6

Gray nodded grimly at the guard, who he knew to be a marine in civilian clothes. "I need to use a secure phone and a computer."

"Roger, sir. Here's your visitor badge. It needs to be in plain sight at all times. Head for the main entrance of that white building straight ahead and park in one of the visitor's spaces. Check in with the front desk, and they'll hook you up."

"Thanks." Out of long habit, Gray glanced around, looking for the security cameras he knew would be recording his every move. In true NSA fashion they were so cleverly disguised that even he, a seasoned operative, couldn't spot them. But then, security was particularly high at this facility. Although its existence was no big secret, its function—gathering every single electronic signal in all of North America and most of South America—was incredibly secret.

Another guard, even beefier and more brusque than the gate guard, examined his credentials again just inside the building. After deeming him not a security risk, this guard pointed him to the first door on the left. No surprise, when Gray opened the door yet another guard met him. This one was reasonably friendly, however, and escorted him down two flights of stairs and into a nondescript hallway. The guy stopped in front of a door and opened it for Gray.

He peered inside what turned out to be a small, no doubt electronically shielded room with a gray metal desk in the middle of it. Sitting on its surface were a black rotary telephone with a series of small, plastic lights mounted along its side, and a reasonably new-looking computer with a flat-screen monitor.

"Take your time, Agent Pierce. Get your fill before you have to go back to the Stone Age out there, eh?"

He grinned at the guard and nodded in commiseration. When the door had safely latched behind him, Gray dialed a memorized number on the STU-3 phone. The secure phone system was old, but reliable. And presumably it didn't give off a whole lot of electronic emissions.

"This is Brighton. Go ahead."

"Hi, sir. It's Grayson Pierce."

"Gray. How are things going in the Black Hole?"

"Interesting." He filled his boss in quickly on Sammie Jo's arrival and their discovery of Luke Zimmer's body. He omitted any reference to Sam's bizarre eyesight. He doubted his boss would believe him if he mentioned it anyway.

"And Winston? What's he up to?" Brighton asked.

There it was. The question of the day. Uncomfortable with the whole subject, Gray answered carefully, "He's worried about Wendall Proctor. I get the impression he thinks there's more to the Proctor group than a bunch of crazies who want to live off the grid."

"Really? Why's that?"

"No idea. Jeff's playing his cards close to the chest."

Brighton asked sharply, "Does he suspect you're investigating him for us?"

"I highly doubt it. We're old friends. Why would he think I'm spying on him?" The words tasted bitter on Gray's tongue. Why, indeed? Jeff had never been anything but upfront and loyal with him. Why should he expect any less from one of his oldest friends in return?

"Can't you weasel what Winston's worried about out of him, Gray?"

"Not without making him suspicious."

"What about his employee, this Jessup woman?"

"I don't think she knows any more than I do."

"Turn the charm on her. Get her to push Winston for more information."

Gray winced. He hated the idea of using her that way. It was bad enough having to spy on one of his best friends. Unfortunately, spies didn't always get to choose who they betrayed. But he'd be damned if he betrayed her, too.

He thought fast. He had to get Brighton to back off the idea of squeezing Sam. He spoke evenly. "It's not that simple, sir. I think I can develop her as a usable asset beyond just this junket in the NRQZ."

"A mole inside Winston Enterprises long-term? Well, now. That would be a coup."

Ahh, the joys of working for the only American intelligence agency with a mandate to spy on its own citizens. For years, he'd been the perfect spy. He had no family beyond his mother with whom he had infrequent contact, no friends to speak of, no close contact with any other human beings. He had no weak spots to exploit.

But in a few days, Sammie Jo Jessup had somehow managed to ignite his long-dormant protective instincts. Here he was, lying to his boss to cover for her, and he barely knew her. Brighton would ask if she was good enough in the sack to be worth ruining his career over. Funny thing was, he hadn't even slept with her. And she'd still gotten under his skin.

Brighton distracted him by saying, "I'm glad you called in. We've been having more signal interruptions."

"Same as before?" he asked. One of the reasons the NSA had been willing to send him on this particular off-the-record assignment was because for some months, periodic short bursts of…something…had been disrupting the supersensitive antennas they relied on for collection of wireless data. The experts in radio interference had been banging their heads against walls trying to find the source, but to no avail. The hope was that a fresh set of eyes on the ground could solve the problem.

"Yup, same as before," Brighton said. "Under a minute in duration, originating from a different location each time. And each time the coordinates of the interference are investigated, nothing's there. Some spot in the woods with absolutely no electronic source to cause the interference."

"Have you guys considered using satellites to look down passively and spot the interference that way?"

"The request is sitting on the desk of the director of the William Byrd Observatory," Brighton answered.

"Keep me apprised."

"Will do. Speaking of keeping you apprised, my people did a little research on the Jessup woman. I've sent their report to your email account. It's an interesting read."

Gray mumbled an acknowledgement, but his gut squirmed in dismay at invading her privacy like this. He would like to know more details about her early life, though. It might give him a better insight as to what made her the complex creature she was. It would give him more ammunition to keep her off balance, if nothing else. And Lord knew he needed all the help he could get in staying one up on her.

He disconnected the call with his boss and stared at the computer in distaste. He really shouldn't look at the report. But sharp desire to know more about her goaded him. Finally, his better self lost the fight with his curiosity. He signed on to his email account quickly and popped up the most recent email from Brighton.

…Joanne Jessup of Hollywood, Florida, has a 98% likelihood of being the mother of subject, Sammie Jo Jessup…

He swore colorfully and closed the email. Now that he knew where her mother was, he couldn't un-know it. How was he supposed to keep that information to himself and not use it against her down the road in a moment of weakness? It was one thing to keep secrets when he surrounded himself with strangers and people who didn't touch him emotionally. But Sam? She had the darnedest way of slipping past his guard and getting him to open up in ways he'd never dreamed possible. Hell, she had him kissing again, and they'd barely known each other three days. He'd sworn off women for good years ago, and to date it hadn't been a problem to stick by that vow.

He scanned through the list of his other email messages quickly. There was a second email from Brighton with an attached file. Presumably that was the background report on Sam. In a belated fit of nobility, he deleted the post and its attachment without ever opening the thing.

Hollywood, Florida. Joanne Jessup. The words rolled through his head over and over, a damning litany of knowledge that was not supposed to be his. If he wasn't careful, he'd wake up tonight shouting the information in his sleep. Brighton was a bastard, and that was all there was to it.

Why was the guy so interested in Jeff Winston, anyway? Winston Enterprises had been nothing but a good friend to the U.S. government. Supposedly, operatives from Winston had taken care of several sticky situations that the government couldn't afford to be directly involved in. Jeff himself had nearly died a year ago on one such operation. And the way Gray heard it, an entire team of Winston operatives had died.

Did Brighton's fascination with Jeff have something to do with the Code X project? Had the NSA gotten a whiff of Jeff's secret research? It would be just like Brighton to want a piece of the action for his agency. The guy was a political climber who played the bureaucratic game exceedingly well.

An urge to warn Sam and Jeff swept over him. But to do so would ruin his career. It wasn't like he needed the money. The insurance payout had been substantial and he could live off it comfortably for the rest of his life. But he needed the work. The purpose. The sad truth was he didn't have anything else to live for.

Predictably, a wave of pain washed over him. It was gentler in its coming than most, but burned like acid as it passed over him. *Twenty-eight days*. He just had to hang on that long. If the pain wasn't better by then, he could release himself from this agonizing grief.

Grateful that no one was coming through that sound-proof door any time soon to disturb him, he gave in to the wave for a change, laid his head down on the desk, and lost himself in the fire of searing memory.

Sammie Jo bounced in her seat as she drove, singing at the top of her lungs to the oldies on the lone AM radio station the Ladybug was receiving. It was a beautiful day, crisp and cool, with achingly blue skies and autumn painting the hillsides around her.

Charleston, West Virginia, came into view sprawling across the valley in front of her. Hallelujah. Modern civilization! As fun as a junket in the NRQZ might be, she was unashamedly addicted to her electronic gadgets. She turned on her cell phone, delighted to have a dozen voice mails waiting for her. She hit the play button.

"Where the hell are you, Sam? We gotta talk."

Ricki the Rocket. She'd made it crystal clear to him the last time they'd talked that she never wanted to see his sorry face again. Why was he calling her?

"Sam? WTF? Are you avoiding me? I ain't done nothin' to you. C'mon, baby. Gimme a call. I gotta see you."

More like he was horny and wanted to bed her. Jerk. At least she'd never consented to sleep with him. Not for lack of him trying, however. But there'd always been something a little bit off about him. She'd never been able to quite shake the feeling that he was capable of being more crazy, and maybe more violent, than he let on.

"All right, you smart-mouthed little slut. Are you hiding from me? If you're giving some other guy what you refused to give me, I swear I'll find you. And when I do—"

Sam deleted the message without hearing the end of it. Ricki could go jump off a bridge for all she cared. Irritated, she listened to his next several messages, which got increasingly angry and threatening. The guy was *such* a loser. What had she *ever* seen in him?

Compared to a man like Gray…well, there was no comparison. It was hard to believe both men came from the same half of the same species.

The last, slurred voice mail from Ricki ran in her ear. "I'm gonna find you, Sam, and I'm comin' after you. You're gonna regret leaving me. You hear me? When I find you, I'm gonna hurt you, bitch. Bad."

A chill shuddered down her spine. Ricki had a vicious temper that had already landed him in jail for three-to-five on assault and battery charges. Only his father's legal connections had gotten the time served reduced to under a year. And when Ricki was drinking, everyone and everything in his path had better beware.

Thankfully, the odds of the jerk finding her in the NRQZ were nil. She had to admit, sometimes it was good to live off the grid. Missing her techno toys a lot less all of a sudden, she tucked away her phone and pulled into the parking lot of a strip mall that boasted its very own internet café.

She gave the clerk a credit card and sat down at a terminal in the back of the joint.

"C'mon, baby. Let's make some magic," she crooned

to the unit. She started typing, quickly moving into a deep web search of one Grayson Pierce.

She wasn't shocked that his employer's name was nowhere to be found. Her guess was he worked for the NSA. If he'd been a CIA field agent, he'd be operating under aliases, and the name Grayson Pierce would completely cease to exist. But she did find the occasional hit on him. He was mentioned as a guest at a charity ball a few years back. That article even had a picture attached. He was dashing in a tuxedo, but looked acutely uncomfortable as a well-preserved and artificially enhanced brunette clung to his arm.

"Don't know who you are, lady, but you're coming on too strong to Gray. He likes his women classy. Reserved. And besides, you're too old for him," Sam announced in disgust to the monitor.

"Okay, Gray. Time to get serious. What didn't Jeff want me to find out about you?"

She dug deeper, accessing private investigation sites and various restricted databases. Well, at least she now knew the guy had superb credit and no debt. She went back further in time, and even broke into a database of police records.

And that was when she got the hit. Or rather hundreds of hits, scrolling down her screen faster than she could read them. She went back to the top of the list and clicked on the Boulder, Colorado, police file that was listed first.

Words leaped off the scanned documents at her: Quadruple homicide. Young mother and three small children murdered in their home. Boy, aged six. Twin girls, aged four. Throats slit. Woman tortured. Sexually assaulted. The list of horrific violations against the woman's body went on to a second page. Emily Pierce was the adult victim's name. Christian, Paige and Payton Pierce were the children. Bodies discovered by their father when he came home from a night shift at work—

Oh. My. God.

Sammie Jo surged up out of her chair and ran for the restroom. She stumbled to her knees and retched into the toilet, emptying the remains of her breakfast violently into the bowl. How long she knelt there, sobbing, she had no idea.

The clerk, a young kid, poked his head in the open door. "You okay?"

She stood up slowly, feeling like an old woman all of a sudden. She ached all over. How had he survived it? To have walked in on the bloody bodies of his entire family…small children…to have seen what had been done to his wife…

Hollow-eyed, she pushed past the clerk and splashed cold water over her face in the sink. It didn't help, but it gave her something to do while she fought to collect herself.

"Is there anything I can do?" the kid asked from behind her.

"Yeah. Bring me a cup of coffee and keep the electrons coming until I'm done. This could take a while."

She'd finally recovered enough from the initial shock for a thousand questions to crowd into her brain. Had they caught the killer? What had happened to the guy? What had happened to Gray afterward? Where had he gone? Was he a spy before his family was killed? Did their deaths have anything to do with his work? Oh, God. How had Gray survived if that was the case?

Grimly, she sat back down at the monitor. If he could live through his family's gruesome murder, she could live through reading about it five years after the fact. She owed it to him as a friend to do this.

But Lord, it was hard. The crime scene photos sent her back to the toilet. And her outrage that Gray was actually a suspect in the killings for a while all but did her in. She couldn't imagine what that must have been like, to be grieving and suffering and then accused of perpetrating that horror on his wife and children. To say she now understood that haunted look in his eyes was an understatement. Frankly, she was stunned that Gray was functional at all. He had every right to curl up in a little ball in a corner and never come out again.

As she dug deeper into the police report, she saw large chunks of it had been redacted—blacked out in such a way that the underlying text was completely eradicated. It was standard procedure for protecting classified information within otherwise publicly available reports. Her suspicion that Gray had been in the intelligence community even before his family's murder became certainty in her mind.

She read around the redacted sections to see if she could guess from context the gist of what had been blacked out. But the missing chunks were too big. It was possible that the investigation had connected the killer to some sensitive or classified work that Gray was involved with.

She was relieved, however, to read that the killer had ultimately been identified. The guy was shot to death in a standoff with police when he refused to surrender. She took dark satisfaction in reading that the bastard had been shot twenty-two times, in fact. Apparently, the Boulder police hadn't been any more amused over the killings than she was and they'd unloaded on the sonofabitch.

There had been an investigation to see if the killer had been working for hire for someone, but almost all of that section of the police report had been redacted. There was no way for her to tell, shy of asking Gray. And wild horses couldn't make her open up his old wounds anew.

At least Gray had the closure of knowing the murderer was dead and would never harm anyone else. But God, the damage the killer had done. She scrolled through pictures of the young family alive and laughing together and cried again, not only for Gray's loss but for the tragedy of promising lives cut short. The kids had been so little. So innocent. Emily had been pretty. Sweet-looking. Obviously head over heels in love with her husband, at whom she gazed adoringly in many of the photos.

Hopefully, the bastard had slit the kids' throats fast, in their sleep, without them ever knowing what had happened to them. But somehow, she doubted it. Not given what the guy had done to their mother. The pain of it sliced through her so hot and sharp, she didn't know how Gray stood it.

She spent hours reading through every last bit of it, not in morbid fascination, but because she cared about the man who'd somehow risen from the ashes of this nightmare and gone on.

And then she found the audio file attached to a police report. It was a recording of the 911 call Gray made to police moments after he discovered his family's bloody bodies in their beds. She put in her earbuds and hit play.

She recognized Gray's voice immediately. He was hysterical, trying to ask for help and describe what had happened in between gasping breaths that erupted from his throat uncontrollably. And then, finally, after he'd

choked out his address and a desperate plea to send
all the police, he'd devolved into one long scream of
primal agony. The sound reached into her chest like a
fist and ripped her heart out with such agony that Sam
had to tear her earbuds out of her ears and run for the
bathroom again.

Eventually, the poor clerk intruded. "Lady, I don't
know what you're doing online, but I think you ought
to stop it now."

"Yeah," she managed to gasp. "I think you're right."

It seemed like a bad joke to pull into the parking lot
of a paint store and buy the brand of floor stain Gray
had sent her for today. Thankfully, he'd written it down
and she only had to shove the paper at an employee to
get what she needed.

She pointed the Ladybug south and drove numbly.
The beautiful day outside seemed like a terrible insult
to the memory of Gray's family. Didn't Nature know
what an atrocity had been committed? How could life
go on as if nothing had ever happened? As if Emily and
the children had never existed?

Sam caught herself looking down at her chest at one
point. Surely, her heart was physically bleeding. It hurt
so bad she could hardly stand it.

A small, green sign along the road announced that
she was entering the NRQZ. On cue, her radio died. She
didn't bother tuning in the oldies station. Who could
listen to music when such senseless violence existed
in the world?

As she neared Spruce Hollow, another serious problem presented itself to Sam. How was she supposed
to look at Gray and not fall completely to pieces? She
couldn't possibly pretend not to know what had happened to his family. But what other choice did she have?

It had been none of her business, and Jeff had explicitly warned her away from Gray's past.

A need to wrap Gray in her arms, to hold him and comfort him, made her empty arms ache. But something in her gut told her he wouldn't appreciate the gesture. His brittle control made perfect sense to her now. If she made a show of sympathy, he might very well shatter.

If Gray ever chose to share his loss with her, he needed to do it on his own terms and in his own time. She owed that to him. No matter how hard it was going to be for her to hold in her horror and grief, it couldn't be a fraction as hard as it was for Gray. And if he could do it, she darned well could, too.

She pulled into the driveway and he came outside to greet her, tall and straight and unbowed. How did he do it? How did he survive? The strength it must have taken overwhelmed her with admiration for this courageous man.

"Everything okay?" he asked lightly. "You look strange."

"Just thinking how handsome you are."

He smiled and lifted the heavy cans of stain out of the backseat. "Let's see if you're thinking kind thoughts about me after you've been staining floors for a few hours."

She let him steer the conversation into mundane instruction on how to properly stain and seal a hardwood floor. She knew now how he was proficient at such things. She'd seen the pictures of a gracious, beautifully restored Craftsman home, its hardwood floors stained obscenely with the blood of his children.

"Look, Gray. If you don't want to mess around with this house anymore, we don't have to. We've probably established our cover enough to keep Miss Maddie talking freely to us."

He shrugged and glanced up at her from where he was brushing stain onto a floorboard. "I don't mind. It gives me something to do to pass the time."

So very brave, this man. It had to kill him to work on this house with her. She couldn't imagine the memories it must conjure. She said lightly, "You could always watch a bunch of TV with me, instead. I'll be happy to fill in your woeful education of American pop culture."

"Gee, thanks. If I get desperate, I'll let you know."

"A rerun of *The Andy Griffith Show* is going to be on tonight. You have to watch it at least once, or be accused of being un-American."

"Fine. It's a date." He smiled, but the expression didn't warm his eyes.

Ah, God. And now she understood why. It broke her heart. "You don't have to try with me," she blurted.

"I beg your pardon?" His eyes had gone dark and alert.

Crap, crap, crap. Her and her big mouth! She stammered, "You seem like a mostly serious guy. And that's okay with me. I just meant that you don't have to pretend to be all cheerful and perky with me all the time."

He frowned slightly. "Umm, okay. Although I doubt I could even pretend to be perky. You're the one who's got that wired."

"Believe me, perky's not particularly in my nature, either."

That caused him to stand up straight and stare at her. "You had me fooled."

She shrugged. "In my experience, life pretty much sucks. You can go through it with your lower lip dragging on the ground, or you can get up in the morning and try to at least act happy you're alive. And that's what I do. Maybe I try too hard sometimes, but I figure faking happy is better than acting suicidal."

Dammit. She'd spoken without thinking *again*.

"I guess I'm not as good an actor as you," he murmured.

"I don't know about that," she replied. "It was just the flannel shirt that messed you up. I think you could've pulled off the jeans and hiking boots. Maybe even a leather jacket."

"Me? A leather jacket? No way," he scoffed.

"Way," she retorted. "You could do it."

"I draw the line at motorcycles, though. Those are death machines."

They smiled at each other in mutual agreement. It was a warm moment. Natural. Normal, even. Yet again, she was staggered that he'd made some sort of peace with the world and could experience a simple moment like that.

"Sam, I've got to run out and pick up the lawn mower we ordered. The guy at the home-improvement store said it would be ready this afternoon. And I can't look at that weed patch out front one more day."

She nodded. "Now that I've got my own wheels, I'll hit the grocery store. If you're up for living dangerously, I'll make supper tonight."

His eyes twinkled as he considered her. "I'm feeling brave."

She had to turn away fast not to burst into tears. How did she stand a chance of helping this man—with this investigation or personally—if she couldn't stop crying all the time? Truth be told, she wasn't at all sure she was strong enough do it. She was too broken herself to ever begin to heal his hurts. But darned if something deep in her heart wasn't determined to try. Thing was, if she failed, if she caused more damage to him than he'd already experienced, neither one of them might walk away from it alive.

Did she dare try?

Chapter 7

Gray pushed his empty plate back, relieved that Sam had confined herself to making a chopped Cobb salad for supper. "That was tasty. Thank you."

"You're welcome." She had been unusually subdued ever since she'd gotten back from Charleston earlier. But he didn't pretend to understand women's moods. As far as he knew, weepy wasn't atypical for her. Although he'd initially pegged her for a more cheerful person overall.

Looking for something natural to say that wouldn't send her into another fit of sniffles, he commented, "How will we get past Miss Maddie undetected tonight to stake out Proctor's compound?"

"Why not tell her we're going camping? We can ask her to keep an eye on the house for us."

Their gazes met, and yet again, the mere act of looking at him seemed to send her into a fit of weepy emotion. "Are you okay?" he asked, thoroughly confused.

"Don't mind me. I'll be fine."

"Are you sure? You've seemed a little…" Damn. What word could he use and not make her mad or hurt her overly sensitive feelings? He finished lamely, "…off."

Oddly, she threw her arms around him and gave him a hard hug.

He tensed involuntarily. It wasn't being touched that arrested him. It was the notion of a female giving him affection like this. He didn't do *female* anything. And certainly not affection. His window in life for that had come and gone. And it was all his fault….

"Thank you for caring, Gray."

Caring about what? Her? Well, of course he cared about her. She was his partner. And if she was upset about something, it affected him. "Uhh, yeah. Sure," he mumbled. Thing was, he hadn't the slightest idea what had upset her. "What's wrong?" he ventured to ask.

"Nothing." She sniffed against the front of his shirt.

It was official: he had no clue what made women tick. Thankfully, Sam seemed to pull herself together and they packed the Bronco for a night surveillance op in the woods. Miss Maddie showed up on her porch about ten seconds into the car-packing process and declared herself delighted to watch their house for them while they were gone.

Shaking his head, he backed out of the driveway. He'd forgotten just how nosy neighbors could be. Truth be told, he'd forgotten a lot of the details of normal suburban life. But Sam was teaching him anew. And it wasn't as bad as he'd thought it would be. She was so different from—

His brain stumbled as a familiar, beloved face leaped into his awareness. He forced himself to complete the thought. *From Emily.*

He tensed as memory of her washed over him. But the usual wave of agony didn't accompany the visual image of her sweet face. Gradually, he relaxed his white-knuckled grip on the steering wheel. Okay, then. That hadn't gone so badly.

"Where are we going?" Sam asked, distracting him.

"I did a little poking around today. Found out the Proctor compound isn't too far from here." It was damned close to the NSA facility, though. Suspiciously so.

"Coolio." She was temporarily back to her usual perky self, apparently.

He reflected on how entirely different from Emily Sam was. Emily had been reserved. Sweet. Quiet. Sam…well, she was a force of nature.

Gray turned onto a narrow dirt road that followed a ridge north for several miles. He'd found this track on the satellite images, too. The ridge itself paralleled a long valley, and Proctor's compound sat on the other side of it. The valley was nearly a mile across. Tonight would be the real test of Sam's vision.

He stopped the vehicle. "From here on out, we'll be on foot."

They'd been hiking rough terrain for about a half hour when she panted, "You know, as dates go, this one's not scoring you many points."

A date? The notion stopped him in his tracks. That was something he never expected to do again. He'd had his shot at dating and falling in love and the whole settling down, happily-ever-after thing.

He spun to face her. Of course, she saw him perfectly well and could've stopped before she slammed into him. But she obviously chose to pretend otherwise. His arms came up around her as her body impacted his. "What'd you do that for?" he demanded.

"Getting your attention. You're distracted, and we're supposed to be working."

Sassy wench. "All right, lady. You've got my attention. Now what are you planning to do with it?"

Shock rolled through him. Was he actually flirting with her? Apparently, he was. He hung on to her until it felt like neither one of them would stumble, but whose balance he was trying to right, he wasn't sure. She rose up on tiptoe and leaned in toward him, and God help him, he didn't stop her. He wanted her to kiss him.

Ahh, Emily. I'm so sorry, baby.

Sam's lips touched his, warm and eager and curving in laughter against his. Her vibrant joy flowed into him and he fed on it like a baby bird opening its hungry throat to food. Maybe not the most romantic notion in the world, he allowed, but he did indeed feel like she was waking parts of him that he'd thought were permanently dead.

Startled, he drew back from her to stare down at her. "What are you doing to me?"

"Kissing you?"

"Now who's distracted from the job?"

"Point taken. You want me to go first? It's pretty dark out here."

"Nah, I'm good. I got myself a pair of night-vision goggles today." And speaking of which, he pulled them out of his rucksack and donned them.

Sam giggled beside him. "You look like an alien."

"Thank you, I think?"

"Wow. Those look pretty snazzy. Where'd you get them? Won't they mess up the telescopes?"

He'd gotten them from the NSA armory. And they were absolutely state of the art. He was curious to see if, with their built-in magnification features, he could keep up with Sam's vision. And he happened to know that these had been calibrated to a frequency that wouldn't interfere with either the astronomical radio telescopes or the NSA's listening post.

"Guy I got them from said they're approved by the NRQZ guys. He's moving out of the area and gave me a good deal on them."

"Everything look lime green to you?" she asked.

"Yup. And speaking of aliens, you don't look very human yourself at the moment."

"Next time, I'll wear my glow-in-the-dark makeup. It cracks up the researchers at Winston Enterprises when they look at me through NVGs."

"Done. I can always use a good laugh." And as he said the words, he was stunned to realize they were true. He liked it when she made him laugh. There'd been precious little of that in his life for the past few years. And he'd missed it. The kids, particularly the twins, had been big clowns and their house had been filled with constant laughter. A twinge of guilt hit him as he realized the sound of it was becoming a dim memory. Dammit, if he didn't remember them, who would?

Abruptly grim, he turned and marched toward the top of the ridge. Sam Jessup was a distraction he couldn't afford. As much as he might want her for himself, he had responsibilities. To his boss. To the memory of his family.

Sam fell silent behind him as if she sensed his change of mood. She was very good at that. But the way he heard it, children in violent and abusive situations were highly proficient at reading the moods of the adults around them as a matter of self-preservation.

Momentary regret for deleting that file on her passed through his mind. What would it have said about her? Although, truth be told, he probably knew already what it would have described. Sam's childhood had been pretty bad, bad enough to force her to leave home. And she struck him as someone with enough intelligence to have understood the gravity of that decision.

The good news was she'd gotten out before she was so damaged emotionally that she couldn't recover. She'd probably made her share of missteps along the way, but she'd eventually gotten an education, found work she enjoyed and knew who she was. Although her taste in men still sucked, apparently.

Too bad she hadn't met a guy like him along the way who didn't treat women like crap. Except she had met a guy like him…now. He stumbled and almost went down to his knees before he righted himself.

"You okay?" she murmured.

"Yeah." He walked on, staring down at the ground. Was he willing to put himself out there, to offer her a relationship if she wanted it? The notion staggered him. He was never going to care about anyone again as long as he lived. He didn't have the strength to withstand any more losses in his life. Loving another person took more courage than he had left.

"Ahh. Nice view," she murmured.

The trees opened up and a panoramic view unfolded in front of them, a carpet of forest rising to meet the mountains around them. He murmured, "The Proctor compound should be directly across the valley."

"Mmm-hmm. I see it."

He glanced back at her and followed the direction of her stare. He spotted a speck of light through the trees. Zooming his optic gear up to its highest magnification, he made out the white boxes of several buildings. A black stripe in front of one of them was probably the silhouette of a guard. "I see some blobs. What do you see?"

"I count two large buildings and ten smaller, two-story ones." She continued the inventory, "Four pickup trucks and one SUV. Chevrolet logos but from this angle, I can't tell you the model. There's an armed guard sitting on a stump in the middle of the clearing. Looks like an AK-47 he's carrying. He's wearing combat boots, jeans and a dark-colored shirt. Beard. Looks to be in his thirties. And he's dirty."

"How can you tell that?" Gray sounded like he was in mild shock.

"He has a smudge on his cheek."

"If I got out a high-powered telescope and pointed it at that clearing, would I see everything you do?"

"If it was high-powered enough, sure. And it would have to have low-light capability, of course."

"Of course." A pause. "See anyone else?"

"A half dozen men are seated around a table inside the nearest large building. There's a kerosene lamp in the middle of the table sitting on top of what looks like a map. And yes, there are limits even to my vision. I can't see what it's a map of from here."

He snorted. "Hell, I can't even see a window. You win."

He was able to see the triumphant smile that lit her features, though. She might make light of her special ability, but in that smile he caught a glimpse of the pride she took in it. He opened his mouth to tell her he got it now, but a twig cracked in the woods behind them and he froze.

To his chagrin, Sam stepped out from behind him to peer in the direction of the sound. Without warning she turned, flung herself at him, tore off his night-vision goggles, and laid a big, hot kiss on him, tongue and all. Was she nuts? There was something or someone out there! He tried to peel her off him, but she clung to him stubbornly.

"Guy with a shotgun," she muttered against his lips.

Then why in the hell was she *kissing* him and not taking defensive action? Unless she thought it was more important to maintain their cover. As if laying a big wet one on him without warning would...oh, wait. She'd seen the guy well before he could see them. When the hostile spotted them, they would already be making out. Okay, this plan could work.

He was still tense, though, listening for some hint of where the guy was. Who was he?

"Work with me," Sam mumbled. "We've got to sell the act."

"Huh?"

"If you don't kiss me with a little more heat, I'm gonna have to stick my hand down the front of your pants," she threatened.

The idea of her doing that rocked his world. Literally. He inhaled hard, and if he thought he'd been tense before, his entire body went rigid. Must focus. Lethal threat nearby. Kiss Sam. Do *not* think about her hand!

Too late. In spite of shotgun guy out there somewhere in the dark, he was suddenly all too aware of her curves against his, of the seductive musk of her perfume, of how good it would feel to have her hands on him giving him pleasure he'd denied himself for far too long.

Nearly growling aloud in frustration, he bent his head to hers and did his level best to kiss her lights out. His attention was torn between the smoking-hot kiss they were sharing, trying to listen for the man in the woods and praying that he or Sammie didn't take a shotgun shell in the back at any second.

Finally, he mumbled against her mouth without breaking contact, "Is he gone yet?"

"Nah. Jerk's enjoying the show. Good news is he looks relaxed and isn't pointing his gun at us anymore."

Gray broke off the kiss immediately, whispering tersely, "I'm not putting you on display for some sick bastard like this. Point me in his direction and I'll go take him out."

"I think if we just move along, maybe head for a clearing so we can gaze at the stars a while, he'll take off."

Without his NVGs, he was as blind as a kitten out here. Sam took his hand and they strolled off through the trees with her leading the way. Unerringly, she took him to a rocky outcropping. They climbed up it and sat down, side by side to stare up at the night sky. The display would be breathtaking were it not for the armed man behind them.

"Still back there?" Gray muttered.

Sam looked around casually, as if checking out the view. "He's moving away from us. Headed generally in the direction of the road."

"Any idea who he was?" Gray asked.

"None. Could be just some bubba whose land we stumbled onto, could be one of Proctor's guys checking us out."

"How would they know we were here? Assuming we didn't trip any motion detectors or the like."

"I didn't see any, nor any weight pads, trip wires or other nasty little surprises," Sam replied. "Normally, I'd say they must have satellite imagery of this area and have picked up our heat signatures."

Gray countered, "But how would Proctor get access to information like that? And heat-seeking sights are electronic. They'd be spotted around here in a minute."

"Unless Proctor only uses them in emergencies. Or unless they're mounted on satellites."

If he had access to a cell phone, he could call the local NSA facility and ask in two seconds if an electronic emission had been picked up tonight in this area. But it would have to wait until the morning.

"So are we setting up a tent and playing house out here tonight?" he asked in resignation.

She gazed across the valley. "It's as good a spot as any. I've got a pretty good view of the compound from here."

"You're kidding." He didn't even see the buildings anymore.

"Told you I'm good."

"You're freaking unbelievable," he muttered.

"And don't you ever forget it," she retorted, laughing.

They pitched their lightweight, nylon tent together, angling the end opening so Sam could see the Proctor compound from inside. He unrolled a pair of sleeping bags and crawled into the longer one of the two. The night was growing cold and damp quickly. Sammie Jo crawled inside her bag as well, but sat up in it beside him and continued to watch the compound. His down sleeping bag warmed to a cozy temperature, and he began to feel drowsy.

Sam glanced down at him and murmured, "Go ahead and take a nap. I'm gonna watch the compound until everyone goes to bed for the night."

He nodded and closed his eyes, listening to a light breeze rustle in the trees outside. Relaxation settled over him and…peace. The sensation was odd. He couldn't remember the last time he'd felt this way. But it was nice. Something he could get used to.

He fell asleep smiling. But when Emily appeared in front of him, looking sad and disappointed, his joy evaporated.

What are you doing, Gray? Have you forgotten me? Don't you love me anymore?

The old guilt rolled through him like acid eating his soul. *Of course I love you, baby. I'll always love you.* Except tonight he was having a hard time making out her face. It was blurred. Faded. Like water had dripped on a watercolor and smeared it.

Only me?

Yeah. Sure. Except his usual certainty in the truth of that wasn't there tonight. More guilt piled on top of the previous guilt. A horrifying realization slammed into him. He couldn't remember what she looked like. No matter how hard he tried, he couldn't bring her face into focus. Panic gripped him. The ghost of his dead wife was slipping away from him. He held his arms out to her, but she was just out of reach and getting farther away by the second.

I forgive you for not being home that night, Gray. For not saving us.

He groaned at the searing pain her words caused. A mountain of guilt that dwarfed all the previous guilt crushed him beneath its mighty weight. *Come back to me, Em! Don't go—*

Something gripped his shoulder. He shook off the interruption. He deserved this pain, this inability to breathe. It was all his fault. They were all dead because of him. Gone…

"Wake *up,* Gray."

"Huh?" He looked up at orange nylon, disoriented. Where was he?

"You were having a bad dream."

Not bad. Emily could never be bad. He welcomed her specter, no matter how painful, for how else would he remember her? Except tonight, he hadn't been able to conjure her face. Frantically, he did his best to picture her. To remember some obscure detail about her. She liked lilies. White lilies of the valley. And lilac-scented candles. And rocky road ice cream. His panic receded slightly.

"Are you okay? What were you dreaming about?" Sam leaned over him in concern, dramatic and bold where Emily was soft and sweet. Mouthy, brash and funny where Emily wouldn't say boo to a mouse. Frankly sexual, where Emily had always been shy almost to the point of painfulness.

"Yeah. I'm okay," he lied. He stared up at the tent ceiling. What the hell was that dream all about? Was Sam erasing Emily from his mind? From his heart? A shocking sense of relief rolled over him, followed quickly by horror. He shouldn't be relieved to forget his beloved wife! It was *blasphemy.* Em and the kids were dead. The least he could do was guard their memories.

He lay there flagellating himself until Sam murmured out of the dark beside him, "Uhh, Gray. We've got a problem."

He lurched upright. "What?" He bumped his head on the tent fabric and ducked instinctively.

"The guy who was following us a while ago? He just pulled into the Proctor compound and was all agitated. And there are about eight men piling into SUVs as we speak. I'll bet he told them about us."

He swore under his breath and scrambled to get out of his sleeping bag. "How much time have we got before they get here?" he bit out.

"You've got to figure it's a twenty or thirty-minute drive around the valley and then along this ridge to our location. Maybe ten or fifteen more minutes for them to hike in from the road to us here."

That was plenty of time to pack up, erase any signs of having been here, and to bug out. Problem was, their Bronco was back behind them, hidden off the same road Proctor's men would no doubt use to come here.

"If they come in on the same road we did, we'll either have to circle around them or sneak right past them to get to our vehicle," he bit out.

"That's why you've got me with you," Sam answered breezily. "Sneaking past folks is no big deal when you can see them long before they see you."

"Yes, but in heavy forest, you've got no advantage on them because of trees blocking your view."

She snorted. "Clearly you have no experience in thinking like an eagle. I don't watch for the men. I watch for squirrels and birds and other critters to move away from the humans. Works like a charm. Trust me."

"Like I have any choice in the matter?" he groused as he stuffed his sleeping bag into his backpack and strapped her sleeping bag onto the bottom of it.

"Have I done you wrong so far?" she asked as she passed him collapsing tent poles to shove inside the pack.

She hadn't. But he'd probably done her a grave

wrong by letting their attraction grow to the level it had. As bad as he wanted her, she was not for him. No woman was.

They took off running through the woods, paralleling the ridgeline a little below it, with Sam leading the way. He had to give her credit. She was in darned good physical condition. Without warning, she screeched to a halt and gestured for him to duck. He crouched beside her, peering through the night-vision goggles at a green world. All he saw were trees and more trees. She gestured that they should head left, toward the rocky high ground that marked the top of the ridge.

He nodded and they moved off quietly in that direction. The trees gave way to a rocky outcrop that was far too exposed for his taste. He opened his mouth to say so, but Sam waved him to silence. Just how close were the bad guys?

They crept along behind the boulders in fits and starts. Sam would stop and stare for a few seconds, nod to herself as if she'd spotted her prey, and then move out. She'd go a few yards until she saw something that made her freeze, and they'd repeat the process all over again. It was maddening. He hadn't the faintest idea what she was seeing, and in spite of his excellent night-vision gear, he felt blind.

Worse, he was dependent on Sam for his safety, which felt extremely weird. He was the protector. The lone wolf who looked out for people in trouble. Not the other way around.

She yanked on his shirt, dragging him down beside her. She held up three fingers and pointed off to her right. Then she pointed her index finger at him like a toy gun. Three armed men off to their right? Damn. He reached for his own pistol. Sam forestalled him with a hand on his forearm and gestured for him to follow her instead. She took off crawling on her hands and knees ahead of him.

Were they not outnumbered and outgunned, he'd probably have enjoyed the view of her pert derriere wiggling along in front of him. But as it was, he spent the long crawl cursing her silently for not letting him take out the guys behind them.

Sam stopped behind a massive boulder topping the highest point along a broad stretch of rocks. She whispered, "They've moved off in that direction. We should be able to watch them from here and when they've moved a little farther off, slip behind them and head for the Bronco."

He stared down at the tree line below, catching occasional glimpses of the men closest to them. Before long, something disturbing dawned on him. The men below were staggered at precise intervals, moving side to side in a highly disciplined search pattern employed by military forces.

He whispered back, "Who are these guys? Where did they learn to search like that? They're using a pattern the army rangers developed."

Sam shrugged. "Maybe they've got an ex-ranger among them."

"It takes more than having a ranger show you the pattern. You've got to train for it, practice it, have a whole team of closely controlled soldiers to execute it properly. I thought these guys were granola-eating hippies. Where'd they learn that kind of discipline?"

Sam glanced over at him grimly. "Same place they learned how to gut a man with a knife, probably."

There was a whole lot more to this Proctor gang than met the eye. What else were they hiding from the rest of the world? No wonder Jeff Winston had sent Luke Zimmer, and now them, to poke around. When they got off this mountain, he was having a serious conversation with Jeff about these guys.

Sam was moving out, picking her way between the rocks. He took a different route that brought him to the bottom of the scree field ahead of her. He might not be able to see a mile, but he knew a thing or two about stealth, and right now that was more important than eagle eyes.

"I'll lead," he whispered. "Let me know if you see anyone approaching."

She nodded.

Whether she liked it or not, he drew his pistol as he eased into the trees. Proctor's men were not amateurs, and Gray had no doubt they wouldn't hesitate to shoot him and Sam. It did beg the question of what they were so defensive of that they'd hunt down a pair of campers nearly a mile from their compound, though.

What was going on at that place? If only Sam had more time to watch it and figure out what Proctor was up to.

He moved swiftly through the trees. The silence around them was heavy with anticipation. Alone, he wouldn't have minded it. He knew how to slide through the night without disturbing it. But Sam was with him and nothing must happen to her. Not like Emily—

He stumbled and his attention snapped back to his footing. He was *not* responsible for Sam. He'd vowed long ago never to be responsible for another human life again. And yet there was no denying his instinct to take care of her.

A tug on his shirt brought him to an immediate halt. Sam was pointing ahead in the gloom and indicating that the road was just ahead. He nodded and moved more slowly, easing toward the as yet invisible opening in the trees.

There. He crept to the edge of the road and glanced up at the tree line overhead, spotting the massive poplar that had been just ahead of the Bronco when he pulled off the road. It was off to their left. Sticking to the shadows, he headed for the vehicle, relieved when its bulk loomed before him. He tossed the backpack in the back, closing the hatch-back with a quiet *snick*. Sam eased into the car beside him and they pulled the doors shut carefully.

He reached for the ignition and Sam bit out, "Wait."

His hand froze. "What's up?"

"Dust ahead."

He tensed, ready to start the car and race away from the approaching danger. He heard it before he saw it. Three pickup trucks raced past them in a cloud of dust. The mini-convoy barreled on by noisily, and the sound of it retreated into the night.

"Are we clear?" he murmured.

"Nothing more is moving out there," she replied.

Good enough for him. He started the SUV and turned it around, heading slowly down the dirt road behind the trucks so he didn't create a dust cloud to announce their presence.

"Well, that was exciting," Sam announced cheerfully.

He frowned over at her. "You don't have to sound so chipper about it. We could've been shot."

"Us? Nah. I'd have seen them pointing a gun at us long before anyone pulled a trigger."

"If you rely too much on your vision to save you, you're going to get sloppy. Make a mistake that could cost you your life." As the words came out of his mouth, dread coursed through him. He couldn't lose Sam, too.

"I'll be fine, Mr. Gloom-and-Doom."

"Don't blow me off. This is important."

"What's it to you?" she retorted. "I can take care of myself."

Stung, he stared at the road ahead. That was what he wanted, right? No responsibility. No commitments. She'd take care of herself. Then why in hell was he so irritated with her right now?

Frustrated with himself, he asked, "Did you see anything at the compound to indicate what they're up to? Anything out of the ordinary. Something that didn't belong."

She shook her head. "If they're up to something, they're probably doing it during daylight hours. It's not like they have to hide their activities if they're going to chase everyone out of this valley at gunpoint. We'll have to come back when people are moving around and working. In the morning, maybe?"

He snorted. "In the morning, I'm calling Jeff Winston and having him call in every favor he has to in order to get satellite surveillance on these turkeys."

"Good call."

"How did you spot them when we were up on top of the ridge? I never saw a thing."

"It was little movements. The tail of a shirt. A handful of gravel rolling. Crickets jumping out of the way."

"And you saw those details how far away?"

"Anywhere from a few hundred feet to several hundred yards."

"Is there anything you can't see?"

"I can't look inside people's heads. Life would be a lot simpler if I could."

The idea of her being able to see his thoughts and feelings appalled him. "I wouldn't like that at all," he blurted.

"Why? What secrets have you got to hide?" she asked.

"Plenty."

"Like what?"

"If I told you they wouldn't be secrets anymore."

"Would that be such a bad thing?"

He glanced over at her. She sounded strangely intense but was staring straight ahead, however. "Depends on the secret, I suppose," he answered.

"In my experience, all secrets are bad."

"Oh, come on. Surely you've got a few skeletons in your closet that you'd be mortified if anybody found out about. Everyone's got them."

She frowned. "Not really. My life's an open book."

The idea of living that way made him shudder. He'd been carrying around his secrets for so long he couldn't imagine laying the burden down. Not to mention his work was all about keeping secrets. But those were different. They dealt with national security and didn't touch him personally. He said slowly, "I wouldn't know how to begin letting go of my secrets. They're part of who I am."

"Memories are part of who you are. Secrets are merely memories you can't or won't share with anyone else."

"Some secrets have the power to hurt other people and are best left unshared," he countered.

"Agreed. But some secrets hurt the person who's keeping them the most. They eat at you from the inside out."

She said that almost like she knew about his most

carefully guarded secrets. Surely Jeff hadn't— Gray cut the thought off cold. His old friend would never betray him in that way.

Bile rose up in his throat. Oh, but he'd betray Jeff Winston, wouldn't he? Sam had one thing right. Sometimes secrets burned their keeper a whole lot worse than the other guy. What had he been thinking to agree to spy on Jeff?

Easy. He hadn't been thinking at all. He'd lived in a fog for years, feeling nothing, caring about nothing and no one. He'd just gone along from day to day existing, but not really living. It had been so much safer that way. And then Sam had to come along with all her energy and sex appeal and make him *feel* again. Damn her, anyway. Except even as he cursed her, he knew it for the lie it was. He couldn't hate her for stripping away the fog. He just hated the man she'd revealed. *The shell of a man he'd become.*

Chapter 8

Sam watched Gray out of the corner of her eye. He looked about ready to shoot someone. She subsided, alarmed. Long experience with men and their violent tempers had taught her to back the heck off when they got that murderous look in their eyes.

They drove all the way back to the house in silence, and when they pulled into the driveway, Gray made no effort to come around and get her door for her. Truly alarmed, she followed him into the house in trepidation. She shouldn't have pushed him. She'd just wanted to give him an opening to bring up the subject of his family's murder if he wanted to. Instead, he'd gone icy cold with rage.

Clearly he wasn't ready to talk about the tragedy. But he really ought to. Sharing grief was one of the best ways to come to terms with it. She knew that one well enough from personal experience. Would Gray never be ready to talk about the loss of his family? She had a hard time believing he'd ever be whole unless he did. What a loss it would be if he refused to heal. He was a wonderful man. He deserved a little happiness. Heck, after what he'd been through, he deserved a whole lot of happiness.

Gray retreated to his bedroom, and she declared herself an official idiot to have driven him into his shell. She couldn't help the guy if he wouldn't talk to her at all.

She parked in front of the television and put on a vintage sitcom. She watched mindlessly through the night, envying the people prancing across the screen their vacuous, uncomplicated lives. Wistfully, she recorded *The Andy Griffith Show* Gray had promised to watch with her.

When dawn broke, she roused herself to cook breakfast. One of the few things she could make was pancakes, and she threw together a batch. She indulged herself and made a berry compote to go with them and topped the whole thing with a small mountain of whipped cream.

"I thought you couldn't cook."

She jumped as Gray materialized behind her. "I can't in general. But I do make pancakes. Want some?"

"Sure."

She moved to get up and he waved her back into her seat. "Eat yours while they're hot. I'll cook my own."

He also fried bacon and scrambled a few eggs while he was at it. She stared at his plate heaped with food as he slid into the chair across from her. "Hungry there, Sparky?"

He shrugged. "I worked up an appetite running around in the woods."

Silence fell around them. She cast about for something normal to talk about to fill the awkwardness. "So. What's on your agenda for today?"

He glanced up grimly. "Calling Jeff Winston."

"Want me to make the call?"

"No. I'll do it. We go back further, and he can't fire me."

Jeff would never fire her. Not only was she part of Code X, but they were family at Winston Enterprises. Everyone there looked out for each other. Which did make her wonder, though, why Jeff had sent her out here completely unprepared for her emotionally wrecked partner.

She'd stood up to carry her plate to the sink when a knock on the front door startled her. It was barely 8:00 a.m. Who on earth would be here at this time of day? Granted, lights were on in the house and someone was clearly awake, but this wasn't a civilized time for a visit.

Gray was already moving down the hall with lethal grace. A pistol appeared in his hand. Where had *that* come from? He opened the front door fast, seizing the element of surprise, no doubt. "Can I help you?"

She frowned and drifted down the hall behind him. A male voice murmured something inane about welcoming them to the neighborhood and making sure they were familiar with the restrictions of the NRQZ. She saw Gray stow the pistol in the middle of his back. He must have some sort of concealed holster in the waistband of his pants.

She yanked out sunglasses—a light brown pair that could pass for regular glasses at a glance and made her eyes look brown if no one peeked around the edges—and slammed them on as Gray stepped back from the door, saying, "Come in." He waved the man in to the living room ahead of him.

Oh, God. She recognized the visitor. He'd been with the group chasing them around the woods last night. This was one of Proctor's men.

She made a production of stepping into the living room. "Good morning," she sang out breezily. "I'm sorry we just finished breakfast, or I'd offer you some pancakes."

She moved to perch on the arm of Gray's chair. She noted that he'd maneuvered their guest onto the deep, low couch. The guy would be at a disadvantage if it came to leaping up and getting the drop on Gray. She slid a hand behind her back and spelled out Proctor in American Sign Language. She had no idea if Gray knew it, but it was worth a try. Gray lounged in the chair beside her, but there was nothing remotely relaxed about him. It probably took knowing him well to see that, however.

"I'm Jim Swenson," the man announced. Sammie Jo noted the clay ground into the fibers of the man's jeans. It wouldn't be visible to the normal eye. She checked his fingernails and saw subtle traces of red clay there, too.

"I'm Grayson Pierce and this is my fiancée, Samantha."

"What brings you to this neck of the woods?" Swenson asked.

"Same thing that brings most folks," Gray drawled. "The radio quiet zone. We're looking to get away from the gadgets and interference in our lives."

"Y'all like the outdoors much?"

"Yup. Pretty country around here."

"Y'all hike? Ski? Camp?"

"All of the above," Gray answered easily.

Poking around about camping, were they? Gee. Subtle much? Swenson launched into a lecture about what sorts of emissions were prohibited in the radio quiet zone. He finished with an explanation of how to apply for permission to use various restricted devices. But the man's eyes were not still while he talked. His gaze shifted all around the room and took in every detail, almost as if he were some sort of trained observer.

Gray finally interrupted Swenson abruptly. "Look. Let's cut to the chase, shall we? I work for the U.S. government and I need to talk to Wendall Proctor. Can you make it happen?"

Sam gaped in shock. But she was no more shocked than Swenson, who stammered, "I beg your pardon?"

What on earth was Gray doing? He'd hated her idea of approaching Proctor directly.

Gray leaned forward. "You heard me. Tell Proctor I want to talk to him."

"Uhh, what government agency do you work for?" Swenson asked.

"If Proctor wants to know, he can ask me directly." Gray stood up, indicating in no uncertain terms that this interview was over. Swenson rose as well and made his way to the front door in obvious confusion.

Sam and Gray stepped out onto the front porch as the man walked to his vehicle in a daze. She glanced at the guy's pickup truck and spotted something on the passenger seat as the guy climbed in that made her frown.

As the truck drove away, Gray herded her into the house without comment. He headed for the kitchen and she followed, stunned. He sat down at the table and gestured her to a seat across from him. She sat.

"Go ahead," he announced.

"And do what?"

"Demand to know if I've lost my mind."

She snorted. "I don't have to ask. I know you have. What made you change your mind?"

"Last night. I don't want armed men pointing their guns at you. This way, I can approach the compound and draw all of Proctor's attention to me. You can stand off and be safe."

"This is about my safety?" she exclaimed. "Seriously?"

"Yes," he answered matter-of-factly.

"Gray, I really can take care of myself. And I don't need you to put yourself in the line of fire on my behalf. In fact, I'd strongly prefer it if you didn't."

"Too late. Proctor's going to be all over me in a half hour or so."

"This is nuts. Let's get out of here. We'll find another way to figure out what Proctor's up to."

"Nope. I'm seeing this through."

"Don't I get any say in this?" she demanded.

"No. You don't."

"Gray, if you have a death wish this isn't the way to do it. Don't throw yourself on your sword for me!"

He went still. "I beg your pardon?"

Crud. She'd almost blurted that she knew everything, that she'd found out about Emily and the kids. But the dangerous glint in his eyes warned her off at the last moment. God, she hated secrets! And if she planned to keep hers, she'd better distract Gray fast. "I saw something on the seat of that guy's truck. A file. With a Top Secret jacket."

"What in the hell is one of Proctor's guys doing with something like that?" Gray responded, blessedly distracted. Her tactic had worked.

She shrugged. "I don't know. I saw the title, though."

"Which was?"

"Does the word *Echelon* mean anything to you?"

The effect on Gray was shocking. He went utterly still. It was as if the man in front of her abruptly turned to ice. He'd heard the word *Echelon* before. And furthermore, he knew exactly what it signified. She'd bet her life on it.

"Okay, Gray. Spill. What is it?"

Nothing. He didn't even blink.

"It sounds like the code name for some sort of government operation. You've already announced to Wendall Proctor and company that you're government, so that cat's out of the bag. What's Echelon?"

He stood up quickly and took his keys off the hook on the kitchen wall. "I've got to go."

"Go where?" She followed him out the side door to the driveway and the Bronco. She glanced down the street and saw something that made her blood run cold. She grabbed his arm when he would have ignored her.

"Listen to me, Gray. There's a man parked about four blocks down. He's got binoculars, and he's watching us. You'll be tailed wherever you go."

That finally broke Gray's bizarre fugue state. "What does his car look like?"

"It's a white Cadillac. Circa 1970. Looks like crap."

"Thanks."

"I'm going with you," she announced.

"No. You're not," he retorted sharply.

"So you're going to leave me here alone to face Proctor's men when they come calling?" It was a mean ploy, playing on what had happened to his family when he'd left them alone. But panic fluttered in her chest and she couldn't think of anything else to get through to him. What in the heck was Echelon, anyway?

He exhaled on a groan like she'd just sucker punched him. Which, in point of fact, she had. "Dammit, Sam. I have to go. But I can't take you, and I can't leave you here by yourself."

"How about I follow you in the Ladybug? I can run interference with your tail."

He shook his head. "Too dangerous."

"Like throwing yourself under Wendall Proctor's bus isn't dangerous?" she exclaimed under her breath.

Gray stared hard at her, obviously frustrated. "How about you go to Miss Maddie's place? Stay with her until I get back."

The idea made sense. Miss Maddie had declared herself an early riser and was no doubt awake. For that matter, the woman had probably seen their visitor and was watching their heated conversation this very minute.

"Okay, fine." Sam relented reluctantly, but she also felt bad about having used his family's murders to manipulate him.

"Promise me you won't be alone until I get back," he begged in quiet desperation.

God, the pain in his voice was almost more than she could stand. She could see the agony tearing at him in his black, dilated gaze. He was thinking about *her* right now. His dead wife.

"I promise. Nothing will happen to me while you're gone."

Relief entered his gaze, but on its heels came confusion. Darn it. He was smart enough to wonder at her particular choice of words. She *had* to be more careful with what she said.

"Go into my bedroom," he instructed. "On the floor of the closet, in the back, there's a box. Get the pistol out of it and put it in your purse. You do know how to use a gun, don't you?"

"Yes, and with my eyesight, I'm a ridiculously good shot."

"I'll wait here until you get back," he announced.

She nodded and did as he'd said. She loaded a clip in the weapon and stashed a second clip in her purse for good measure. Sure enough, Gray was sitting in his truck when she came back outside. He pointed at Maddie Mercer's house and she nodded. She gave him as cheerful a wave as she could muster and tromped across the dew-laden grass to the retired teacher's home.

Gray started the Bronco and made a slow production of backing out of the driveway as she knocked on their neighbor's door.

"Why, hello, dear. Lover's spat?" Maddie asked sympathetically. "Come in and tell me all about it."

Sam smiled bravely as the Bronco accelerated behind her. Where was he going? What had her mention of the word *Echelon* made so blazingly important for him to do this very second?

Gray would have driven blindly were it not for the white Caddy behind him. As it was, he had to lose the car before he did anything else. Since he'd already announced to Proctor that he was a Fed, it did no harm to demonstrate his government training. He floored the Bronco and threw the vehicle through several offensive driving maneuvers that shook the Cadillac off his tail in about two minutes flat. The good news was the driver behind him couldn't use a cell phone to call in reinforcements.

Still, to be safe, he spent a few extra minutes evasive driving to be certain his tail was clean. When he was sure he was no longer being followed, he headed for Shady Grove. The guards recognized him today, but still made him go through the same security checks as before.

In a few minutes, he was seated in the little room again, staring at the secure phone. Who, exactly, did he plan to call? By rights, he should report in to Brighton at NSA headquarters. But he'd rather call Jeff Winston. Torn, he stared at the black phone for long, agonizing seconds. Where did his loyalty lie at the end of the day? With his friends or his job? Both had been there through the worst days of his life.

He picked up the receiver, determined to do his duty. To call his boss. But Sam's laughter rang in his ears, and memory of her gazing at him in compassion and caring came to him. He'd thought he'd divorced himself entirely from the human race. But maybe not. Maybe he'd had it wrong all along. Maybe in the final analysis it was people who made life worth living.

Emily's soft voice flowed over him. *Of course it's the people, silly. Family and friends love you no matter what. They stick with you through thick and thin. Jobs come and go but people stay in your heart forever.*

Oh, how he knew that to be true. Even when they'd been dead and gone for years. He could feel his children's wriggly bodies in his arms, smell their sticky sweetness, hear their squeals of laughter as he tickled their ribs. He gasped in agony. Slammed the phone down.

He couldn't do it. He couldn't pretend his family wasn't always with him. Couldn't deny the love they'd all shared. Once he'd opened the floodgate just a crack, other memories, long denied, came rushing back to him. The way Jeff Winston had been at his side in a matter of hours and not left him for weeks. The guy had walked away from a billion-dollar company at the drop of a hat to be there for his old friend.

And his mother. She'd stayed with him for *months*. An entire string of family and friends had mounted a round-the-clock suicide watch on him, in fact.

For the first time in years, he allowed himself to remember their compassion. Their pain. Their shared suffering. How could he have forgotten all of that for so long?

The answer was simple and obvious. He couldn't allow himself to remember it until now. He hadn't been ready to deal with their pain before now. Hell, he wasn't sure he was ready to deal with his own pain yet.

The shrinks had told him he would come to terms with things in his own time and to be patient. Right. Because he just loved feeling like an ungrateful bastard. He hadn't been kind to the people around him when they'd prevented him from joining Emily and the kids in death. Even now, he wasn't sure they'd done him a service or not. But at the end of the day he was still here. And he still had a decision to make.

Although truth be told, he'd already made it.

He picked up the phone and dialed Jeff Winston.

"Hey buddy," Jeff's voice boomed. "How's tricks?"

"Complicated."

"How so? Sam's not wigging out on you, is she?"

Gray frowned. "What do you mean?"

"Let's just say her life hasn't always been a bed of roses. The word *complicated* definitely applies to her."

"I'd gathered that," Gray replied dryly. "Actually, she's been rock-solid."

"Really?" Jeff sounded surprised. "Well, good for

her. I figured after that psycho she just broke up with she'd be a bit of a mess."

Was that why Jeff had sent her to West Virginia? As therapy? Gray snorted. Some pair the two of them made.

"Look, Jeff. I've got a confession to make. And first, I need to apologize to you."

"For what?"

"I was an asshole to you after…" he took a deep breath and forged ahead "…after Emily and the kids died. And you were a better friend than I deserved."

Jeff was silent like he didn't quite know what to say. Then he burst out, "You don't owe me any apology! I just hope I was some help. I didn't feel like I did a damned thing for you."

"No one could've helped me. I had to make the journey to hell and back on my own."

"Does this mean you think you've made it back?" Jeff asked cautiously.

He sighed. "I don't know if I'll ever make it all the way back. But I'm finally figuring out a few things."

"Yeah?"

"Yeah. I think I owe you my life." Jeff made a sound of denial, but Gray pressed on. "About that confession I need to make to you. The National Security Agency wants me to spy on you for them. In fact, they think I'm doing that very thing right now."

Jeff was silent at that.

"But I can't do it, man. You've been a true friend and stood by me through everything. I owe you better than that."

"Thanks." A long silence. "So where do we go from here?"

Gray took a deep breath. "Have you ever heard of Echelon?"

"Whoa. Yes. But I didn't expect you to talk to me about it!"

For good reason. The Echelon Program was about as classified as anything could get in the United States government. It was the name of the operation to collect every bit of electronic communication that happened in this hemisphere. All of it. Every phone call, every wireless signal, every email, every internet transmission. *All* of it.

"So it really exists, then?" Jeff asked.

"Oh, yeah. And Wendall Proctor knows about it."

"I *knew* it."

Gray was shocked. That was the real reason he and Sam had been sent here? To protect Echelon from Wendall Proctor? Holy crap. He asked Jeff tersely, "So here's the big question. What does he plan to do with the information?"

"No idea. That's what I was hoping Luke Zimmer could find out for me."

Gray said grimly, "Give me a day or two. I'll either be dead or get the information for you myself."

"What have you done, Gray?"

"I told one of Proctor's guys I'm a government agent and I want to talk to Wendall. Either the guy will shoot me, or he's going to talk to me."

"And *then* shoot you!" Jeff exclaimed.

"Probably. Unless I can convince him I'm of more use alive than dead."

"How do you plan to do that?" The worry in Jeff's voice warmed Gray's gut.

"I'm going to have to act like I know more about Echelon than Proctor does or than I'm telling Proctor."

"It's too dangerous. You and Sam should get out of there. We'll find some other way to peel this onion."

"How, Jeff? It's not like you can point a satellite at the guy and watch him from space. The NRQZ makes that impossible. Only way to use a satellite is to shut down the telescopes, and that takes permission from the observatory. It's going to take feet-on-the-ground, eyes-on-the-guy surveillance to figure out what Proctor's up to. With my training and her eyesight, Sam and I are the best team for the job."

"I don't like it."

"Hell, I don't like it, either. But we've got no choice. This is the sort of stuff Sam and I might have to sacrifice our lives to protect, if it comes to that. What more can you tell me about Echelon that'll help me string Proctor along?"

Jeff answered in a hush that he probably didn't realize he was using. "There are at least a half dozen antenna arrays around the world that collect signals data for the program. It's a known thing that they collect radio and wireless transmissions. These are no doubt fed into supercomputers and analyzed. But what's not widely known is that the Echelon Project has tapped the internet."

"How?" Gray asked.

"There are only thirteen nodes around the world that absolutely every internet transmission has to pass through. I have received information that they've been tapped and that their data is also being fed into government supercomputers for analysis. My source says *all* the nodes are being harvested, even the Chinese one, and I have no reason to doubt my source."

Gray shuddered to even think about how highly placed a source Jeff had to have to know this information. "Okay, so Echelon is watching pretty much everyone everywhere. What else?"

"Like that's not enough?" Jeff blurted.

"We're talking my life, here. The more information I have, the more chance I stand of staying alive."

"Or of having it tortured out of you," Jeff grumbled.

There was that.

Jeff continued reluctantly, "I have reason to believe the computer array that takes in and sorts Shady Grove's data is in Maryland, sixty miles or so east of the antenna array. I'm told it's comprised of acres of supercomputers housed in an underground facility."

"How does the data get from the antennas to the computers?" Gray asked.

"Buried fiber-optic cables."

"Anything else?" he asked.

"Interference automatically knocks the radio telescopes offline. It's a safety feature to keep the sensors from being overloaded and blown out. There've been rumors of unexplained interruptions in the collection of radio data at the Byrd Observatory. And if their antennas are getting knocked offline by something or someone, I'm betting the NSA's antennas are getting messed up, too."

Damn, Jeff's sources were good. Someday, they'd have to have a talk about where the guy got his information.

Jeff was speaking. "—dig up anything else, I'll give you a call."

"Let me call you," Gray replied quickly. "Our house is under surveillance, and I wouldn't be surprised if our phone lines get tapped pretty soon."

"Be careful, eh?" Jeff didn't say the words, but Gray heard them in his friend's voice. *And don't let anything bad happen to Sam.* Right. Like he was the guy to look out for yet another woman's safety since he'd done such a great job with Em and the kids.

He closed his eyes and gave his heart over to the knives imbedding themselves in it.

"Don't die, Gray. It's not worth it. If this approach doesn't work, we'll find another way."

"I hear you." He didn't make any promises to Jeff. He *couldn't* make any promises. Life had taught him that much. One thing he did know—he'd die before he let Sam get hurt. That much he could promise. And he did, silently, to himself.

Chapter 9

Sam made up some silly argument between her and Gray that launched Miss Maddie into an hour's worth of advice on marriage. Which was ironic given that the woman had never been married herself. After a little while, Sam concluded that the woman had learned everything she knew about relationships from soap operas. She tuned out her neighbor entirely after that.

She'd positioned herself in a chair beside Miss Maddie's large living room window so she could see outside. The woman had a surprisingly good view of a hefty chunk of Spruce Hollow from here. The man in the white Cadillac had followed Gray out of town, but had been replaced in about a half hour with a dusty pickup truck. She didn't recognize the man inside, but he looked impatient at having been stuck on surveillance duty.

How long was Gray going to be gone, anyway? She

didn't know how much more of Miss Maddie's prattling she could take.

Finally, in desperation, she asked the older woman, "By the way, would it be possible for you to tell me how you make that amazing macaroni and cheese of yours? I swear, Gray still hasn't stopped talking about it."

Miss Maddie simpered. If she weren't pushing eighty years old, Sam might be jealous of the woman's obvious crush on him. "Honey, I'd be glad to give you the recipe."

Sam did her best to blush. "Actually, I'm a terrible cook. A recipe won't be much help to me. I was wondering if you could show me how to make it."

"Why, I think I have all the ingredients. How about we whip up a batch of it right now? A peace offering for your handsome young man," she added slyly.

"You're amazing." She gave the woman a genuine hug of gratitude. For all her gossiping, Miss Maddie had a good heart.

Thankfully, the conversation turned to cooking, and Sam actually did her best to pay attention. No one had ever bothered to teach her anything about functioning in a kitchen. Her own mother had been too drunk or too stoned to bother, and none of her mom's long string of boyfriends had cared much for cooking.

Sam had been too busy running around being an idiot, and then trying to get an education and right the listing ship of her life to slow down before now and learn for herself. But Gray appreciated good food, and a desire to be able to provide it for him coursed through her.

Good grief, he'd brought out a domestic streak in her. Horrors! Except actually, it felt kind of nice. Normal, even.

Miss Maddie made them cups of tea while the macaroni and cheese baked, and Sam limited herself to looking at her watch every three minutes or so. But as time ticked by, she grew more and more concerned about Gray.

"Don't worry, sweetie," Miss Maddie patted her hand. "I've seen the way he looks at you."

That captured Sam's attention. "How's that?"

"Like he's adrift at sea and you're his anchor."

The insight of that remark staggered Sam. "His anchor?" she echoed in a small voice.

"Just so, child. That man loves you. It's all over his face when he looks at you."

Gray? Her? Love?

Nah. He was just a great actor. But a tiny part of her—okay, not so tiny a part of her—wished it was true. To have a decent, kind, intelligent man like Gray love her…that would be beyond her wildest fantasy come true. And it didn't hurt that he was smoking hot. She'd never dared even imagine a relationship with a man like him. But then, she'd never really imagined a stable, long-term relationship for herself, either.

The oven timer dinged and Miss Maddie got up to take the golden-brown, cheesy masterpiece out of the oven.

Just then, the front doorbell rang. Sam leaped to her feet. "I'll get it." Please, God, let it be Gray. She grabbed her purse as she approached the door and slung the strap over her shoulder. Plunging her hand inside, she gripped the cold, heavy pistol as she opened the door.

It was Gray. She sagged in relief as he stepped inside quickly and swept her up in his arms. Who kissed who first, she didn't know and didn't care. All that mattered was he was holding her and kissing her back nearly as desperately as she was kissing him.

"I hate being away from you," he whispered against her lips.

"I hate it, too," she whispered back.

"Ahh, the lovebirds have made up," Miss Maddie crowed from behind them. "Guess you won't be needing that macaroni and cheese after all, Samantha."

Gray looked up, laughing. "Oh, yes, she does."

Miss Maddie wrapped the steaming dish in a towel and handed it to Sam, who cradled it carefully as Gray hustled her across the front lawn to their own house.

"So. What did you—" she started. Gray cut her off with a sharp wave of his hand.

She headed for the kitchen to dish up bowls of the macaroni and cheese while he headed for his bedroom. He emerged carrying a small handheld device about the size of a cell phone. She recognized a scanner for picking up electronic surveillance.

"Won't that trigger some sort of alarm?" she asked under her breath.

"It's a passive scanner. It'll merely register if there's output," he breathed back.

She waited impatiently while he scanned the house for bugs. He partially took apart the telephone and even disappeared outside briefly to check the phone box on the pole behind their house.

"Clean," he announced.

"I bet it won't be that way much longer. White Cadillac guy was replaced with a truck about a half hour after you left. He's still there."

"We've definitely got Proctor's interest," Gray agreed.

"So. What did you find out? I assume you talked to somebody about Echelon?"

"Yeah. Your boss."

"Really? Did Jeff know anything?"

Gray filled her in briefly, and her jaw was hanging open by the time he finished. "You're telling me that every phone call I make, every email I send, every internet site I visit is recorded by the government and scanned by them?"

"That's most likely correct."

"Man, the conspiracy theorists would have a field day with this information. At a minimum, though, it seems like invasion of privacy on an epic scale."

"Hence the intense secrecy surrounding the Echelon Program."

"Isn't it blatantly against the law?"

He shrugged. "Well, if we spy on the Brits and they spy on our people and we happen to exchange anything interesting that we happen to hear—as a favor between friendly governments, of course—"

"Of course," she interjected sarcastically.

"—then nothing illegal has technically taken place."

"I highly doubt it would hold up in court."

"It doesn't have to. The National Security Agency has permission to spy on Americans in the name of homeland security. And besides, such a case would never make it to court. The plaintiffs would disappear long before they managed to actually press charges."

She shuddered at how casually he said that. He, of all people, knew the price of murder, government sanctioned or otherwise. There were human faces behind state-sponsored assassination. Families. Loved ones.

But then she took a good look at him. He looked… ravaged. "Rough morning?" she asked.

"You have no idea."

"I don't like fighting with you."

"Me, neither," he said quietly. He reached across the table and squeezed her hand.

"Whatever happens, we'll face it together," she announced. "And speaking of which, is the plan for both of us to visit Proctor, or do you want me to stand off and watch you from afar?"

"I'd prefer to have you stand off. But we may not have any choice in the matter. If they make you come along, your job is to convince Proctor and his people that you know absolutely nothing about my work. You don't even know exactly who I work for."

Which was mostly true, anyway. She nodded.

"And for God's sake, don't let them know how intelligent you are."

"Or that I see like an eagle?" she added wryly.

"That goes without saying. How will you hide your eyes?"

"I have the brown contacts I used before. Don't worry about me. I'll survive."

"You always do, don't you?" he asked reflectively.

She blurted, "What did Jeff tell you about my past?"

"Nothing you haven't already told me. He did mention that the most recent boyfriend was a psycho."

"That's no lie. At least I got wise before I got too deeply involved with him." Although that series of voice mails he'd left for her flashed through her mind and called her statement into doubt.

She leaned forward. "Okay, so I'm the sex-kitten girlfriend without two brain cells to rub together. Anything else?"

"If this goes bad, you're to get yourself out. Don't worry about me. Just save yourself."

She leaned back hard in her chair. "Not happening, big guy."

"Sam. I mean it."

"So do I."

"I'm trained to deal with situations like this."

"And if it goes bad, you'll be a hell of a lot better off if I have your back," she retorted.

"I'm not arguing about this—"

"Good," she stated forcefully. "Because I'm not discussing it. I have your back and that's that."

He opened his mouth to make a fight of it and she cut him off with an intensity that matched his. "I'm an adult. I know how to defend myself. I've been in some bad situations before and I'll fight like a maniac if it comes to it. No one's going to sneak up on me and do something horrible to me."

He went pale.

She continued, "You are not responsible for my safety or my decisions. I choose to be there for you, and I can tell you right now I will never abandon you or leave you. Got it?"

He looked ready to throw up.

"I care about you, Gray. Deal with it."

The summons came in the form of a phone call. Gray, still shaken by his earlier argument with Sam, answered it and was not surprised to hear an anonymous male voice say merely, "Come now. And bring the woman."

Apparently, Proctor was into power plays and intimidation. Good to know. Not that such amateur tactics would work on a trained operative like him. Still, he was worried sick about Sam. Stubborn, brave, foolish Sam.

Gray glanced at her as she waited anxiously in the doorway of the kitchen for a report from him. She knew him too well and had recognized this was the call they'd been waiting for. He hung up the receiver without bothering to answer the man on the other end. Let Proctor stew a little.

"Looks like you're coming along," Gray told her grimly. Truth be told, he was relieved not to be going in alone. Sam's eyesight was an invaluable asset to have on his side, as long as he managed to keep her with him and safe. Knowing Proctor, though, that would be a bit of a trick. But Proctor would inevitably underestimate Sam, and that was what made her such a valuable weapon.

"Wear something outrageous," he instructed her quietly.

A grin broke across her face. "Roger that." She disappeared into her bedroom, still grinning. Part of him cringed to see what she came up with, but a secret part of him was wildly eager to ogle her in something sexy.

She didn't disappoint. She came out wearing a sheer, black lace bodysuit with random geometric leather shapes sewn onto it at strategic points. On top of that she wore leather chaps that barely qualified as decent. A loose tank top that hung off one shoulder suggestively and a skimpy little black tulle skirt completed the ensemble.

The outfit made it clear that her figure was as perfect as he'd suspected it would be. The post-apocalyptic triangular sunglasses were back, along with the high-heeled stiletto boots. She looked like a goth roller-derby queen. "This work for you?" she asked cheerfully, spinning around for him. He nearly choked on his coffee at how those chaps cupped her lace-clad derriere through the semitransparent skirt.

"Uhh, sure," he managed to croak.

"Spectac-ulous!"

Apparently, she was in full-blown, bouncy-beach-girl mode, as well. In fact, if anything, she was trying too hard. *She was scared.* "You don't have to go."

She planted her hands on her hips and her hair swirled around her in a glorious display of crimson. "We've already had this fight, and I won. I'm going with you."

He took a different tack. "Tell me this, then. Why are you afraid? What worries you about this outing?"

"I've been in a cult compound before. It's the place I ran away from and left my mom."

Her voice didn't give away a thing. Immensely frustrated at his inability to read her, he reached out and gently removed her sunglasses. Her golden gaze met his in anguish. As he'd thought. She did hide behind her shades.

"Tell me about it, Sam."

She shrugged, but the casual gesture obviously wasn't casual at all. "They were an 'end of the world is nigh' bunch. My mom was a true believer and I wasn't. I didn't want to stick around and drink the cyanide fruit punch."

He sensed her holding back. "What else happened there?"

She huffed. "Well, there was the cult leader who decided to make me his thirtieth or so wife, and at fifteen years old, I didn't feel like having sex with a fat, bald guy in his fifties. So sue me."

A fragile, hurt quality clung to her as he glimpsed

the girl she must have been. "And your mother did nothing to protect you?"

Sam shook her head, and he stepped forward to wrap her in his arms. "I'm sorry, baby."

He froze. *Baby.* That's what he used to call Emily. It had just slipped out. But shockingly, the world didn't end. Sam snuggled closer against his chest. He drew his next breath. The pain didn't shred him. One second ticked into the next. Was it just a word after all? He hadn't uttered it in five years. Had thought he'd never say it again. But lo and behold, the impossible had happened.

"Your mom failed you, Sam. You know that, right?"

"Yes." She sighed against his chest. "I know it in my head. But it feels an awful lot like I did something wrong and she abandoned me."

"You took action to defend yourself from rape. Action your mom should have taken for you. You were brave and strong."

She laughed without even a hint of humor. "I'm not strong. I've just been faking it long enough to get good at it."

He knew the feeling. "Had me fooled. And you really don't have to go to Proctor's place with me. You can stand off at a distance and keep an eye on me perfectly well."

"But then I wouldn't have your back if things go bad."

"I don't want you there if things go bad." The words came out of him without his volition. He couldn't live with himself if something terrible happened to her.

"And I don't want *you* there if things go bad," she retorted, "so we're even."

He leaned back far enough to smile down at her.

"Fair enough. We take care of each other and get out of there pronto if things get ugly. And speaking of which, I need to put an emergency exit plan in place."

"How's that?"

He kept one arm around her as he reached past her for the phone. Her hands roamed up and down his back and he all but moaned with the pleasure of having another human being touching him.

He spoke into the receiver. "Hi, Novak. If I don't call you guys in the next four hours and use the phrase 'peachy keen' in the call, I need you to send in the cavalry to the Proctor compound to rescue me and Sam."

"One dead-man switch up and running, Gray," Novak replied jauntily.

He hung up the phone and looked down at her. "Ready to do this?"

"As ready as I'll ever be."

He couldn't resist. He kissed her, inhaling the strength that defined her. It was a novel sensation being with a woman who could stand beside him as an equal.

The drive to Proctor's place was quiet. As they turned onto the driveway with its prominent sign warning that trespassers would be shot, he looked over at her. "I won't let anything bad happen to you, Sam. I promise."

She smiled back gamely. "And I won't let anything bad happen to you."

He did believe she meant that, too. She'd fight like a mother bear to defend him if it came to it. Yet another novel sensation for him.

Miss Maddie hadn't been exaggerating when she said the place had huge fences and armed guards. They had to wait for a razor-wire-topped gate to be rolled back while surly guards glared at them. He guided the

Bronco inside. As the gate swung closed behind them, he gauged the Bronco's ability to crash through the heavy barrier in a crisis. He didn't like the odds.

He glanced over at Sam and saw her mouth had gone tight. "You're a bimbo sex kitten," he reminded her under his breath.

That made her grin. "I'm gonna make you regret those words," she threatened playfully.

For once, she waited for him to come around to the passenger side of the SUV to open her door. Apparently, it took armed men threatening her to teach her proper etiquette. He opened her door with a flourish. She stepped out and an audible silence fell around them. Ahh, the sweet sound of men underestimating his partner.

Huh. She really *was* his partner. He hadn't had one of those since before the murders. He held his arm out to her with a murmured caution to watch her footing on the loose gravel.

"Honey, I've been walking in heels since I was three," she replied breezily.

"This way," someone said gruffly from behind them.

He looked around the compound curiously. It was neat. The buildings looked newer than he'd expected. Freshly painted. Perhaps a dozen men stood around, wearing jeans and jackets for the most part. There were no women or children in sight, however.

A man led them to the main building in the center of a ring of what looked like dormitories. The building turned out to be a dining hall about half-filled with rows of tables and benches. Gray spotted Wendall Proctor immediately. There was no mistaking the lean build, short crew cut and pale, intense eyes of a zealot. The man was all but holding court in the open area at the far end of the room with an array of his disciples sitting on benches in a half circle in front of him.

Sam tensed, and Gray gave her hand a little squeeze of support. She squeezed back and relaxed fractionally.

They were led to the middle of the circle of benches and left there like sacrificial lambs. Proctor ignored them, looking down at a sheaf of papers for nearly two minutes. Gray's lips twitched in humor. This guy didn't miss a trick when it came to intimidation tactics. For her part, Sam appeared to be staring fixedly at the papers. Probably reading them. His amusement increased. Little did Proctor know the mistake he was making by having those papers out in front of her.

Finally, Proctor looked up. "Who are you?" he barked without preamble.

"My name is Grayson Pierce. And who are you?"

Proctor momentarily looked startled as if everyone ought to know who he was. *Uh-huh. Big ego.*

"I'm Wendall Proctor. I run this place."

"And what is this place, exactly?" Gray replied. Might as well keep the offensive as long as he could.

"It's a cooperative of like-minded souls," Proctor replied. The men around him nodded like proper sycophants. Big, physical, soldier-like sycophants. If he wasn't mistaken, a shudder passed through Sam. He found the vibe in this room shudder-worthy, too.

"Why did you want to talk with me?" Proctor threw out.

"Because you and I need to have a conversation about Echelon."

The word galvanized the room. An almost electric tension zinged in the air. "And you know about Echelon how?" Proctor snapped.

"I work for the NSA," Gray snapped back. He wasn't yielding one inch to this egomaniac.

"So talk."

Instead, Gray glanced down at Sam. "Baby, why don't you go outside and take a little walk?" It helped her girlfriend cover if he didn't want to talk business with her around. And, if he sent her out before Proctor's men took her into custody, maybe she'd get the run of the place instead of being a prisoner. After meeting Proctor in the flesh, he needed at all costs to keep her out of the bastard's clutches.

She looked vaguely stunned but smiled and trailed a hand down over his rear end as she turned to leave. Every male gaze in the room riveted on her derriere as it twitched out of the room. He'd lay odds she was doing that intentionally. Amusement coursed through him. He loved her ballsy courage. And the beauty of it was nobody suspected a thing. In ten minutes, she'd know more about this compound than they could begin to imagine.

He turned back to face Proctor. "Echelon has to be stopped."

Sam strolled outside, startled at the complete lack of women and children. Where were they? She spied the roof of a tall structure well beyond the ring of apartment-like buildings and headed for it. She'd just passed the last living facility when she was startled by movement off to her left.

A little girl, maybe five years old, peeked out from behind a straggly bush where she'd obviously been hiding. Notable was her fair skin and brilliant orange hair.

Sam stopped and smiled. "Hi. My name's Sam. What's yours?"

"I'm Molly. Is that your real hair color?"

"Yup," Sam replied. "How 'bout you? Is that *your* real hair color?"

The little girl giggled and nodded.

"Do you live around here, or are you just passing through?" Sam asked.

Molly pointed at the building behind them, which Sam assumed meant that was where she lived. "Where is everybody this morning?" she asked the child.

"Working at the farm."

"What farm?"

"The one right over there."

"Show it to me?" Sam held out her hand and Molly took it confidently. They strolled past the buildings and a large, plowed field opened up before them.

"So how do you like living here?" Sam asked the little girl.

"It's fun. Except I don't like weeding the garden. Or making my bed."

"I hate making my bed, too," Sam confessed.

"Really?"

"Really. It must be a redhead thing."

"The other kids call me Carrot Stick. I don't like it."

"Aww, they're just jealous of us gingers. My hair wasn't much darker than yours when I was your age."

Molly looked up at her with wide eyes. "Did they call you Carrot Stick, too?"

"Mostly they called me the Great Orange Pest." That was one of the few repeatable names she'd been called as a kid.

The child looked sympathetic. Sam stopped and knelt down to bring herself to eye level with the little girl. "So here's the thing, Molly. Redheads are special, and other people get jealous of us."

The girl's sky-blue eyes grew even larger.

"They say when God gets tired of looking down at green everywhere he pulls out his magic paint and magic brushes, and he paints the mountains all of his favorite colors." She gestured at the autumn finery rising across the valley from them.

"And sometimes, when he's feeling especially artistic, he picks out a really special baby and uses his magic to paint that baby's hair a color as special as they are. You and me, we're God's particular favorites. That's why he gave us our beautiful hair in his favorite color." She reached out to tug at a stray strand of orange from Molly's ponytail.

"When you grow up, your hair's going to darken a bit and turn into the most amazing shade of auburn. Other girls would die to have it, and boys will fall all over themselves to get your attention."

"Really?" Molly breathed.

"Cross my heart and hope to die." Sam stood up and they commenced walking again. "So tell me about this farm, Molly. What do you grow on it?"

"Plants and pigs."

"You grow pigs in a garden? This I have to see."

"No, silly," Molly laughed. "We grow plants in a field. We raise pigs in a barn. They stink."

"So I noticed," Sam replied dryly. The stench was a bit overwhelming, in fact.

"We're downwind," Molly announced wisely. "If we go through the apple orchard it won't smell so bad."

"Take me to your apples," Sam declared.

"We help hurt wild animals get better, too. And then we turn them loose."

That tidbit surprised Sam. It seemed awfully humanitarian of Proctor. The guy surrounded himself with armed guards and concertina wire, after all.

"Right now, we've got a deer, and a fox and some squirrels we trapped. Wanna see 'em?"

"I'd like to see the whole farm. What do you grow?"

"Pretty much everything. I hate brussels sprouts."

"Me, too." Sam laughed.

Several acres of low plants in long rows were dotted with men and women bending over, harvesting various species of squash and pumpkins from dying vines. A large barn stood wide open, and teenaged youths carried baskets of produce in from the field and appeared to be sorting it. A second, smaller barn across the field was tightly closed up, however.

"Can we go into that barn over there?" Sam asked her guide.

"Oh, no. That's the secret barn."

"What do they do in there?"

"Dig."

Sam frowned. "Dig what?"

"Don't know." Molly's voice dropped to a half whisper. "I think the grown-ups play in there and don't want to share with us kids. They come out all dirty."

Even with her extraordinary eyesight, Sam didn't pick up any clue as to what was going on inside the building. She heard the faint rumble of a diesel generator beside it, and a large bundle of power cables went from the generator into the building. A multitude of tire tracks in front indicated that there was plenty of activity in and out of the structure. Hmm. Interesting.

"So, Molly. What do you do for fun around here?"

"Play with my friends. Go fishing. Watch movies on Friday night."

The child actually sounded pretty well-adjusted.

Maybe this wasn't the kind of messed-up cult Sam had experienced as a kid, after all, but a true commune. "Do any of the teenagers sneak off and drink beer in the woods?"

Molly shook her head and replied earnestly, "Oh, no. Beer's bad for you. We eat all 'ganic foods here. Stuff we grow ourselves, mostly."

"You're really lucky, Molly. Do any of the grown-ups smoke stuff they grow?"

"Nobody's allowed to smoke here. It's bad for you."

"Right you are, kiddo." Hmm. So, this place was really populated mostly by health nuts, after all. She glanced back at the closed building curiously. "Do funny smells ever come out of that building?"

"Nope. Just dirt."

"What happens to the dirt?"

"They dump it in the fields where we grow stuff."

What on earth? It didn't sound like a still or a marijuana-drying operation was hidden in the mysterious structure. "How do folks around here make money to pay for stuff?"

"Mr. Proctor gives us all allowances. Grown-ups get a hundred dollars a month apiece, and the big kids get twenty dollars a month. But we get all the food and wood we want."

"Wood?" Sam echoed, startled.

"Yes. Food and boards."

Laughing, Sam continued pumping the child for information. "Do you get an allowance?"

Molly stood tall and proud. "I get fifty cents a week."

"Wow. That's a lot. What do you do with it?"

"I buy candy. Joey says that's why my front teeth fell out."

Sam grinned. "Your baby teeth fell out to make room for your grown-up teeth. Joey's teasing you."

Molly scowled. "I knew it! I'm telling my mom on him."

"You do that. So, tell me. How does Mr. Proctor get his money so he can give it to you?"

Molly shrugged.

"Do you all sell any of the food and pigs you grow?"

"Sure. Whatever we don't eat."

"How many people live here?"

"Sixty-seven and a half."

"And a half?" Sam queried.

"Miss Krista has a baby growing in her tummy. Do you know how it got there? I want one to grow in my tummy."

Sam choked back a crack of laughter. "Maybe you should ask your mom that one." She calculated fast. She didn't see enough land under cultivation to do much more than keep up with sixty-seven mouths.

"Does anyone do anything around here besides farm?" she asked Molly.

"Not really. The grown-ups sit around and talk an awful lot. I wish we had a TV in our apartment. But the 'lectricity's bad for the big 'scope."

"Does every family have its own apartment?"

"'Course they do."

"How many bedrooms does yours have?"

Molly held up three fingers. "One for Mommy, one for my brother and one for me."

Wow. This place was a whole lot more prosperous than the cult Sam and her mom had lived in. But then, that earlier cult had expected the world to end and everyone to die any minute. Prosperity and productivity were a waste in that context.

"As much as I'm enjoying my walk with you, Miss Molly, I probably need to head back toward my friend."

"I heard your friend made Mr. Proctor hatchitated."

Sam mulled that one over. "Do you mean agitated?"

"Uh-huh."

She'd bet Gray had agitated ole Wendall. That shot he'd fired at Proctor about needing to end Echelon as she'd walked out the door had probably hatchitated the guy all the way to his toes.

While Proctor stared at him in open disbelief, Gray mentally chalked up a score for himself. He glanced around at the flunkies and commented to no one in particular, "Someone get me a chair."

One materialized beside him and Gray sank onto it, stretching his legs out casually. The ball was firmly in Proctor's court and he waited patiently for the re-turn volley.

"Why do you want to kill Echelon?" Proctor finally got out.

As he'd suspected, the guy knew exactly what the program was. Gray shrugged. "I happen to think the U.S. Constitution isn't broken. It guarantees the right to privacy for all citizens."

The men around him nodded. Also as he'd suspected. It was a refrain Proctor had sung to these men already.

"What do you propose we do about it?" Proctor asked cautiously.

"The logical course seems to be to gather evidence and expose the program to the public. Of course, the challenge will be to avoid being silenced by Uncle Sam before you tell all."

A few grunts of agreement around him told him he was on the same logic track Proctor was on.

"What can you do for me, Mr. Pierce?"

Gray shrugged. "I'm an insider. I've got security and identification credentials. I can get inside Shady Grove. You tell me what you need."

Proctor leaned back, studying him intently. Not ready to show his hand to a stranger, huh? Cautious man.

Gray leaned back as well. "Of course, I don't expect you to tell me what you need right now. You have no idea who I am, after all. You'll want to do your homework on me. Check out my employment record and the like. Take your time. And be careful, by the way. The National Security Agency tracks down hackers aggressively."

Proctor made a face like that wasn't going to be any problem. Duly noted. The guy had a top-notch hacker working for him.

Gray continued, "When you know I'm for real, and you figure out how you plan to use me, give me a call."

He reached into his back pocket, pulled out his wallet and fished out a business card. He scrawled the house phone number in Spruce Hollow on the back of it and flipped it across the space between him and Proctor. It fluttered to the man's feet. Proctor's black, snake-like gaze didn't so much as flicker downward toward the card. Creepy dude.

Gray stood. "It's been nice talking with you, Wendall."

Consternation rippled through the room. Apparently, one did not get up and walk out on the great man without permission. *Government agents did.*

Two burly men stepped forward as if to detain him. Gray ignored them and made eye contact with Proctor.

"Surely you know I'm not dumb enough to walk into a place like this without a dead man's switch."

Proctor scowled and made a hand gesture to his thugs. They fell back from Gray.

He turned on his heel and walked out of the room, his shoulder blades itching the whole way. When he stepped out into the sunshine, Sam was just rounding the corner of one of the far buildings with a small child in tow. Abject relief that she was safe and moving around freely roared through him. A powerful need to get her out of here as fast as possible spurred him forward.

"Who have we got here?" he asked Sam while he smiled at the little girl.

"This is my friend, Molly."

Gray's heart broke as he gazed at the child. His own kids had been about this age when their lives were stolen from them.

Sam, thankfully, filled in the gap as his throat closed up. "We were out looking at the farm. Did you know they have pigs here?"

"And they stink," Molly added earnestly.

He managed a lopsided smile, but it cost him every ounce of self-control he had.

"Sam says us redheads are 'mazin'. Did you know God painted my hair orange special to match the mountains?"

"He did, indeed," Gray affirmed solemnly. And then an errant thought popped into his head. If he and Sam ever had a daughter, this is what she'd look like. A sudden, fierce need to have another child ripped through him, nearly bringing him to his knees.

"You okay?" Sam murmured.

Ever perceptive, his eagle-eyed Sam. "Yeah. Sure,"

he mumbled. He couldn't see her gaze on him, but he felt her intense regard. She wasn't fooled for a minute that he was all right.

"Ready to go?" she asked him.

"Yes."

"Skip to my car with me?" she asked Molly gaily.

The pair skipped along ahead of him, swinging their clasped hands between them. Their exuberance almost did him in.

Thankfully, one of the guards stepped forward to take charge of the child as Gray started the Bronco and guided it to the front gate. Sam rolled down the window and waved wildly to Molly as they pulled out.

"So how'd it go?" she asked him as she rolled up the window and he accelerated away from the compound.

"Like I want to check this car for bugs before I answer you."

On cue, her voice climbed back into the beach-bunny register. "Wow. Cool. Spy stuff. Such a turn-on!"

He grinned over at her and rolled his eyes. "Hold that thought, babycakes."

It was her turn to take her shades off long enough to roll her eyes at him. He grinned and headed for home. All in all, it had been an interesting encounter. Proctor was definitely out to destroy Echelon. Now he and Sam just had to figure out how and then stop the guy.

Chapter 10

Sam watched a classic Hitchcock movie that ended at nearly 3:00 a.m. Gray had been quiet since their return from the Proctor compound and hadn't actually wanted to talk much about his conversation with Wendall Proctor. From what she gathered, though, Gray had dangled the bait, and now they just had to wait for the man to take it. But it was more than that making Gray quiet. He'd gone ghostly pale at the sight of Molly and had all but fallen into a catatonic state.

Not that she blamed the guy. To have lost all three of his children at about that age—heck, she'd never been a parent and she could hardly contemplate it. Echoes of Gray's terrible screams on that 911 call resonated in her ears.

She blinked and looked around the living room. A faint echo of that horrible, gasping grief resonated around her right now, in fact. Oh, God. That was because the sound was real! And it was coming from Gray's bedroom. She raced down the short hall and burst into his room, prepared to do battle with whoever was attacking him.

He was curled into a fetal position under the covers clutching a pillow against his chest.

A raw keening sound slipped out of his throat. Three guesses what he was dreaming about, and the first two didn't count. She stepped forward and touched his shoulder.

"Gray, honey, wake up. You're having a bad dream." Although calling what haunted his nightmares a bad dream was rather like calling the Grand Canyon a small hole in the ground.

Gray jolted upright, flailing violently to free himself of the comforter.

"Easy there, Sparky. It was just a dream."

He rasped, "Not just a dream."

Yup, he'd been dreaming about the murders. The ones she wasn't supposed to know about. "What, then?" she asked gently. "Tell me about it."

He shook his head and his entire body shuddered. She couldn't help it. She stepped to the edge of the bed and pulled him close. He grasped her waist as if she was a lifeline in a terrible storm and he was lost at sea. She wrapped her arms around his head and hung on tight, hurting for this man like no one she'd ever known before.

After a minute, it dawned on her that the shaking racking him was Gray sobbing silently. She was humbled by him sharing his private grief like this. His suffering called to her at the deepest level of her being. A need to take his pain into herself, to share it and heal it, filled her.

When the tension finally left his body a long time later, she murmured, "Scoot over." She slipped into the bed beside him without ever letting him go and plastered her entire body against his from forehead to ankle. She let go with one hand long enough to draw the fluffy comforter up over both of them. Gradual warmth cocooned them.

She didn't bother asking him to tell her what was wrong. This pain went far beyond words to express.

How long they lay there, hanging on to one another for dear life, she had no idea. But very slowly, she felt Gray become aware of her. Recognize her. The tenor of their embrace changed to one of gratitude and then to a hug born of desperation.

"I can't do it," he rasped. "Can't make it twenty-six more days."

Huh? She didn't know how he went on living, either. She doubted she would have the strength in the same situation. Soberly, she replied, "Nothing can make it better. But other things can fill in some of the empty spaces in your life. New things. Different things." She added fiercely, both in conviction and desperation of her own for her words to be true, "Happiness *is* possible."

She *had* to be right. If she was wrong, then there was no hope for this wonderful man, and she refused to believe that.

"How?" The single word sounded torn from the bottom of his soul.

Like she knew the answer to that one. She was no shrink. Heck, she'd messed up her own life by the numbers, and no one she'd loved had been horribly murdered. Completely out of answers and at a loss for words to make his pain better, she did the next best thing. She lifted her chin and kissed him.

He kissed her back with terrible desperation. She shoved her hands under his T-shirt to get to skin. Warm, living, human flesh. It was as much to reassure herself that he was alive as anything else.

He reciprocated, all but tearing her tank top off and stripping away her flannel jammie bottoms with equal violence. In moments, they were both naked, body to body, an affirmation of their mutual humanity and mutual survival.

Their legs tangled together, Gray surged up over her, all but inhaling her darkly.

She opened her soul to him and gave him every bit of herself—her joy, her laughter, her toughness, even her sorrow. And he took it all, sometimes gently, and sometimes roughly, his hands and mouth moving across her skin without finesse. Tonight wasn't about skilled lovemaking. It was about finding a way to go on for one more day. One more hour. Maybe even one more minute. It was raw and painful and ugly.

He whispered no endearments, said nothing to indicate he was even aware of her identity. He merely fed on her soul and took everything she offered and more. And she let him. Oh, how she let him. If she had more to give him, more strength to hold him close, more fierce desire to pour out to him, she'd have done it.

He handled her with a near violence that would have frightened her if it had come from any other man. But she opened her heart and her body to him without reservation and drew him into her both physically and emotionally. The abyss within him sucked her down into its sad, despairing embrace, and she let it. If this was what he needed, so be it. She could forego casual pleasure in the name of exposing the demons within Gray.

He made an angry sound, and she couldn't tell if it

was directed at her or him. Probably it was directed at both of them. She gripped him tightly, forcing him to acknowledge the physical reality of their sex. She rocked her hips against his, demanding his attention in the most primal of ways.

Thankfully, instinct took over. He moved within her, bitterly, roughly, at first. She absorbed his darkness gladly, hoping to lighten his emotional load for a few minutes. Nature found its rhythm, though, and her body accommodated itself to the invasion. The slide of flesh on flesh became slick. Deeply pleasurable. A different intensity began to build between them.

And finally, finally, the act itself took him over, clearly erasing all thought. All memory. His violent eyes glazed over and a faint sound of pleasure escaped his throat. Overjoyed, she surged beneath him, urging him to find more pleasure, driving him toward release, begging him to lose himself in her.

He planted his elbows on either side of her head and, staring down at her, he hammered into her over and over, faster and faster. His eyes drifted closed. His thrusts took on an element of finesse, as if he were savoring the sensations between them. She continued to stare at him, drinking in the sight of the infinitesimally small smile that passed across his face. She'd done it. She'd broken through to his private hell.

And then the pace changed. Increased in intensity once more. But this time it wasn't angry or desperate. This time he raced pell-mell toward the pleasurable release she offered him. The moment overwhelmed her, and her body broke on an orgasm of such shattering power she thought she might pass out. She cried out her release and Gray's shout joined hers as their bodies and hearts exploded together.

His body relaxed against hers. Heavy. But she reveled in his weight. Eventually, he propped himself back up on his elbows to stare down at her. Normally, she'd make some flippant comment about how great the sex had been. But this time, with this man, she had no idea what to say. There were no words. They'd just been to hell and back together. Literally.

He broke the silence. "Are you all right?"

She smiled a little. "I'm fine. Better than fine. How about you?"

"I don't know. I feel good right now. But I'm waiting for the guilt to hit."

"Guilt's a choice. Choose not to go there."

He laughed shortly and without humor. "You say that like I've got control of my thoughts."

She wriggled her arms up to place a hand on either side of his face. "You have more self-control than any human being I've ever met. You're alive. And for the record, I came to your bed voluntarily. I'm the one who started this. There's nothing *at all* for you to feel guilty about."

"But—"

She shook her head, cutting him off. "Life is for the living, Gray. You're breathing. Walking and talking. You're *supposed* to live."

Gray stared down at Sam in shock. She said that almost like she knew…

But then the message of her words penetrated his sex-fogged mind. Was she right? Was it that simple? His heart wished it was so. But his head wanted to reject the notion. Just live, huh? God, that sounded so easy. So terribly simple.

More sex with Sam? He could definitely go for that.

But at what cost to his soul? At the moment, that price was not making itself known to him. But he knew himself well enough to know the reckoning *would* come.

"What were you dreaming about?" Sam asked, startling him out of his grim thoughts.

"Excuse me?" he mumbled, trying frantically to buy time. Time to come up with a plausible lie to tell her. He rolled to his back beside her and stared up at the ceiling in the dark. Except Sam and her eagle eyes would see right through any lie he tried to foist off on her.

"When I first came in here and woke you up. What were you dreaming about?" she persisted.

A flash of his nightmare came back—blond children, bloody and crumpled on the floor, their throats gaping open obscenely. Funny how that hadn't been the part that freaked him out. It was when the gory images he was so familiar with faded into a laughing redheaded child skipping toward him that he'd lost it. If he didn't remember his own children, who would? He was the last and only keeper of their memories. If he failed them, then the kids would be well and truly gone.

Nausea rolled through him. Sam had erased their memories effortlessly with sex.

And he'd let her.

Oh, God. He'd let her.

"Go ahead and say it," Sam murmured in resignation beside him.

"I beg your pardon?"

"Tell me what we just did can't happen again. That for whatever fill-in-the-blank professional or psychological reason, you can't let yourself experience happiness like that again."

He cursed mentally. For all the world, it sounded like

she *knew*. Why else would she make a remark like that? Cautiously, he asked, "Why do you say that?"

"Because I know you. You're bound and determined to deny yourself happiness at all costs."

He turned his head to stare at her. She was right. Why should he be happy when Emily and the kids would never know happiness again? They'd *all* been robbed of a lifetime's happiness. In some ways, he was nearly as dead as they were. A dead man walking.

Sam sat up beside him, hugging her knees. Her body was sleek and sexy and he wanted her fiercely, even though he'd just had her. He shouldn't look. Shouldn't lust. But damned if he didn't do both.

She spoke carefully. "You're as much a victim as the real victim if you let a tragedy rob you of your life, too."

She *did* know. Why else would she say something like that? Horror rolled through him. The only way he dealt with the rest of the world was by knowing that they didn't have any idea his terrible secret existed. That he was the only one carrying the burden. But if she knew, how was he supposed to keep up even a thin facade of normalcy with her?

"What have you done?" he asked in icy rage.

"I haven't done anything," she declared. "I'm just saying that I think you have a subconscious death wish."

He snorted. There was nothing subconscious about it. Twenty-six days remained in his current bargain with himself. Twenty-six days until he had permission to kill himself and end this agonizing travesty of a life.

"Don't snort at me," she snapped. "I'm right and you know it."

"Of course you're right. I freely admit it. I want to die."

She wilted like a balloon that had just had all the air let out of it.

Furious with her, he bit out, "What? You thought one night of mind-blowing sex with you would make everything in my life okay? You have no idea what I've been through. Nothing—no one—will ever make it better, and certainly not you."

She flinched at each hurtful word he flung at her, going even paler than her usual porcelain self. But stunningly, she said nothing. Where was the mouthy, tough chick that let nobody push her around, thank-you-very-much? She was supposed to get pissed off. Lash out at him. Tell him to go to hell.

But no. She just sat there, all curled into a tight little ball, and absorbed his anger and accusations as if she deserved them all.

His fury climbed out of all proportion to the moment until the truth finally hit him. He wasn't mad at her. He was enraged at himself.

"Get out," he told her tiredly.

She nodded like a lost little girl and climbed out of his bed. She bent down to retrieve her torn clothing and, when she straightened, said quietly, "I'm sorry. It won't happen again."

Chapter 11

Sam stared into her coffee cup hollow-eyed. She felt… empty. Understanding the complex psychology of what had happened between her and Gray last night didn't do a darned thing to make it hurt any less. She'd overstepped her bounds with him on an epic scale. She'd *known* she should wait and let him make the first move. She'd *known* not to rip away the thin veil of normalcy he hid behind. She'd *known* better than to push him faster and further than he wanted to go.

But her own lust and need to comfort the man had overtaken her better judgment. As usual, she'd leaped before she'd looked. And now she was paying the price.

That, she could handle. But what about Gray? Had she just set his recovery back by years? Forever? Funny how he'd been the one talking about guilt last night. This morning, she'd lay odds her guilt was even greater than his. And that was saying something.

She heard stirring in Gray's bedroom and dread filled her. A burning need to run away and hide nearly sent her out the back door. If only all those damned counselors over the years hadn't pounded it into her head that no problem was solved by running away from it!

Frankly, in her experience, she'd found that some problems *were* best solved by simply leaving. But, she was forced to admit—reluctantly—that Gray was not one of those problems. She'd made this mess, and she could just suck it up and tough it out.

She had a job to do. They both had a job to do. She would do her best to figure out what Proctor and his cronies were up to, stop them from doing something awful, and then she and Gray would go their separate ways—him more broken than ever, and her sadder but wiser about messing with other people's hearts and minds.

Gray walked into the kitchen looking more handsome and patrician than ever. His polo shirt and khaki slacks were impeccable, his hair perfect, his expression as cool and distant as she'd ever seen it. Wow. He'd really put on some suit of emotional armor this morning. Funny how all that physical perfection he cloaked himself in now looked like nothing more than the mask it really was.

"Good morning," he intoned.

"'Morning," she mumbled.

"Aren't you usually asleep at this time of day?" he asked as he poured himself a cup of coffee.

It was exceedingly obvious that she couldn't sleep or else she'd be back in her bed snoring right now. She shrugged and didn't bother to answer the question.

He sat down across from her and reached for the

newspaper she'd already driven down to the convenience store to purchase. She'd read the thing cover to cover, and nothing notable or conversation-worthy had happened in the world overnight.

Unable to stand the tension hanging thick and silent between them, she got up, put her cup in the sink, and headed for her bedroom. She crawled into bed and pulled the covers over her head. She was a blazing idiot. This was all her fault. She'd ruined the easy relationship between them by being so sure she could make everything all better for him. Gray was a grown man. If falling into bed with some chick would fix his heart, he would have done it long ago. Or maybe he'd already tried that and knew it wouldn't work. Yup, she was officially a ginormous idiot.

She listened in agony to the sounds of Gray making breakfast for himself and cleaning up afterward. Even from in here, it sounded like the careful routine of a man on the brink of shattering. She heard a jingle of car keys and a door opening and closing. Deep silence settled over the house, and she had no idea if he was ever coming back. Black depression filled her, and she stared sightlessly at a wall for a very long time.

Only the sound of the phone ringing roused her from her stupor. In hopes that it might be Gray, she tore out of bed and raced for the kitchen, snatching up the receiver on the third ring. "Hello?" she said breathlessly.

A male voice she didn't recognize replied, "Uhh, hello. Is Grayson Pierce available?"

"He's not here right now."

"When do you expect him back?"

She confessed uncomfortably, "I have no idea."

The man swore under his breath. And then, "Could you give him a message?"

"Sure."

"Tell him Brighton called and his employment records have been hacked."

"Ahh. That would be Proctor," she responded.

"Wendall Proctor?"

"Who am I speaking to?"

The man replied sharply, "Give Gray another message for me. Tell him Proctor's a dangerous sonofabitch and don't underestimate him."

"I will."

The man hung up without bothering to identify himself or to say goodbye. She stared at the phone. Who in the world had that been? Yet again, frustration at not being able to jump onto the internet and find out who Brighton was filled her. No doubt about it. She was a creature of the twenty-first century.

She also wasn't the kind of person to sit around moping, and do nothing for long. The walls were closing in on her fast and she had to get out of here. She packed a quick snack in a rucksack and headed out. She drove the Ladybug back to the ridge across the valley from Proctor's compound. The faster the mystery of Wendall Proctor was solved, the faster she could get away from this crazy place. Away from Gray and his broken soul, and the mess she'd made of everything.

Cognizant of the response their last junket to this hillside had caused, she was careful to stick to the cover of trees as she worked her way close enough to observe the Proctor compound. The day was overcast, but still horribly bright to her. It was a good-news-bad-news scenario, however. The bad news meant she had to wear her darkest sunglasses and put up with the pain. The good news was the daylight meant she saw details with blinding clarity.

She focused her attention on that mysterious barn Molly had known so little about. She'd been watching it for maybe ten minutes when a truck approached its far side and paused. A moment later, it pulled forward and disappeared inside the structure. She swore under her breath. If the door only faced this way, she would have gotten a look straight into it!

Frustrated, she eyed the fields next to the barn. There was pretty heavy tree cover beyond the plowed acreage and past the tall hurricane fencing. Who'd paid for that snazzy fence, anyway? Probably whoever bankrolled the generous allowances Proctor passed out.

It would be risky getting close to the compound, but if she were on the other side of the valley, she'd be able to maneuver into a position to see into the mystery barn. Decision made, she hiked back to the Ladybug and drove around the far end of the valley to approach the Proctor property from the back side. Navigating mostly by feel—Lord, what she wouldn't give for a nice GPS navigation system right about now—she pulled the Beetle off a small dirt road and hid it behind a stand of blackberry bushes that no doubt scratched the heck out of its paint job. With a silent apology to the little car, she set out into the woods.

The underbrush was thick and the going was slow. Plus, she had to keep a watchful eye out for trip wires, pressure plates, motion detectors or other gadgets Proctor might have placed out here in defense of his privacy. She'd call the guy paranoid if she didn't happen to be sneaking up on his compound to spy on it at this very moment.

Eventually, she spotted a dull glint of aluminum through the trees ahead. *The fence.* She slowed down and approached it cautiously. She hugged the darkest shadows of a giant spruce tree, peering around it just far enough to spot the mystery barn perhaps a quarter mile away at the other end of a long field of plowed dirt.

She'd been standing there, motionless, for perhaps two minutes when she heard movement nearby. Really nearby. She looked around frantically, but saw no one. The trees were too close, the undergrowth too thick for her vision to penetrate. And she didn't have a bit of cover within diving range, either.

Desperate, she looked around for options and saw only one. It wasn't ideal, but what other choice did she have? She grabbed the tree trunk beside her, hugging it for all she was worth. Scratching her cheek and bloodying her hands as she scrambled up the rough trunk by main force, she grabbed for the lowest major branch.

She swung her feet around the limb and levered herself up to a sitting position on it. From there, she was able to stand and reach for the next big limb. She climbed as fast as she could, working her way high in the mighty tree before the limbs were too flimsy to support her weight.

And then she prayed. She didn't have a lot of cover from anyone below who happened to look straight up into the tree. But hopefully it would be enough.

She watched in dismay as a man passed by the tree, toting an AK-47 and moving aggressively. What had she done to set off a trap? She hadn't seen *anything*. It was almost as if they had heat-seeking technology out here or something. But that wasn't possible. Not deep in the heart of the NRQZ.

Voices called back and forth below and she listened in tense disbelief as they talked about the intruder's possible escape route. How in the heck were they spotting anyone who even came near them?

Not that it was going to matter if they found her now.

Once he'd signed into Shady Grove, Gray emailed Jeff Winston's private address immediately. All he typed was *Did you tell Sam?* No need to spell out exactly what he was talking about. Jeff would know.

A reply came back in under a minute. The answer was a single word. *No.*

Gray leaned back, staring at the word and thinking hard. Had he overreacted to the things she'd said last night? Did she really have no idea what had happened to Emily and the kids? Some of her comments made it seem so clear that she knew everything. The stuff about not letting himself be a victim, too. About him needing to actually live...

She was wrong about that, of course. His life had effectively ended the same night his family's had. For a while, he'd told himself he would live for vengeance. That had been enough to keep him going until the police caught the bastard.

He and most of his superiors were convinced the murderer was a hit man for hire, but every lead to who might have hired the bastard had died with the guy in a shoot-out with the Denver police. After a couple of years, even he'd been forced to admit defeat in tracking who'd paid for the hit.

He'd made plenty of enemies over the years in his work for the National Security Agency. He would probably never know which one of them had gone after him through his wife and kids. And after a few years, he'd realized he didn't need to know. Emily and the kids were dead, and that was all that really mattered.

When he'd given up on vengeance, he'd already been back at work for a while and was deeply involved in several cases. He'd turned his focus to his job and made that his reason for living.

And then Sam had come along and challenged everything he'd become. How dare she trick him into having sex with her like that? She'd taken advantage of him in a moment of extreme weakness—

It wasn't her fault, dammit. He'd wanted the sex. He could've stopped at any time. But he hadn't. He'd let her past his guard. As much as he'd love to blame her for last night, he couldn't honestly lay it all at her feet.

She was right about one thing. It must never happen again. And the best way to make that happen was to get as far away from her as he could as fast as possible. To that end, he made a phone call to a very specialized working group within the NSA and plowed through a lengthy identification process before he was allowed to speak to an actual human being.

"Barrett here," a voice finally announced.

"Agent Grayson Pierce. I need a real-time satellite surveillance report on a location."

"Contrary to popular belief, Agent Pierce, we don't keep eyes-in-the-sky on every square inch of terra firma."

"I bet you have eyes on the spot I want to look at. The way I hear it, a request for satellite surveillance of this area was in the works a few days ago."

"Where's that?"

"Shady Grove, West Virginia."

Silence met that announcement. And then, "Stand by."

Uh-huh. That's what he'd thought. The NSA darned well did keep an eye on one of its most important and secure installations from above.

One minute stretched into two. And then five. Finally, Barrett came back on the line. "Say priority access for your request."

Gray pulled out the big guns and gave the highest emergency duress code he knew. It was the one that indicated a field agent was in mortal danger and in need of immediate assistance. It wasn't like anyone was holding a gun to his head, exactly, but if he didn't get this thing done and get away from Sam damned soon, someone might as well just shoot him.

Barrett spoke into his ear. "The telemetry is coming up now." A pause. "Visual scans show no unusual activity. All roads within the search area are clear of hostile equipment."

No surprise. Tanks and armored personnel carriers didn't drive around West Virginia on a regular basis.

"By the way," Gray asked while the guy at the other end of the phone scanned the area, "have you guys had any luck nailing down the source of the bursts of electronic interference that have been shutting down the NRQZ antennas?"

"Nope. Stuff's coming out of thin air. Or more precisely, the middle of the damned woods—" The guy broke off. "Well, hello, there."

"Have you got something?" Gray asked when the guy didn't elaborate.

"Infrared scan shows a cluster of humans moving in what appears to be a concerted search pattern."

"Zoom in on that," Gray said, interested. Were Proctor's boys chasing some hapless hiker away from their compound this morning?

"Roger. Stand by." Then, "I've got a stationary human within the search perimeter. My assessment is that's the likely target of the search."

"State location of target," Gray instructed.

The guy rattled off a pair of lat-long coordinates practically on top of the Proctor compound. "Can you send me a link to the imagery?" Gray asked.

"Yes. Give me the ISP address of the computer you're sitting at, sir."

The lengthy alphanumeric sequence was written on a piece of paper taped to the desk. Gray read it off quickly. In a moment, his monitor flickered to life and an image that looked a lot like weather radar popped up.

A white arrow cursor tracked across the screen, stopping on a blob of yellow. Barrett was speaking again. "Here's the target. If you'll notice, these eight hot spots are moving right to left across your screen in a standard search pattern."

He watched for a few seconds. "How is it they haven't spotted the target? They all but walked on top of him."

"He must be hidden."

Gray pictured the forest surrounding the Proctor compound. There were stands of brush here and there, but not thick enough cover to hide an adult from a determined search effort. Besides, he'd bet Proctor's men knew every square inch of the area. They'd know exactly where to look for a hidden observer.

"Is it possible to zoom in on the target?" he asked Barrett.

A snort was his only answer. The image zoomed in

rapidly until the yellow blob nearly filled the screen. It resolved into a distinctly human shape. Although, the guy's posture was strange. Gray stared at it for several seconds until it dawned on him that the guy was hugging something.

"Looks like he's up a tree, sir," Barrett commented.

Of course. Questions exploded across Gray's brain. Who else was out there spying on Wendall Proctor? Did he and Sam have an ally they didn't know about, or was this an enemy of Wendall's, maybe the real problem behind the goings-on at the Proctor compound? He asked tersely, "Can you get a visual on the guy's face?"

"I'll have to switch feeds. Stand by."

Gray's screen went black for several seconds. It flickered to life again, and he was momentarily disoriented by a gray-green blob. A pine tree.

Barrett zeroed in on the evergreen tree in the middle of the screen, quartering it methodically from base to tip. In the third screen shot of foliage, Gray glimpsed a flash of color. A speck of neon yellow peeked out from below a branch. The person in question was high up in the tree, clinging to the trunk, mostly hidden in shadow and overhanging branches. But a light breeze ruffled the needles and a brief flash of a face came into view.

"Can you capture that image?" Gray asked quickly.

"Already on it." The surveillance operative was working quickly as various pixilated images flashed across the monitor and disappeared as fast as they loaded. Finally, a slightly fuzzy image began to form on the screen. Tree branches, pine needles and then white skin. And then…red hair.

Holy—

Gray leaped up out of his chair, knocking it backward into the wall violently.

"Sir? Agent Pierce?"

Gray was out of the room and tore up the stairs without hearing anything else Barrett said.

Chapter 12

Gray alternately begged Sam to be safe and cursed her for her stupidity. What was she thinking, strolling right up to the fence of the Proctor compound by herself like that? She knew Wendall was paranoid and security-crazed. Did she want to get caught? Hell, she was going to blow the whole operation. He was going to kill her when he got his hands on her.

Please, God, let him get to her first. He didn't even want to contemplate what would happen to her if Proctor got a hold of her. Was the bastard sick enough to torture a prisoner? Gray recalled that unblinking, almost reptilian stare of Proctor's and shuddered. All the guy would have to do was put Sam in a brightly lit room and take away her shades.

Would she actually go blind or just be debilitated by blinding pain? He'd seen the strength of the numbing eye drops she sometimes used, and they were ample testament to just how painful bright light really was to her. Not that she ever complained about it. He'd been dragging her around all over the place during the day without giving it a second thought. Just how much had he hurt her?

He flinched as last night came back to him in all its inglorious detail. Lord knew he'd hurt her last night. Not physically. She'd been at pains to assure him of that. But emotionally? It would be a long time before he forgot the devastated look in her golden eyes as she'd slipped out of his room and out of his life. He was a born-again bastard, all right. He didn't deserve a girl like her.

Almost as quickly as the thought occurred to him, its absurdity struck him. He didn't deserve any woman. He'd utterly failed his wife. Let her be tortured and killed on his watch. Even now, he shied away from remembering the horrendous things the killer had done to her before she died. He could only pray that soft, fragile Emily had passed out fast.

The road topped the ridge and dipped into Proctor's valley. The Bronco fishtailed as it hit a bad patch of loose gravel at high speed, but he wrestled it back under control and kept his foot on the gas pedal. Surely Sam had the sense to approach from this direction and not drive right up the guy's driveway.

As the road narrowed and twisted closer to the Proctor property, he was forced to slow down. He didn't spot the Ladybug, but that didn't mean it wasn't out here. He approached as close to the area currently being searched as he dared and hid the Bronco quickly. He opened the spare tire storage compartment and took out the sawed-off shotgun hidden there. He filled his pockets with spare shells and headed out.

Where are you, Sam?

He took his bearings from the tallest mountaintops around him. She and the men hunting her should be off to his right. He didn't relish having to slip past the tight line of men to reach her, but it wasn't like he had any choice.

The farther into the woods he moved without hearing or seeing any of Proctor's men, the more nervous he got. Had the bastards already found Sam and left the area with her? Dread made him so jumpy he could hardly force himself not to take off running toward her.

He glimpsed a bare flicker of movement ahead. And then another. And another. The search team was lined up practically shoulder to shoulder and moving directly toward him. No way was he getting past these guys to reach Sam. And no way could he outshoot them all. There'd been eight men on the satellite imagery.

Time for Plan B. He looked around frantically for some soft soil. There. He ran over to it and stomped his right foot down on the patch of dirt, his toe pointed back toward where he'd just come from. He dashed a few yards farther toward the Bronco and broke a few stems of dead grass. Another dash and he picked a thread off his shirt and draped it over a tree branch at shoulder height.

The trick was not to make the trail too obvious. The men behind him would have to have a decent tracker with them to follow his trail. Satisfied he'd laid down a big fat arrow for the bad guys to follow, he shifted course and sprinted at a ninety-degree angle to the trail he'd laid down, making sure to leave no tracks at all. Now he just had to get around the end of their search line.

He'd run for nearly five minutes when he judged

he'd passed well beyond the last man in line. He angled back toward the Proctor compound and Sam. She was *so* dead when he caught up with her. A cry went up. His trail had been spotted.

He headed back toward her last known position, peering up into the trees overhead for some glimpse of her. It was hard watching his footing, keeping an eye out for more of Proctor's thugs and trying to spot his tree-climbing partner, all while leaving no tracks and making no sound. Oh, yeah. She was a dead woman when they got back to the house.

He'd paused, frustrated at his failure to make contact with her and unsure of where to head next when, without warning, something hit him sharply on the top of his head. He ducked, and only long years of field experience kept him from crying out in surprise and pain.

Something hit him again, this time bouncing off his shoulder and falling to the ground. He looked down. A small pine cone. He looked up just in time to see another missile flying down toward him. He dodged it, but not before he saw Sam grinning in the tree above him. *Dead. Woman.*

She scrambled down out of the tree quickly and jumped to the ground beside him. "What brings you to this neck of the woods?" she breathed casually, as if they'd bumped into each other on some random street corner.

"You," he bit out. "C'mon." Looking around, he headed away from the Proctor compound at an oblique angle he prayed would keep them clear of the search party.

They'd almost made it to where he judged the road he'd been on to come out, almost gotten away unscathed, when a shot rang out behind them. He dropped to the ground instinctively and took quick inventory. High-powered rifle. Fired at several hundred yards, even accounting for the muting effect of the heavy trees and brush around them. All his limbs worked. He wasn't hit.

"Stay low," he ordered under his breath. "Move out."

Sam grunted behind him, which he took for assent. They'd been spotted, hence speed was a hell of a lot more important than stealth at this point. Crouching, he headed for the road crashing through the underbrush heedlessly. They burst into the clear all of a sudden. The road. He turned right to make a run for the Bronco, but Sam grabbed his left arm, stopping him.

"What?" he snapped quietly.

"Ladybug's this way. And close." She gestured to the left with her chin.

"So's Proctor."

"I hate to argue, Gray, but I have a little problem."

Frowning, he looked at her fully for the first time. She was standing funny. Slightly bent to the left. "What's up?"

"I'm hit. I got shot."

The words were like a bucket of ice water dumped on his head, stealing his breath away. He looked down at where her left hand was pressed against her side. Blood soaked her shirt and her fingers were bloody. A little voice in the back of his head started screaming. *Nononononononononono—*

Stop. He ordered the voice away, and it worked. At least for the moment. He had to keep functioning. Keep moving. Take care of Sam. The voice started to swear, started to remind him of another woman covered in blood—

Shut. Up!

"How far is your car?" he asked quickly.

"Maybe a hundred yards."

"Need me to carry you?"

"Not yet," she answered. He couldn't tell if she was joking or not and his panic ratcheted up another notch.

"Give me your backpack. And you set the pace." He refrained from telling her that Proctor's men had to be close by now, given how close that shot had been and how long they'd been standing here.

She took off at a limping run and he kept pace beside her, frantic with worry and need to do something to help her. Thankfully, Sam veered off the road in under a minute, and he spotted a flash of red where she pointed.

"I'll drive," he bit out. She fumbled for the car keys in her pocket and held them out. But when he reached for them, she refused to let go. Instead, she frowned at the Ladybug behind him.

"What now?" he asked.

"Something's wrong," she mumbled.

She didn't sound good. And she looked like hell. She was noticeably more pale than usual and the bend to the left was more pronounced. He listened for pursuit and was worried that he heard nothing. Proctor's men surely had to be all but on top of them by now.

"Give me the keys, Sam."

"Something's wrong," she repeated. The words were slurred enough to worry him even more.

"What, exactly?" he asked with thin patience.

"Someone's been here." A pause. "I see tracks. By the doors."

"That's probably how Proctor's men figured out you were watching them. They spotted the Ladybug."

"But I hid it." She squinted as if she was having trouble seeing him. Just how badly was she hit? How much blood was she losing? She mumbled, "Even I couldn't see it."

"Obviously, someone was out on a patrol in the woods and spotted your car that way."

She shook her head as if it was getting fuzzy and she couldn't clear it.

"We don't have time to stand here arguing," he declared. "Get in the car." He opened the passenger door and all but shoved her inside. He raced around to the other side and jumped into the cramped vehicle. He reached for the ignition, and a bloody hand gripped his wrist with shocking strength. He jolted, startled.

"I see fingerprints," she gasped. "Steering column."

"So? You've put your hands on it and left some marks."

"Not. Mine."

They didn't have time for this. But she gripped his wrist stubbornly and seemed determined to make him have a look at the damned fingerprints. He was too tall to bend over and see anything, so he opened the door, jumped out, dropped to his knees and looked under—

Holy mother of God.

"Sam, I need you to get out of the car. Head for the road. As fast as you can go."

"Why?"

"There's a bomb under here." No wonder Proctor's men weren't approaching them. They knew he and Sam were going to be blown to Kingdom come the second they started the vehicle. Intruder problem solved.

And the two of them would have been killed, too, had she not had such incredible eyesight. Which gave him an idea. It would be dangerous, but worth the risk. He took a look inside Sam's rucksack and was amused to see she had stuffed in at least as much handy gear as

he would have. He fished out the length of nylon rope
he spotted. It wasn't perfect, but it would work. He tied
the end of the rope to the car key then looped the rope
around the steering column and through the steering
wheel. Then, extremely carefully, he slipped the key
into the ignition. He played out the rope, backing the
full twenty-five feet of its length away from the Ladybug. He crouched behind a tree and very carefully
pulled at the rope. It went taut. One more tug—

Boom!

Concussion and heat slammed into him. He took off
running in roughly the direction Sam had retreated. He
found her a few feet from the road, sitting down and
leaning against a tree. Her eyes were closed.

"Are you still with me?" he asked her quietly.

She nodded slightly without opening her eyes.

"Can you stand up if I help you?"

Another nod, but smaller. He reached down for her
and she let out a soft cry of pain as he lifted her under
her armpits and put her on her feet. "I'm going to pick
you up now, baby."

He swept his arm behind her legs and lifted her in
his arms. She was heavy, but he didn't care. She was
hurt, and he'd do whatever it took to get her to safety.
No doubt Proctor's men would move in to check out
the Ladybug and make sure he and Sam had died in
the explosion. But the car should burn hot enough for
the next ten or fifteen minutes that the men wouldn't
be able to get near enough to realize the two of them
hadn't been inside the car.

He crossed the road quickly and moved off through
the woods parallel to the narrow track. Sam passed
out almost immediately and scared the hell out of him.
When he judged he was far enough from the Ladybug

that Proctor's men wouldn't see them, he stepped out onto the road and broke into a clumsy jog.

He laid her out flat in the back of Bronco and used his pocket knife to cut away her shirt from the wound. There was a small entrance wound in the fleshy part of her side and no exit wound. The bullet was still in there, then. The good news was the bleeding wasn't extensive. He ripped open his first-aid kit and slathered her side with antibiotic cream. Slapping several large gauze pads over the wound, he quickly taped them in place.

"Hang on, baby," he murmured as he tucked her legs inside the vehicle and closed the door. "I won't let you die."

He bent down to peek under the steering column and was relieved to see it free of any extraneous wires. He jumped in and drove like a bat out of hell.

The nearest major hospital was in Charleston, a full hour away. Pocahontas County Memorial Hospital in Buckeye was closer, but still a ways away. He pointed the Bronco toward Shady Grove instead. Where there were marines, there were field medics. And where there were field medics, there was fast, competent care for a gunshot wound.

He screeched up to the guard shack, relieved to recognize the guard on duty. "My partner's shot," Gray bit out. "Where's your best medic?"

The guard pointed at a building Gray hadn't been inside before. It was smaller than the main office and off to one side. "I'll let them know you're coming."

Gray accelerated toward the facility and was relieved to see a kid come outside carrying a bulky field medic's kit. Gray parked in front of the marine and raced around to the back of the Bronco. He wasted no time with niceties. "She's in here. Unconscious. Entry wound. No exit wound. Not much bleeding."

The medic efficiently removed the dressing and, after a brief examination of Sam's side, looked up at Gray. "I can pull the bullet here, or I can stabilize her and you can take her to a real hospital."

"Is this life threatening?" he bit out, tense.

"Nah. Bullet's lodged in the muscle of her hip. She was lucky."

If he took her to an emergency room, the identity of the person who'd been shot watching Proctor's compound would become public knowledge. Gray made a quick decision. "Do it here."

The medic nodded. "I don't have great drugs to knock her out with. If she comes to, you're gonna have to hold her down."

"She's tough," Gray replied. He climbed inside the Bronco with Sam. The medic worked with quick efficiency, occasionally asking Gray to pass him something.

"You done a few of these before?" Gray asked to distract himself from how the guy's fingers were buried in Sam's side.

"Yeah. Couple dozen. Four tours in Afghanistan. Saw my share of gunshots. Pass me a gauze pad, will you?"

"Sure."

Sam moaned faintly and shifted weight, and the medic snapped at Gray to hold her still. He planted both hands on her shoulders and she went still once more.

"I saw more damage from IEDs than bullet holes," the medic commented. He made a face and then announced, "Got it."

A lump of metal thumped to the floor beside Sam.

And all of a sudden there was a lot more blood. Gray asked anxiously, "Is something wrong?"

"Nah. Just letting it bleed a little. Cleans out the wound."

A little? It looked like her entire blood supply was draining out of her! But then the medic inserted what looked like a small deflated balloon on the end of a piece of surgical tubing. The guy used a bulb-like hand pump on the end of the tube to inflate the balloon inside the wound.

"What's that?" Gray asked, relieved as the blood flow diminished greatly.

"Nifty little gadget we invented in Iraq. Puts pressure on bleeders inside a wound. Stops the bleeding a lot faster than surface pressure. Saves a ton of lives. I hear the first time the technique was used, the medic stuck a condom in a wound and blew it up like a balloon with his mouth."

Gotta love that Yankee ingenuity.

The medic continued, "We're gonna let the balloon sit for fifteen minutes or so, then we're gonna check for bleeding again. If it's stopped, we'll stitch the wound and load up your girl on antibiotics and painkillers. How'd she get shot?" the guy asked conversationally.

"We were somewhere we weren't supposed to be. A guy with a rifle took exception to our presence."

The medic nodded without comment. He'd probably dealt with enough Special Forces men over the years to be used to vague answers.

The next fourteen minutes ticked by so slowly Gray wondered if time had stopped. Sam had to be okay. She just had to. If the bleeding didn't stop…if she had complications because he didn't take her directly to a hospital…if she died…

No! He couldn't even think about *that*. But his mind insisted on circling back to it. He was a complete mess before the medic finally pulled the bulb off the end of the surgical tube and deflated the balloon in Sam's side. He eased the device free of the incision.

"See? No bleeding. Cool, huh?"

"Fantastic," Gray commented sincerely. Funny how he'd been able to watch the entire surgery, but when the medic commenced stitching up her flesh, he had to look away hastily lest he pass out.

He passed the medic bandages and tape and breathed a sigh of relief when it was all over.

"Keep her quiet for a few days. If she shows any sign of fever, redness or swelling around the wound, any drainage or foul smell, get her to a hospital ASAP. The bullet was small caliber and didn't go deep, so the wound should heal fairly fast. She should be ambulatory in a couple of days and back to normal in a few weeks."

Gray nodded, listening carefully. The worst of it was probably going to be keeping Miss Maddie away from the house until Sam was back on her feet. As quickly as it had begun, the crisis was over. After thanking the medic profusely, Gray drove carefully out of the Shady Grove facility and headed for home. It was a risk to go back to the first place Proctor would look for them. But if the guy wanted a direct confrontation with a federal agent and the force Gray could rapidly bring to bear on him, Wendall could go ahead and bring it. At this point, Gray was all over any excuse to have Uncle Sam blow the guy to Kingdom come.

Sam woke up somewhere along the way and mumbled from the back, "Where am I?"

"In the back of the Bronco," he answered over his

shoulder. "Don't move. The bleeding's stopped and I want to keep it that way."

"What happened?"

"You got shot. I took you somewhere to get the bullet removed and get stitches. You're going to be fine, but I need you to be still and not tear anything open."

"I remember…a tree? Did I climb a tree? And throw pine cones at you?"

"Yes to both."

"My car!" she exclaimed.

He saw her lurch upright in his rearview mirror and he said sharply, "I just told you not to move. Lie back down."

Whether she actually followed his order or was merely laid out flat by pain, he didn't know. But he was relieved to see her disappear from sight once more. The rest of the drive home was silent. He backed into the driveway and used the house itself to hide Sam from Miss Maddie's prying eyes as he helped her out of the back of the SUV.

"Are you going to be able to walk inside?" Gray murmured to her.

"Sure."

But there was a white line around her mouth by the time they reached the front door, and he guided her straight to the sofa, where she collapsed gratefully onto her side. He spent the next few minutes bringing her pillows, blankets, the TV remote, orange juice, water and one of the pain pills the medic had given him.

"Really, Gray. You don't have to fuss over me like this."

He asked her blandly, "Do you want me to take all this stuff away, then?"

"Well, no."

"Then clearly I do need to fuss over you. Why don't you try to get a little sleep?"

She turned on the television and did, indeed, fall asleep quickly. He collapsed in the chair next to the sofa and finally gave in to the emotional overload of nearly losing Sam. Had that shot been a few inches higher, or a few inches to the right, the outcome could have been entirely different. Hell, if the bullet had even just nicked a major artery, she'd have died on his watch.

He closed his eyes and visions of other blood, another beloved face frozen and contorted in agony, came to him. He opened his eyes fast and stared at the television screen blindly.

This was not the same. Sam was fine. She'd been winged by a bullet. No more. It was not his fault. It was just a bit of bad luck.

But no matter how many rational reasons he gave his brain not to freak out, he was completely, totally, 100 percent freaked. He dozed off, but the moment Sam shifted slightly and made a small noise, he was wide awake and at her side.

"Are you in pain?" he asked in a hushed voice. She blinked her eyes open. "A little. I've experienced worse."

Sympathetic pain sluiced through him. "Are you saying you've been shot before?"

"Nah. But a good beating hurts a lot more than this."

Rage enveloped him. "Who?" was all he managed to bite out past the red haze obscuring his eyes and his brain.

"Hey. It's past history. I'm done with violent boyfriends, be they mine or my mom's." She tried to sit up but grimaced at the movement. He reached out to help her move to a slightly more upright position and to put another pillow under her shoulders.

"Sam, I'll never let anyone lay a hand on you again."

She reached out, smiling, to touch his face with cold fingers. "My knight in shining armor, huh?"

He blinked several times. He was nobody's knight, armor or otherwise. "Can I get you anything?" he mumbled, flummoxed.

"I'm fine. I'm not used to having someone hovering over me like this."

He shrugged. "Get used to it. I'm not going anywhere."

She gave him a funny look that sent him to the kitchen to process. Now why had he said that? He only meant he wasn't going anywhere in the next few days until she was recovered from her injury. Right?

Except the idea of returning to his regularly scheduled life seemed like a distant impossibility. He barely remembered what things had been like a mere week ago before Sammie Jo Jessup blew into his life. What on earth was he going to do with her?

Chapter 13

Sam watched Gray beat a hasty retreat and her heart fell. If he still felt a compulsion to run away from her when mention of anything more permanent than the next few days came up, she had no chance with him. None at all. She was stupid to hope that he might ever get past his issues enough to try out a relationship with her. The only reason he was being nice to her now was because she was injured.

Her side didn't feel that terrible, considering. It felt like whoever'd treated it had put some kind of numbing substance on the wound. She hoped they'd given some of the stuff to Gray for later. Every now and then when she moved without thinking, the wound burned enough to hint at discomfort to come. But she would suffer the fires of hell before she'd complain to Gray about it. He was so messed up already that she'd gotten hurt on his watch he could barely see straight.

She watched television and dozed well into the evening. Yet again, Gray poked his head in from the kitchen to ask if she needed anything.

She replied, "Yes. I need you to go to bed and get some sleep. You look exhausted."

He stepped fully into the room. "I'm fine. Can I get you something to eat? Another pain pill?"

"Gray, come here."

Frowning, he tossed a dish towel on the table behind him and came over to the sofa. She shifted slightly and managed not to grimace as she did it. She patted the cushion in front of her belly. "Sit."

"No. I'll hurt you."

"I'm going to stand up and drag you down here if you don't sit, and that *will* hurt me."

Frowning, he perched on the very edge of the sofa.

"Look at me," she ordered. He glanced at her and then away. "No. Really look at me."

"What for?" he mumbled.

"I'm alive. I'm going to be just fine. It was an unlucky accident that I got hit at all. I'm sure that gunshot was meant to herd us toward the Ladybug and nothing more. It'll never happen again."

"Darn straight it won't. I'm putting you on a plane out of here as soon as you can travel."

She took his large hands in hers. "I love you for worrying about me like this. But I need you to stop. I'll be *fine*."

"You lo—" He broke off and jumped to his feet. "Don't love me, Sam. Ever. You hear me?" Hope and horror warred in his gaze.

"Why not?" She hadn't exactly meant the words to be a grand declaration of her feelings, but she supposed she did love him a little for real. He was a remarkable man. And that glimpse of hope in his eyes told her that, at some subconscious level he couldn't acknowledge yet, he really did want her to love him. Or was that just her being a self-deluded idiot?

"Just *don't*." He turned and raced out of the room like a ghost was chasing him. Which she supposed wasn't far wrong. How was she supposed to convince him he was worthy of her love or that she was worthy of loving him if he wouldn't let her even begin to try? Although why she was still beating her head against that brick wall, she had no idea. He'd made it perfectly clear last night that he neither wanted nor appreciated her interference in his life.

Just because he was being kind and solicitous of her now didn't mean he wanted happily ever after with her. So he felt guilty that she'd been shot. Fine. Let him. Who was she to talk him out of such stupidity?

She lay back against the hot, uncomfortable pillows in frustration. She *knew* she had to let go of him, but she was having a heck of a time convincing her heart of that. She had to find a way. That was all there was to it.

Gray tossed and turned for much of the night, listening to the faint drone of the television in the living room. Whether or not Sam was watching it or merely sleeping in front of it, he didn't have the courage to get up and check. If he knew what was good for him, he would stay as far from her as he could within the bounds of polite behavior. But since when did he do what was good for him?

Finally, when the first dim gray of dawn began to creep around his curtains, he climbed out of bed, grateful for an end to a sleepless night and being forced to be alone with his thoughts.

He tiptoed to the living room and was relieved to see that Sam was out cold. In sleep, she looked younger. Softer. Vulnerable. Sometimes he forgot how pretty she was behind the sheer force of her personality and those extraordinary eyes of hers. Her red hair spread out on the white pillowcase like a waterfall of every autumn color from gold to chestnut to burgundy. How had she described it to that little girl? God's favorite colors? He liked the notion. How had Sam learned to love herself when so few people in her life had loved her along the way? In another life, he would have liked to shower her in enough love to make up for her rotten childhood.

But that wasn't the hand he'd been dealt.

And in the meantime, he had to figure out what Wendall Proctor was willing to blow up cars and shoot people to protect. Gray refilled the water bottle next to Sam, laid out another pain pill and her morning anti-biotic, covered a plate of cut fruit with plastic wrap to keep it fresh and set it beside her, and eased out of the house on silent feet.

As much as he'd love to confront Wendall and sug-gest in the strongest possible terms that the next time the bastard tried to kill Sam the man would not like the results, Gray refrained. Punching Proctor in the nose would accomplish nothing other than pissing the guy off and letting him know who'd been watching him.

It was time to call in the big guns.

Sam blinked awake to painfully bright light stream-ing past the curtains. She shoved on a pair of sunglasses and squinted at the offerings Gray had left for her. She popped the pills and then called out, "Gray? Are you here?"

Silence was her only answer. She got up painfully

and made her way to the bathroom. Her side looked okay around the bandage, and she eased into clean clothes carefully.

Even she could only take so much television before her brain turned to mush. She sat down gingerly at the kitchen table with a pad of paper and a pencil and began to doodle. The exercise usually helped her organize her thoughts as she jotted down names and started drawing lines between them.

The one thing that made everyone involved with this case jump was Echelon. Whatever Proctor was up to clearly involved Echelon. She highly doubted his intent was as simple as wanting to expose the program. He could've done it before now if he'd wanted to. Based on that folder she'd glimpsed in his guy's truck, Proctor obviously had a fair bit of information on the program, possibly even a fair bit of classified information.

The obvious assumption was that Proctor wanted to destroy Echelon. How would she go about doing that if that were her goal?

Blowing up the antennas would be difficult. The dish antennas at the nearby William Byrd Observatory weighed many tons apiece, and the way she heard it, the NSA antenna was actually a massive array of sensors and wires spread out over a huge, circular area.

Not to mention, the security around the NSA's Shady Grove complex would no doubt be extremely tight. At the other end of the Echelon pipeline, she expected the security around a massive array of supercomputers used for sorting and analyzing data would be just as heavy, if not more so. But the antennas and the computers had to be connected somehow. Underground cables, no doubt. A person could definitely go after those.

The mystery barn on the Proctor compound sprang

to mind. In all the excitement of fleeing yesterday and getting shot, she'd temporarily forgotten about what she'd seen inside the structure. In between panicking about the armed men below, she'd gotten unobstructed views inside the barn twice as vehicles left the building.

A pair of state-of-the-art computers sat on a large table inside the barn, which didn't entirely surprise her. But the workbench beside the computers had surprised her. Bits and pieces of small radios lay all over the bench. It had strained the limits of her eyesight to identify the components, but there was no doubt about it. The big secret in the barn, or at least part of it, was little radios. What on earth could Proctor be using them for? She'd seen just about every brand of bug and surveillance microphone in the business, and these weren't that small or sophisticated. They frankly looked crude and homemade.

Additionally, she'd spotted the heavy cables that came into the barn from the generator outside. They snaked across the floor toward some unseen target within the barn. If the generator wasn't powering just the computers, what else, then? She'd also caught sight of the edge of some piece of large equipment. It was about four feet tall and had a curved metal case. She sketched it as she remembered it, trying out various possibilities to complete the shape.

Her best guess was an industrial-size fan. One of the big floor models that moved massive amounts of air through warehouses or factories. Now why would Proctor have one of those in a relatively small building? Did it have something to do with the dirt Molly had mentioned?

Something else Molly had said clicked in Sam's brain. The child said the grown-ups were dumping dirt from the building in the fields. That meant a *lot* of dirt was coming out of a small building. And that, combined with the giant fan, could mean only one thing. Wendall was digging a tunnel. The dirt was coming out of it, and the fan was being used to ventilate it. Those power cables could be powering lights or even something like a jackhammer.

Was it possible Proctor was targeting Echelon's underground cables? But surely if the signals were interrupted the NSA would be all over it immediately. And besides, cut cables could be quickly repaired, would give away Proctor's sabotage and would get the guy sent to jail for the rest of his life.

Was it possible to do something less obvious, like siphon signals off the cable? She'd read an article from the CIA a few months back that had to do with photon leakage off fiber-optic cables. But she doubted such leakage would be enough to deliver any meaningful intelligence to Proctor's people. What else could Proctor be up to?

A car engine's noise made her look up sharply from the kitchen table. She started to leap to her feet to check it out, but a sharp knife of pain in her side forced her back down onto the chair. Whoops.

She breathed fast and shallow, willing the pain away, and wilting in relief as Gray's voice called out from the front hallway, "Sam?"

"I'm in the kitchen," she managed in a relatively normal voice that didn't give away the shooting pain in her side.

He joined her quickly, concern on his face. "You're not trying to cook, are you?"

She grinned up at him wryly. "Does that worry you

because you don't want me to overdo it or because you've tasted my cooking?"

He rolled his eyes. "Does your side hurt?"

"Nah. I'm fine," she answered cheerfully. And now that he was here, she *was* better. He just had that effect on her.

"I didn't know you could draw," he commented as he moved around the kitchen, whipping up egg salad sandwiches.

She shrugged.

"You've got talent. Maybe you should think about developing it."

"And get out of the field where bad guys shoot guns at me and blow up my car?" she asked lightly.

"What's wrong with wanting you to be safe?"

"Nothing. It's just not going to happen. I've got this crazy eyesight, and I'm supposed to use it to help people."

"Yes, but…" He trailed off.

"If you finish that with some snarky comment about my being only a girl, I'm going to have to beat you up, stitches or no stitches."

"Don't you dare tear those out," he threatened. "You could get an infection."

They glared at one another in one of the standoffs that were becoming commonplace between them. This time, he looked away first. "Fine. Girls can play superhero if they want to. Just not you."

"Why not?"

He burst out, "I don't want you to die!"

She was a little taken aback at his intensity. "I have no intention of dying anytime soon, thanks."

"I'm serious, Sam."

"So am I. I like being alive, thank you very much."

He shook his head. "If you hadn't spotted those fingerprints in the Ladybug yesterday…if you'd been just a little more out of it…that would've been it for us. Life is so damned fragile—" His voice broke and he stopped speaking.

"You think I don't know that?"

"No, I think you don't."

"But you do?" she challenged.

For once, he met her gaze and said grimly, "Yes. I do. I know all too well how easily life can be snuffed out. When you least expect it, poof. Done."

"Tell me what happened, Gray." She winced as the words slipped out. She knew better than to ask. He wouldn't tell her. Besides, it felt almost as if she were lying to ask like she didn't already know the answer.

"I lost someone I loved. Terribly. Tragically. Without warning."

She stared at him in shock. He'd actually offered her an answer of sorts! "I'm sorry for your loss," she managed to choke out.

"Thanks." The pace of his chopping increased and he spent the next few minutes pulverizing lunch. She left him alone to work out his agitation.

Gray spent most of the afternoon working feverishly around the house before his overall tension seemed to ease. He made a delicious vegetable stew for their supper and then slipped outside to have a look around.

He was back far too quickly, however, and wearing far too grim an expression. "We've got a problem, Sam."

She looked up in alarm from the newspaper spread across her lap. "What's up?"

"Someone's watching the house, and I don't think it's Proctor."

"Man, if even you can spot them, they must be making no attempt at all at stealth."

"I'm not blind," Gray retorted, "and I do have a little training. I know what to look for."

"And what did you see?"

"There's a truck down the street. Not the usual pieces of crap Proctor's guys drive. This thing's big and in great condition. Diesel model. Darked-out windows."

"Show me." She started to get up from the sofa by herself, but Gray was beside her instantly, lifting her gently to her feet. His hands felt so good on her skin. Her body craved more of him, and memory of their intense passion flooded her mind.

Gray stepped back hastily. She sighed, deflated. "Turn out the lights, please, so I can look out the window."

He turned off not only the lights but the television, too. She moved to the side of the curtains and peered down the street. The truck might as well have a neon sign over it announcing that a bad guy was inside and watching them.

As her eyes adjusted to the dark, she was able to make out the face of the driver and recoiled sharply. "Oww!" She couldn't help but cry out.

Gray's arms went around her immediately. He lifted her off her feet and carried her quickly to the sofa. Despite her protests, he turned on a lamp, lifted her shirt and checked her bandage.

"You didn't tear your stitches," he announced in relief.

"I know who's watching us."

"Who?"

"My ex," she answered sourly.

"The psycho?"

"Yes. Ricki the Rocket. He earned that nickname by having a volatile temper, by the way. It goes off like a rocket."

Gray sagged in relief. "I thought it was someone out to kill us."

"Ricki probably plans to kill me at a minimum. I don't know if he'll go after you or not."

Gray's eyes went hard and cold. "I welcome him to try."

"Don't underestimate him. He spent a year doing hard time and probably learned some nasty tricks in jail. It would be his style to use the time in the slammer to become even more dangerous and violent."

"Don't underestimate me, either, Sam. I'll do whatever it takes to protect you." An unspoken promise of death to the ex hung in the air between them.

She smiled weakly. "Okay, then."

Gray looked surprised. "You're not going to fight me on this? You're actually agreeing to accept protection?" He added dryly, "Will wonders never cease?"

"I'm hurt, buster. As soon as my stupid side's healed, all bets are off."

Gray grinned. "There's my girl."

She scowled back at him. "What are we going to do about Ricki?"

"Perhaps a small conversation with the fellow might be in order."

She clutched his arm in concern. "Promise me you won't provoke him. He's really nuts when he gets mad."

"All right. If you insist. But it might be easiest if I just march down there, pull him out of his truck and teach him a lesson in manners."

"Please, Gray…"

"Fine. I won't pick a fight with the guy tonight. He

gets until tomorrow morning to leave and never come back."

She subsided, relieved. Her tummy was doing the strangest little flips, all fluttery and girlie-feeling. What was *that* about? Was she seriously getting all worked up because some big strong man was looking out for her? Except it wasn't just any man. It was Gray. She didn't care what he said. He was definitely knight-in-shining-armor material. She gave him a lopsided smile.

He met her gaze for just a single, naked second of understanding, and then he predictably made a beeline for the kitchen. She listened to him banging around and knew it for the stress it was. She smiled indulgently. At least he hadn't openly denied that he was a good guy this time. Maybe there was hope for him yet.

When midnight rolled around and Gray announced that he was turning in, she decided to move to her bedroom for a change of scenery, too. She put up cheerfully with Gray fluffing pillows and tucking in blankets and generally making her feel about five years old. He really was being sweet to her. The guy was a natural family man. How he'd denied this side of himself for so long was hard to fathom. Maybe he'd just lost this part of himself for a little while. She was happy to help him rediscover it.

More optimistic than she'd been since he'd kicked her out of his bed, she snuggled down to sleep.

Chapter 14

More terrified than he'd been in a long time, Gray lay in bed staring up at the ceiling in the dark. It would be so easy to fall into the comfortable relationship Sam represented. His bed—and his arms—felt empty tonight, and it was a fight not to get up, go fetch her and carry her back here. But he'd pretty much blown up that particular bridge when he'd thrown her out of his bed and his heart two nights ago.

Or at least he'd tried to throw her out of his heart. The way he was feeling right now, he clearly hadn't succeeded. But it wouldn't be fair to her to even suggest engaging in a relationship. He wasn't remotely close to whole emotionally, and Sam ought to have someone who could give her everything she needed and deserved.

A faint scrape from what sounded like the kitchen drew his attention, and irritation flared that Sam was traipsing around getting things for herself instead of asking him to do it. He climbed out of bed and headed down the hall to tell her so.

She'd left all the lights off—must be nice to be able to see in the dark—but his eyes were also adjusted to the darkness. He drew breath to scold her and prepared to round the corner into the kitchen…and froze.

He backed quickly into the shadows of the hallway, his entire being screaming a warning at him. *Intruder!*

Ricki the Rocket thought he was going to scare Sam, huh? Gray's eyes narrowed in satisfaction that the jerk had handed him this golden opportunity to kick some psycho, ex-boyfriend ass.

Gray spun into the kitchen low and fast. He drove his shoulder hard into the guy's back and slammed Ricki to the floor. The guy grunted in surprise and something thick and black skittered away from his grasp. Gray recognized the shape in shock. Ricki'd been carrying a gun?

But then Ricki twisted fast and hard in his grasp and kneed him viciously. Pain exploded in his crotch as the guy ripped away and rolled to his feet. Gray forced his body to move, to ignore the breath-stealing agony, and rolled to the other side of the kitchen table, springing to his feet as well.

A blond, mature man with a square jaw and military crew cut stared grimly across the table at him. *Not Ricki.*

The knowledge exploded across his brain, so unexpected it almost didn't compute. Who in the hell was *this* guy? The intruder's gaze dropped down and to his left for just an instant. But it was enough. Gray lunged, not to race the guy for the gun lying by the stove, but to slam his foot up and into the guy's face as he bent down to scoop up the weapon. The blow connected solidly, and the intruder staggered back, holding his face. Definitely a busted nose.

Gray jumped forward to grab the man. He had a few questions for this character. But the guy was fast and leaped away, racing down the hallway toward the bedrooms…and Sam. Spurred by sheer, raging terror, Gray sprinted after the guy.

The intruder raced past Sam's bedroom door, careened into the bathroom and slammed the door shut. Gray rattled the lock and slammed his shoulder against the panel. The door was old and made of solid wood. He heard the bathroom window squeak open. The intruder was getting away!

Swearing, Gray turned to head outside.

Sam's bedroom door swung open. "What's going on—"

"Lock yourself in your room," he bit out as he ran past her. He yanked open the front door and tore outside. But he was too late. A dark-colored car peeled away from the curb, its taillights retreating fast. Too fast for him to catch a car model or license number.

Sam spoke up from directly behind him. "*Y-Q-R-3-5-4.*"

"What's that?"

"License plate."

God, he loved her eyesight. "I thought I told you to stay in your room and lock yourself in."

"You looked like you might need help."

"I had it handled," he bit out.

"And what was 'it,' exactly?" she asked as he retreated inside the house, herding her before him.

"Make that a 'who.' We had an intruder. I thought

it was Ricki, but it wasn't. The guy looked more Proctor's style."

"Would you recognize him again if you saw him?" Sam asked.

"I don't know. Maybe."

"Can you describe him to me? I might be able to make a sketch of him. I'm assuming you don't plan to go to the police over this?"

"Not until I figure out if our intruder is connected to Proctor and his gang."

"How can a break-in to our house not be connected?"

"Exactly. Let's see if we can come up with a sketch, and I'll show it to a few people. Maybe we'll get lucky and get a hit."

If nothing else, keeping the house lights on and staying awake awhile would ensure that the bastard didn't try to come back and finish whatever it was he'd started.

Gray found the legal pad Sam had been drawing on yesterday morning and scared up a couple of pencils. He carried them to the living room and sat down on the sofa beside her. She roughed out a human face, and then made changes as he described the guy. He leaned closer to point out what he meant about the man's nose shape, and she nodded, concentrating intently.

Her hair smelled good. She used some sort of fruity organic shampoo, but it was tangy and a little sassy, like her. Her elbow bumped into his side and he started to move away.

"Come back here," she murmured absently.

Startled, he scooted close so their thighs pressed against one another. He draped his left arm across the back of the sofa cushion so he could lean in closer and point out little tweaks to the unfolding sketch. She was a talented artist. Another benefit of her enhanced sight, he supposed, was that she had such an eye for fine detail.

Finally, he nodded down at her. "Perfect. That's the guy." Sam's drawing was so detailed it looked more like a photograph than a pencil sketch.

She tore the sheet off the pad and handed it to him. "Maybe your NSA database will be able to make a match off that."

It still felt weird to have her calmly mention his association with the NSA. It had been such a big secret for so long that he had no idea how to react to hearing it referred to by anyone else. But that was the story of his life these days. He kept secrets, and Sam casually ripped away every one he tried to hide behind.

He glanced down at her. "How are you feeling?"

"Okay. Why?"

Usually, she replied with some perky adjective like "superlicious" or "fantabulous." Translation: "okay" meant she was doing rotten, in a lot of pain and not about to admit it. "I'll go get you a pain pill."

He brought her both pill and water to down it with. When she'd emptied her glass, he took it from her and made to stand up.

Her hand parked on his knee, effectively freezing him in place. "Don't go."

His hand itched to creep forward off the sofa cushion and rest on her shoulder. "What's up?"

"Who do you think that guy is?" She glanced at the sketch lying on the tray table beside her.

"No idea."

"What's your gut telling you?"

Gray frowned. "That he was too good a fighter and too fast a thinker on his feet to be some flunky of your ex's. He's one of Wendall Proctor's elite guys. Ex-military if I had to guess."

She nodded soberly. "It always comes back to Echelon, doesn't it? Is it possible Wendall's not the only guy out to destroy Echelon?"

"How do you know Wendall's out to destroy the program?"

"It's the only goal that makes sense."

But as she spoke the words aloud, something in Gray's gut rebelled, denying the truth of her assumption. He spoke slowly. "What if destroying Echelon isn't what Wendall's after?"

She frowned up at him, her golden eyes almost bronze with worry. "What does he want, then?"

"Did you see anything that could help us figure that out while you were up in that tree chucking pine cones at me?"

She grinned unrepentantly. *Wench.* "I took a bunch of notes about that while you were out earlier." She filled him in briefly on the computers, small, home-made radio transmitters, and evidence that Proctor was digging a tunnel.

Dread settled in Gray's gut. Whatever she'd seen, he was sure it all had to do with the heart of Proctor's true operation.

Sam continued thoughtfully. "The thing I don't understand is why he hasn't already cut the cables. He's been in the area for years, and that barn has rust around all the rivets. It has been there for at least a couple of years. Wouldn't they have been able to tunnel their way down—or across or whatever—to the cables long before now?"

He stared at Sam. "What are you saying?"

"I'm wondering what else they could do with those

cables. Assuming they could even actually intercept a signal, the NSA must encrypt the living daylights out of any signals intelligence it wants to move from Antenna A to Computer Array B."

He nodded numbly, not liking her logic, but reluctantly acknowledging its accuracy.

"So why do they need access to those cables?" she continued. "What's so important about them?"

What, indeed? One thing he knew for sure. Whatever Proctor was up to, it couldn't be good. And the guy was willing to use whatever means necessary to hide it. A shooting, a car bomb and now an armed intruder who fought like a trained soldier…or a spy, like him.

"Did you see anything else? Anything at all?" Gray asked urgently. "No matter how trivial or unimportant it seems."

She closed her eyes, obviously picturing remembered sights. She murmured, "I doubt it's important, but the day we went to visit Wendall, I saw what he was reading when we got there."

Gray remembered the pointed way Proctor had ignored them and cruised through that stapled sheaf of papers.

"It was a study by a wildlife biologist about using radios to track the migration patterns and feeding habits of wolverines in Alaska."

"Now why would something like that interest Proctor?" Gray speculated. "There aren't any wolverines in this part of the country."

"No, but Wendall's guys are building those little radios. Could they be for use on animals?" Another piece of information obviously clicked into place in Sam's brain as her face lit up and she snapped her fingers. "Molly told me the folks in the compound rehabilitate injured wild animals. I don't recall what all she told me they had, but they apparently heal up deer, foxes and even little critters like squirrels and return them to the wild."

He stared at her in surprise. "Wendall Proctor rescues bunnies?"

"I know!" she exclaimed. "I couldn't believe it, either."

No way could Gray reconcile the cold, calculating man he'd met with anyone who'd rescue wild animals.

Sam shivered beside him, the ripple of movement traveling through her thigh and straight to his heart. He did wrap his left arm around her shoulders then. "Cold?" he murmured.

She leaned into him before she remembered and jerked away from him, stiffening.

"I'm not going to bite you."

"Too bad—" she started cheerfully. Her gaze snapped up to his in dismay and then slid away guiltily. "I'm sorry. That was out of line."

Remorse speared through him. It was his fault she was this jumpy and awkward with him. "Sam, I don't want you to be uncomfortable around me. I was an ass the other night, and I'm sorry."

"For which part?"

He frowned. "The part where I kicked you out. Is there something else I should apologize for?"

She went even more stiff. "Gee, I don't know. You tell me."

Emily had never stood up to him like this, and he frankly had no idea how to handle a prickly female. He went for the blanket, I'm-a-big-fat-jerk apology. "Whatever I did or said to hurt you, I'm sorry."

She shifted to face him and he caught the momentary wince that crossed her face. "You *are* in pain," he accused. "I'm carrying you back to bed right now."

He stood up, but she did the same. They were abruptly chest to chest with one another. The passion and fury of two nights ago slammed into him like a freight train. He craved the physical and emotional release he found in her arms so much it nearly drove him to his knees.

"Sam, I—"

She put her hand over his mouth. "Unless you plan to kiss me again very soon, please don't say anything. Let it be."

He didn't want to just kiss her. He wanted to inhale her. To pull her inside his soul and absorb every bit of the laughter and attitude and joy she had to give. It was insane to even contemplate. But his head was tilting down.

He'd already made the break with her, already shattered her hopes and maybe her heart by declaring in the strongest possible terms that he didn't want a relationship with her. He'd be a cad to offer her renewed hope that there could be anything between them. But his arms were tightening around her.

He shouldn't want this. Shouldn't want her. But without question, he did. Her fingers slipped away from his mouth and their lips touched. She moaned softly in what sounded like distress.

"Did I hurt you?" he muttered, startled.

"Not in the way you think. Please. Kiss me again, and don't ever stop."

He simply didn't have it in him to say no. Not to her, not to himself. Not to his loneliness, nor his empty soul. He could call himself every name in the book—weak, selfish, cowardly—but it all paled in the face of her effect on him. She ripped away everything from his past and left him reborn into a new life. A new soul. How could any sane person say no to that?

He kissed her gently at first, but she leaned into him impatiently, grabbing his shirtfront to drag him closer, to demand more. And, God save him, he gave her everything he had to give. Not that it was enough. It would never be enough. But he couldn't hold back anymore.

Carefully, he scooped her up in his arms, never breaking the contact of their mouths. She tasted like the fresh pineapple he'd cut up for her earlier and mint toothpaste. He strode down the hall, checking his steps momentarily in front of her room, but then continuing on to his bedroom. Kicking open the door with a foot, he carried her over to his bed where she belonged. He eased her down to the mattress, but as he laid her down, Sam wrapped her arms around his neck and made it clear she had no plans to let go. He stretched out on the bed beside her, cautious of her wound.

"I don't want to hurt you," he mumbled.

"Then you'll have to distract me," she retorted. She rolled fully on top of him and he smiled up at her boldness. He'd never been with a woman like her, and he definitely liked it. He loved her confidence and her willingness to express her desire.

"Are you sure about this?" he asked her.

"Well, I'm not sure exactly how I'm going to get my pajamas off, but I thought I'd leave that to you."

He grinned up at her. "I've got it handled." He hooked his hands inside her flannel sheep jammies and eased them down over her bandage. Once they were bunched down around her thighs, it was an easy matter to push them the rest of the way off. Her tank top was a breeze to lift over her head.

His hands connected with satin flesh, and he sighed in pleasure. The curves of her body were quintessentially female, and he savored the luscious shape of her derriere. Her breath caught in the back of her throat, and he wished he could see her face more clearly. As it was, her eyes practically glowed in the dark as she stared down at him, their yellow-gold catching the faint streetlight from outside and reflecting it back at him.

"I'm sorry about the other night," he murmured. "I didn't mean it."

"Which part?"

"The part where I threw you out of my bed. I've never wanted anyone to stay as badly as I wanted you to stay then."

"Then why—"

"You scare the hell out of me!" he blurted.

She made a sound that vaguely resembled a laugh. "Yeah, I know the feeling."

"I scare you?" he asked in dismay.

She went still, straddling his hips, and stared down at him thoughtfully. She nodded slowly. "You scare me worse than anyone I've ever known."

In the context of the bastards and outright psychos she'd spent much of her life with, that wasn't much of an endorsement. Disappointment rolled through him. Had he really blown it with her that badly? He lifted his hands carefully away from her thighs. "I'm sorry, Sam. I didn't mean to frighten you—"

She cut him off quickly. "I'm not frightened of you in that way. I know you'd never, ever lay a hand on me." She amended hastily, "At least not with intent to do harm."

"How do I scare you, then?"

"You're...the real thing."

He snorted. He was a complete fraud. He might act like a walking, talking, living man, but he was nothing more than a hollow shell going through the motions of living.

Sam was talking again. "...could see myself with you for a long time...be happy, even...never thought I'd find someone like you...decent...kind..."

"Aww, honey. I'm not the right guy for you. You deserve someone with a heart as big and open as yours. Someone who makes you laugh. I always seem to put you on the verge of tears."

"Yeah, but that's because of—" She broke off.

He started to ask her because of what, but she leaned down quickly and silenced the question by kissing him. Or more accurately, by practically having carnal knowledge of his mouth. Her lips were full and soft, her teeth even and sharp, her tongue as quick as a mink and terribly clever. He'd never known kissing could be such a frankly sexual thing. He groaned his pleasure and surrendered without bothering to put up a fight. He'd lose, anyway.

But he had to admit, surrender had never felt so good. Her hands roamed over his body, and she made little sounds of approval that drove him crazy. He returned the favor carefully, dragging his fingertips over her skin lightly. The last thing he wanted to do tonight was hurt her.

Funny how last time they'd made love he'd felt a compulsion to push her, to test her resolve. He realized now in a burst of shocked clarity he'd been trying subconsciously to drive her away and prove she didn't really want him. But tonight, the exact opposite was true. He wanted to lure her to him, to draw her in, to seduce her. More to the point, he wanted her to love him just a little.

"I'm sorry for how I've treated you," he murmured.

"So far, I'd say you're doing pretty well." She sighed against his neck where she was currently nibbling her way toward his ear and making him a little crazy.

"You deserve so much more than me."

She propped herself up on his chest to stare down at him with those incredibly observant eyes of hers. "Yes, but I want *you*."

"Are you sure?" he asked quietly.

"Let's see. I'm naked and in bed with you—this after you rather rudely tossed me out of it a few days ago. I think about you every waking moment. I got shot and watched my car get blown up by a bomb, and yet I have no desire to leave this place if it means leaving you. Yes, I'd say I'm sure. I'm a goner."

"Ahh, baby. Now I really am sorry."

"Shut up and quit thinking so much. Just make love to me."

That, he could definitely do. Carefully. Treating her like a piece of hand-blown crystal and being mindful of her wound, he lay her down on the bed and proceeded to make love to her the way he should have the first time. With hands and mouth, heart and soul, he showed her everything he could not bring himself to say about what she meant to him.

It was so easy to lose himself in her. To let go and feel alive again. To forget, even if just for a little while, all the reasons why it was wrong for him to be happy. Even when he lay with her cradled in his arms a long while later, both of them limp and sated, the feeling didn't abate.

"Ahh, Sam. You are a wonder."

"My, you're black tonight, Mr. Kettle," she murmured sleepily.

A comfortable silence settled between them. It was the sound of peace.

"I should move," she sighed. "But I'm so comfy."

She was warm and relaxed and draped across his chest, and he didn't want her anywhere else anytime soon. "Don't move. Sleep. I'll keep watch over you."

"My knight in shining armor."

He didn't dispute her, even though he would steadfastly maintain he was no such hero if he were more awake.

He thought she'd fallen asleep, but then she mumbled semiconsciously, "How do you do it?"

"Do what?"

"Keep going. After…you know."

Abruptly, he was quite a bit more alert. "After what?" he asked, careful to keep his voice sleepy and slow.

"After losing your family."

His entire being went utterly still. She knew? She *knew?* Jeff Winston had given his solemn word he didn't tell her. And she sure as hell didn't know about it when she'd arrived in West Virginia—

His train of thought jumped the tracks and leaped ahead. Her road trip to Charleston. She'd been a mess when she got back from that. And it had taken her an inordinately long time to pick up a few buckets of varnish. That had to be when she'd researched him on the internet. He'd seen what was available online, which meant she knew *everything*. It felt like she had just ripped all his clothes off in front of a crowd of people.

Jaw clenched until it ached, he said, "I told you to leave my past alone."

Nope, not slow on the uptake, Sam. She popped upright beside him immediately. "Oww." She clutched at her side, but at the moment, he didn't give a damn if she had a knife sticking in it.

"It wasn't like I had any idea what I'd find," she explained. "You were so freaking mysterious about your past. How was I not supposed to poke around a little? It's what I do for a living. I'm so sorry for your loss—"

"Stop," he snapped, cutting her off. "I don't want your pity."

"Why the heck not? Aren't I allowed to feel sympathy for your tragedy?"

"No! I don't want your sympathy!" Unreasoning rage bubbled up inside him at her intrusion into the most private part of his life.

"Fine," she snapped back. "I'll just give your wife and kids my sympathy, not only for dying horribly, but for having to put up with a jerk like you." She threw back the covers and stormed—albeit gingerly—out of his room, naked.

A tiny, detached corner of his mind noted that it really was a magnificent exit. It also noted that she might have a point. But then his anger flared again. He would have stayed where he was and nursed his outrage except he heard Sam's voice coming from the kitchen. Foreboding that she was doing something extreme drove him to his closet for jeans. He pulled a shirt over his head as he strode down the hall toward the kitchen.

"—right now. I don't care if Jeff's been up for two days straight and just got to sleep. Wake him up," Sam was saying forcefully.

Gray barged into the kitchen and demanded, "What are you doing?"

"My job," she bit out.

He was about to make a sarcastic comment about

whether having sex with him was part of her job, when she spoke into the phone. "Jeff, it's Sam. An intruder with military training broke into the house a little while ago. I've got a sketch of him. I'm going to fax it to you, and I need you guys to get me an ID right away."

There was a brief pause where Jeff no doubt reminded Sam that there were no fax machines in the NRQZ.

She said fiercely, "I bet there's one at the sheriff's department. And if the right deputy's on duty tonight, I'll have no trouble getting him to send the sketch to you," she said.

Gray ground his molars together. That deputy had practically drooled on her shoes.

His irritation was interrupted by her speaking again. "Proctor's guys shot at me and blew up my car yesterday. It's time to end this."

Funny how she left out the bit about being hit by a bullet. Didn't want Jeff to pull her off the job, huh? He couldn't wait to tell Jeff about her injury and get her yanked out of here.

"What are you going to do?" Gray kibitzed at her. "March into Proctor's compound and demand to know what he's doing?"

She covered the phone's mouthpiece, her eyes glittering with yellow fury. She looked like a tiger about to eat him. "That's exactly what I'm going to do."

"That's insane," Gray hissed as she stuck a finger in her free ear and listened intently to whatever Jeff was saying.

"Really?" she said with interest. "That gives me an idea. What are the odds you can send a field operations unit out this way, like now?" A pause. "Yes, fully armed. I think Proctor's more dangerous than we thought."

,Gray's jaw threatened to sag. What in the hell was she doing?

She said, "Keep me up-to-date on the signal interruptions, eh? I think they may be more important than we'd realized."

She hung up the phone and brushed past him without speaking.

"Where are you going?"

"To pack."

"Why?"

"I'm done here."

"You're leaving West Virginia?" It was the very thing he'd been anticipating a minute ago, but something sharp and hot twisted in his gut at the reality of her leaving him.

She sniffed. "You wish. No, I'm seeing this thing through." She added with a hint of bitterness, "In spite of you."

He hated having to ask her what she had in mind, but he was specifically tasked with keeping an eye on her by the NSA. "What are you planning?"

She spun to face him, grimaced as she gripped her side, but did not utter a sound. "I'm sneaking into Proctor's compound and having a look down that tunnel he's dug."

"You'll never make it. Hell, no one can move within a mile of that place without his guys swarming out like angry fire ants to chase off the intruder."

"And how is it he always seems to know when someone's nearby?" she demanded. "I *know* he doesn't have on-the-ground sensing devices in that valley. I spot stuff like that in my sleep."

"I have no idea."

"Well, I do. There's a leak inside your precious NSA. Someone's feeding the guy satellite telemetry. I'd bet my next paycheck the NSA has a camera pointed down at the NRQZ all the time."

He knew not to take that bet. But…a leak? "NSA employees are thoroughly vetted out before and after they're hired. The odds of Proctor slipping one of his followers past one of our background checks are pretty slim."

"He doesn't have to slip a human past you. All he has to do is find the right wire and tap into the signal. The U.S. government just had to shut down a major satellite surveillance facility because the contractors who built it installed a second, shadow wiring system and were bleeding off satellite signals and selling them on the black market. Same thing could've happened here."

His stomach dropped heavily. Was she right? Had his agency been compromised?

"Heck," she continued, "after H.O.T. Watch got shut down, I'll bet there's been a giant scramble to find an alternate source of satellite intel by bad guys around the world."

"That's not the kind of signals intelligence Shady Grove collects, Sam. They pick up phone calls here."

"Agreed. That's why we have to have a look in that tunnel and find out what Proctor's really doing."

"If the guy is getting leaked telemetry, how do you propose to get into his tunnel?"

"Have your people turn off the satellites watching Shady Grove."

"You seriously think I have that kind of power?"

She gave him a considering look. "Yes. I do."

He just shook his head.

"Make the call, Gray. Buy us a window of time to get in there and have a look around."

"I'm a trained field operative. You're not. I'll go in. But I'm not taking you with me."

Infuriatingly, she shrugged. "Fine. I'll go in on my own. I'm confident Jeff and his grandfather have the clout to get the satellite turned off for a little while. I'll just ask Leland to call the president—"

"I'll make the damned call." He couldn't begin to imagine the mess that would roll downhill and land on his head if the Winstons involved the White House in this investigation. "But you're still not going in with me."

"Like I said. I'll just go in on my own."

He huffed in exasperation. "Sam. You're hurt. You can't do it."

"I'm betting it'll take you a few days to make the arrangements, and I heal fast. I'll be ready to go."

"No."

"I'm not asking for your opinion or your permission, Gray. I'm going in and that's that."

"But you don't even like danger!"

"I'll do what's necessary. This investigation needs to end so I can get away from you and quit hurting you."

Her declaration stopped him cold. She thought she was the one hurting him? He was the one who kept lashing out at her in his pain and grief. Not that he wasn't still furious that she'd poked into his past without asking him first. And not that his saying no would have stopped her.

His thoughts derailed. Truth be told, nothing would have stopped her. She was a researcher for a living. Did he seriously think she wouldn't eventually want to know what made him such a head case? He'd been deluding himself to think he could keep his past a secret from her. What had Jeff Winston been thinking to send someone like her to help him? Sure, her eyesight had been enormously helpful, but Jeff had to know she would ultimately pry into his personal—

Of course. That was exactly why Jeff had sent her. Mentally, he called his old fraternity brother every foul name he could think of. Gray tried to stay angry at Jeff, but enough of him could understand Jeff's impulse to help that he couldn't work up a real head of steam against the guy. Jeff should've stayed out of it. Left well enough alone. Gray had been doing fine without his frat brother's interference. Or Sam's.

He walked down the hall to her bedroom, which was already a tornado of half-packed clothes. The woman didn't waste any time once she'd made up her mind. "Don't go, Sam."

He couldn't believe he was saying it, but the words had unquestionably come out of his mouth.

"Why shouldn't I?" she asked tersely.

No doubt she was hoping for an apology and a declaration of how much he cared for her and couldn't live without her. His jaw tight, he answered, "Because Miss Maddie will ask questions and start all kinds of rumors. And given how closely Proctor's scrutinizing us, it could tip him off that we're heading for the endgame."

"Right. The mission," she replied bitterly.

As he'd thought. She'd been hoping for the whole I-can't-live-without-you speech. He was assailed by the same feeling he got when perched on the edge of a cliff. One part of him wanted to back away very carefully. But a tiny part of him was tempted to take one more step forward. To leap off the cliff and see what it felt like to fly, even if only for a few seconds.

His old friend and comfort, Suicide, wasn't getting the job done this time around. Somehow, it seemed like an empty gesture now. Dammit, Sam had ruined even that for him. How was he supposed to go on without the safety net that the prospect of killing himself provided? If he did it her way, he would have to live with the pain. Live with the grief. Hell, how was he supposed to find a way to go on? Sam made it sound so damned easy. But he knew—he *knew*—it wasn't easy at all. Yet, she seemed to believe he was capable of it. Was she right? Was he strong enough, after all?

He backed away from the cliff in more haste than grace and headed back toward the kitchen. She wanted this thing over? So be it. He picked up the phone with grim determination and dialed a number from memory that would set the wheels in motion. One way or another, he'd either be dead or rid of Sam in a few days. He'd never have to face her and the things she made him feel again.

Chapter 15

Sam was losing her mind. Being in the same house with Gray, who'd become a total stranger to her overnight, was killing her. The revelation that she'd found out about his family's murder had completely shut him down emotionally. She didn't have the faintest idea how to scale the walls of the fortress he'd thrown up around himself. Finally, in desperation, she called her boss.

"Jeff, I have a confession to make. Gray's in bad shape, and it's my fault."

"Did you poke into his past?" Jeff asked immediately, startling her mightily.

"Uhh, yes. I did."

"Excellent. I knew you would."

"But you ordered me not to!"

"Sam, I've worked with you for a long time. What's the one way to be absolutely sure you'll tackle a problem with everything you've got?" She mumbled something inaudible as he answered his own question. "Tell you something can't be done. If I told you in no uncertain terms to leave alone something that had to be killing you with curiosity, there was no way you'd follow that order. You'd run in the opposite direction as fast as you could. And you did. Good girl."

"Not good. I think I've really hurt Gray. He's a mess. He won't speak to me and just sits and stares out the window like he's contemplating the most efficient way to kill himself."

"He was already a mess. I needed someone to shake him up. Give him a swift kick in the pants and force him to come out of his shell."

"I'm pretty sure I drove him way deep into his shell, boss. He about took my head off when he found out that I knew."

"He yelled at you?" Jeff asked in surprise.

"Yes. He was really angry."

"Outstanding!" Jeff exclaimed.

"Excuse me?"

"He hasn't shown a real emotion since the day Emily and the kids died. He's been holding it all in. And it's killing him. I knew you could draw him out. Force him to finally feel something again. To start living."

"I don't know about the living part, but I definitely made him feel some things. Like rage and betrayal. He hates my guts."

"That's fantastic!"

"Speak for yourself," she grumbled.

Jeff fell silent. "Oh, no. You like him, don't you?"

"He's a pretty great guy when he's not being all stoic and withdrawn."

"I just assumed…you being fresh off your breakup

with that Rocket guy that you wouldn't fall for him...
Oh, jeez. I'm so sorry, Sam."

She squeezed her eyes shut in mortification. "Hey.
I'm an adult. I knew what I was getting into. I just bit
off a little more than I could chew with this guy. He's
too damaged for me to fix. I just hope I didn't make a
bigger mess of him than he already was."

"Sending you to him was a last-ditch effort on my
part, Sam. If you can't reach him, nobody can. Don't
beat yourself up over it."

Yeah, well, she was. But for all her self-flagellation,
she didn't have a clue how to make it up to Gray. He'd
retreated further into his own private little hell than she
was able to reach. She'd lost him. And she feared he'd
lost himself for good this time.

She asked Jeff, "Do you know anything about this
business of him counting down days?"

Jeff swore under his breath. "Where is he in his
count?"

"Nineteen."

Her boss answered heavily, "He's counting down the
days until he can kill himself. He makes these bargains
with himself where he sets a date that, if things haven't
gotten better by then, he gives himself permission to
commit suicide. He said it helps him deal with the pain."

Great. She'd made the guy suicidal. She hung up,
more depressed than ever.

Three more days counted down while they waited
for the NSA to approve Gray's request to turn off the
satellites pointed at the NRQZ. Jeff had recalled an ops
team from somewhere overseas, and they were due in
any minute but had yet to arrive.

Sam began to suspect she was obsessing about
Gray's countdown more than he was. Sixteen. The

number loomed huge in her mind as she woke up near sunset. A little over two weeks. They had to finish this case, and soon. Give him time to get far away from her and get some breathing room to recover from the hurt she'd caused him before he got to zero.

She couldn't take it anymore. She jumped out of bed, dressed and barged into the kitchen to confront him. "Gray, I've had it. I can't take this anymore. I'm calling Jeff and getting that satellite shut down now."

"What can't you take anymore?" he asked emotionlessly.

"You!"

He frowned. "What have I been doing?"

"Nothing. And that's the point. I'm not sitting around here one more day watching you wait to die. I can't do it. You're making a stupid decision, and I won't be part of it. If you plan to kill yourself, you can bloody well do it on your watch."

His eyes flashed briefly, the first sign of life she'd seen in them in days. Maybe that was the key to breaking him out of the funk he'd fallen into. Maybe she ought to pick a massive fight with him. At least then he'd feel *something*.

She picked up the phone.

"Wait."

Hark. He'd spoken to her. It was a single word, but it was more than he'd said to her for the past several days. She looked over at him expectantly.

"The NSA approved the shutdown a few hours ago. It goes offline at 2:00 a.m. tonight. A memo's gone out that the satellite is being taken offline so a software upgrade can be installed."

"And when were you planning to share that information with me?"

"I wasn't planning to."

"You were going to try to sneak out and leave me here?" she asked ominously.

He shrugged.

"Has anyone told you recently what a self-centered jerk you are?" she snapped.

His mouth quirked for just a moment. "Not recently."

"Well, you are. I get that a horrible thing happened in your past. But you don't have the corner on that particular market, Sparky. My life hasn't exactly been a picnic, either, but you don't see me moping around counting down the days until I can slit my wrists."

She *knew* she got a rise out of him. Irritation glinted in his eyes and his shoulders went tense, but still he said nothing. Frustrated nearly to the point of screaming, she battered at the walls he'd built around himself. "Do you think you're the only person who's ever suffered a terrible and violent loss? Pick up a newspaper. Terrible things happen to good people all the time. It's not pretty, but it's part of being human. But you know what people do? They grieve and they suffer…*and they go on*."

Gray shifted in his chair uncomfortably, but she wasn't about to let him get up and leave. Not until she had her say. She aimed a glare at him and dared him to try to walk out on her. He subsided in his seat.

"People who've lost every bit as much as you get up in the morning and they paste a smile on their face and wait for the day when it becomes a real smile. And it does, eventually. Sure, it takes time. And the hurt never leaves entirely. But that hurt also adds a sweetness to the good times to come. You learn to appreciate life a little bit more. But you have to let yourself live again first."

He opened his mouth. Closed it.

"Don't give me some crap about not deserving to be happy. You didn't kill your family. Some psycho, probably paid by another psycho, did it. You couldn't have stopped the killer. If not that night, he'd have waited for some other time, some other night you worked late, to murder them. The guy was a pro, and you had no idea he was out there waiting to strike."

Gray threw up his hands. "Do you seriously think you're the first person who's ever said any of this to me?"

"Of course not. But I am the first person who could've made you happy again. We could've had something really good together, Gray. But you wouldn't let yourself reach out and take what was right in front of you. I have no need to replace your wife and kids, and I know not to bother trying. I'd have been okay with their ghosts being part of our family. You really could've had it all."

She turned to leave and stopped in the doorway only long enough to add, "I'm going with you tonight. And then I'm out of here. I give up, Gray. If you want to count all the way down to zero and give in to your cowardice completely, you're going to have to do it without me."

Call him a coward and then sail out of the room like a queen, would she? Gray was so furious he could hardly think, let alone breathe. But a tiny part of him had to admit that this fire in his belly felt better than the ice-cold nothingness of the past few days. Lord, that woman knew how to make an exit.

Why couldn't she leave well enough alone? But then, that wasn't her style. At all.

His irritation gave way to amusement as he headed

for his room to check and pack the gear he'd need tonight. He was going in armed to the teeth, particularly if Sam was coming—

The thought startled him. What did she have to do with anything? How could he still feel protective of her, even after she'd made it crystal clear she was out of here the minute this op was concluded? Obviously, logic had nothing to do with his impulse. But then logic rarely had much to do with Sammie Jo. She'd made him feel a hundred different sensations in the past several weeks, but anything remotely resembling reason was not one of them. Mostly, she made him crazy.

He stocked up his rucksack with freshly wound rope and new cyalume sticks.

She made him mad, too. And frustrated.

He sheathed a freshly sharpened field knife in a side pocket and tucked several flares into a waterproof pouch sewn into the pack's lining.

Of course, she also made him laugh. And got him all hot and bothered....

He slammed his hand against the wall. The stinging pain in his palm snapped him out of his ridiculous ruminations. He could *not* afford to be this messed up in the head hours before a dangerous mission. He checked over his night-vision goggles and put fresh batteries in them; he had faith he'd need every bit of help he could get to keep up with Sam tonight.

He was not wrong. Promptly at 2:00 a.m., she climbed out of the Bronco without saying a word to him and set a blistering pace through the woods around the north end of the Proctor compound. They'd never approached from this direction before. It required more time in the woods, but it also put them beside the fence closest to the barn that was their target tonight. They'd still have to traverse an alarmingly wide patch of tilled soil without being spotted. But he'd decided that speed might ultimately be more important than stealth. The satellite would be out of commission for approximately two hours. It was the best the NSA could do for him without compromising other security needs.

Sam had insisted on going first, and her head swiveled constantly as she marched along. She seemed relieved when she stopped abruptly and pointed out a trip wire to him. He stepped over it gingerly. Had Proctor been warned about the coverage gap tonight and taken additional precautions?

She spotted two more trip wires as they approached the fence, and they easily avoided both. Gray consoled himself with the notion that he'd have spotted the wires on his own. Of course, he'd have been moving at a fraction of this pace.

Finally, they crouched at the fence. There'd been a brief debate at the kitchen table over cutting their way through the fence or digging under it. He'd wanted to cut through, Sam wanted to dig. As they examined the fence, though, the bottom was sunk in concrete buried in the ground. Cutting it was.

He pulled out wire cutters, already taped and padded to ease the job, but Sam put a restraining hand on his arm. His biceps tensed involuntarily at her touch, and she jerked her fingers away.

"There's a sensor wire," she whispered. "I'll reroute it while you cut."

He nodded and got to work while she efficiently pulled out a spool of wire and claw clips to reroute the sensor. He was shocked at how good it felt to cooperate with her on something for a change. They'd been pulling against each other so hard the past few days he'd almost forgotten what it felt like to be on the same team with her.

She nodded her readiness, and he snipped through the sensor wire. No sirens or floodlights exploded to life.

"Are we good to go?" she whispered.

He shrugged. "No way to tell except having company in a few minutes. And we're on a short timetable. No time to sit around and wait." He pulled back the panel of hurricane fencing and held it for her while she crawled through. He passed the packs to her and then followed, pulling the panel back into place behind him.

As they'd agreed upon, Sam took a quick look around. When she signaled an all clear, they took off running across the field. The dirt was soft and deep, and they left footprints a three-year-old could track. But there was no help for it. And hopefully, they'd be out of here long before it mattered.

He and Sam dived into the shadow of the barn, breathing hard. Now for the padlock on the door. That was his field of expertise, and Sam played lookout while he picked the lock.

He almost had it when Sam whispered, "Routine patrol passing between the dormitories." He froze as she continued under her breath, "One guy. On foot. And he's out of sight now."

Gray's pulse pounded nonetheless as he finished the lock. It clicked open quietly. He eased the big sliding door open just far enough to slip inside. Sam pushed it shut behind them, and they both froze in horror as it gave a hefty squeak.

"Keep moving," he murmured. "If someone heard it, there's nothing we can do about it."

Sam nodded, but she looked scared. "I can buy us a

little time, just in case." She looped the lock through a hasp on the inside of the door to prevent anyone from opening it from the outside. They'd decided she would search the computers while he checked out the rest of the building, and they both set to work.

She draped a piece of black fabric over a computer monitor and ducked under it to boot up the system. Using his night-vision goggles, he popped a tiny, two-inch cyalume stick and used its scant light to have a look around.

He jolted as five pairs of red eyes glared at him out of the darkness. He pointed the cyalume stick at them and two rabbits, a squirrel and a fox stared back at him from a line of cages. Proctor's inexplicable wild animal rescue program was alive and well.

"I'm in," Sam announced quietly.

Dang. That password-decrypting gadget she'd received in the mail yesterday was as good as she'd said it was. The device was something Jeff's people had designed and Sam swore by. He moved over to her side and ducked under the black hood with her. The intimacy of it caught him by surprise, but he forced his intense awareness of her aside. Still. It felt good to stand close to her again.

She was scrolling rapidly through a file directory.

"Just copy the whole mess. We can look through it later," he ordered.

She nodded, plugged in a flash drive and typed a series of commands. While she did that, he continued his search of the building. Storage cabinets and toolboxes didn't yield any interesting finds.

"Any luck on the tunnel?" she asked quietly.

He snorted. The thing was impossible to miss. A huge bundle of orange extension cords led right to it, and a big fan stood not far from the opening. The tunnel was a good eight feet in diameter and headed straight down into the ground. "It's over here."

He expected her to join him, but glanced over at her when she didn't. She was standing in front of some sort of workbench, examining something small and electrical-looking. Whatever it was, she jammed it in her pocket and continued over to him. Even clothed entirely in black, nondescript leggings and a turtleneck, she was stunning, a shapely shadow in a sea of lime-green.

"There's a ladder," he murmured. "I'll go down first."

The vertical shaft turned out to be short, four feet or so down to what turned out to be a ledge. Another ladder led down to a second, lower level. And it was off this that a tunnel extended away into the dark.

He started forward into the blackness. The scale of the tunnel was staggering. Although it wasn't much more than shoulder-width for him, it was easily seven feet tall. He had plenty of headroom, even with wires and air ducting overhead.

Moving cautiously and keeping a sharp eye out for booby traps, they made their way forward. They'd been walking for maybe ten minutes when the tunnel widened out into a small room of sorts. They flashed their lights all around the space but saw nothing special about it.

"I think this is just a turnaround or rest area," he announced.

"Let me go first. We'll move faster," Sam replied.

He nodded and she took off down the tunnel quickly. They'd been striding along briskly for maybe five minutes when another area opened up. And this one had electric lights installed. They found the switch and a widely spaced row of bulbs illuminated on down the tunnel. More interesting, a set of steel tracks wound off into the gloom. A small cart not much larger than a wheelbarrow sat at the end of the track.

"Wanna ride?" Sam asked.

"May as well. There's no telling how far this thing goes."

"It's quite the excavation project," she commented as they climbed into the little railcar. He picked up the remote control lying inside it and pushed the green button. The cart lurched into motion, dumping Sam in his lap. "Uhh, sorry," she grunted as she scrambled to right herself and push away from him all without touching him any more than she had to.

"Oh, for Pete's sake. Stop squirming."

She froze against him.

"Just turn around and sit down in my lap. It'll be more comfortable for both of us because I'll have somewhere to put my legs."

She did as he suggested without comment. And all of a sudden, the train ride seemed to go on forever. She smelled good. Even though she was tense against him, she felt as feminine and sexy as ever. The only sensible thing to do with his arms was to put them around her waist. If he wasn't mistaken, she snuggled a little closer before she went ramrod-stiff against him.

"Relax already," he muttered. "I won't bite you."

She drew a quick breath, no doubt to make a snappy comeback, but then said merely, "How long do you suppose it took them to dig this thing?"

"They must have worked on it for months. Years, maybe. That scaffolding supporting the ceiling looks like they expect the tunnel to be here for a while, too."

She nodded, looking up. "They wouldn't go to all

this trouble if they were planning a one-time sabotage of the computer cables."

Sam was absolutely right. What on earth were these people up to? As the ride continued, she wiggled in his lap without warning. For an alarmed and thrilled second, he thought she was making a grab for his male parts. But sadly, she was only digging in her pocket for something.

She said eagerly, "Look what I found."

He pointed his cyalume stick at a small object she held out in her palm. It was no larger than his thumbnail. "What's that?"

"A radio," she announced triumphantly.

"What do you suppose it's for?"

"This." She pulled a second object out of her pocket. It was a thin pile of nylon with a buckle. She held it up and it resolved into a harness-like contraption a person might walk a dog in, but smaller. Rabbit-size. Or squirrel-size. And it had a tiny pouch sewn onto it where a radio could ride the wearer's back.

"Proctor's attaching radios to the animals he rescues?" Gray asked.

"They're not just radios. They're jammers."

"Come again?" he asked, surprised.

She flipped the tiny radio over. "This is a signal jammer. It emits a specific frequency in a concentrated burst that would totally jam one frequency or a small range of frequencies."

That would explain all those radio bursts randomly knocking out the Shady Grove and Byrd Observatory antennas. And when investigators went to the source of the signal, they always found nothing. *Animals* were wearing the radios. Proctor was turning the radios on somehow, probably remotely, and then turning them off after a minute or two. The harnessed animals would move on to a new location, and nobody was the wiser as to where the signal had come from. It was actually ingenious.

"What kind of range do you think those radios might have?" he asked.

She grinned up at him. "If a short in a heating pad can kick the big antennas offline, these wouldn't have to be powerful at all to screw up the antenna arrays at the observatory and at Shady Grove."

"Okay. Then why does Proctor want to screw up the antenna arrays?"

The cart chose that moment to lurch to a stop, throwing him forward against Sam. "Sorry," he mumbled.

"No sweatskie. Let's find out what's at the end of the line, shall we?"

Her enthusiasm was contagious. They didn't have all the pieces yet, but he could feel Proctor's plan falling into place around them. The tunnel ended maybe a dozen yards beyond the track in a third widened area in the tunnel.

More lightbulbs were clustered in metal cages here, and Sam put on a pair of sunglasses. While she adapted, he took a look around. A rough table to one side of the space held two surprisingly state-of-the-art computers and a tower that would hold a good-size computer server. He glanced up at the ceiling at the far end of the room.

"Bingo," he announced.

"What've you got?" Sam moved over beside him to gaze upward. "Ahh."

Yup. Ahh. A twelve-inch steel pipe had a gaping hole cut in it, revealing rubber lining and cables. Lots and lots of cables. And some sort of small box was nestled among the mass. Thin wires led from the box directly into the backs of the two computers on the table.

Sam leaned in, studying the connections closely. "How weird! That box is not actually tapping into any of the cables. It's just sitting beside them. But Proctor has stripped away the insulation around the fiber-optic cables next to the box-thingie."

"Any guess as to what the box-thingie does?" he asked dryly.

Frowning, she moved over to the table. "Let's see if we can find out." She turned on one of the systems and it booted up without needing a password. Proctor must be pretty confident of his security if he didn't bother protecting these systems. Sam browsed the computer's contents for a minute or two when a strange screen popped up in front of her.

"What's that?" he asked.

"Correct me if I'm wrong, but doesn't this look like a power monitoring program?"

He frowned. "Yes. It does."

And then it hit him. "They're not breaking into the information flow from the antennas to the computer arrays. They're only watching when the information is flowing."

"Now why would they care about that?" Sam mumbled.

He frowned. Radios that would jam signals. Computers that would tell when the signals were stopped or not. "Why would someone shut down the antenna arrays intentionally and go to all this trouble to check that they were down?"

Sam stared at him, her sunglasses giving away nothing. "What are the two things nobody can do in range of the big antennas without getting caught?"

"Use electricity, for one. What's the other?"

"Easy," she answered. "Send messages. No phone call or wireless signal in North America can get past Shady Grove's antennas."

A chill rushed through him. They were on the right track now. The next obvious question was, "Who does Proctor want to call so privately that he's gone to all this trouble to knock the antennas offline and verify that they're offline?"

"No idea. Let's see if there's an answer in here," Sam offered as she began to type.

He waited and watched while she typed. Finally, she stopped on what looked like the readout from a seismic sensor. It was a wildly varying scribble that crawled across the screen. "I don't know if this is important, but it looks like this might have to do with a radio signal. I can't tell what it's measuring, though."

As a longtime NSA employee, he took one look at the screen and knew precisely what he was looking at. "That's a record of signal bursts from satellites. They send an initial signal—this blip here—then pause to align themselves with the ground station. Then, after this short delay—the flat line here—they commence the body of the transmission, which is done in a microwave relay. That's all this electronic activity here. When the satellite's done talking, it sends this final burst to show it's done. The ground station sends a termination reply—here—and voila. One complete satellite transmission."

"Who's making the transmissions?" Sam asked.

"That's a hell of a good question. Can you find any kind of signature that can tell us what specific satellite this program is tracking?"

Sam poked around for a minute. "Does GSAT-12 mean anything to you?"

He swore softly. "Yes. That's a state-of-the-art communications satellite."

"So why is Proctor watching a communications satellite?" Sam asked.

Gray stared at her and she stared back. He reached out with both hands and gently removed her sunglasses so he could look directly into her eyes. Worry made them dark gold.

She spoke slowly, clearly thinking as she went. "If I wanted to make phone calls that wouldn't be monitored by Echelon, I'd have to turn Echelon off, right?"

He nodded, appalled. His intuition shouted that she was spot-on.

"So how would I turn it off?" she continued. "I'd cause interference that kicked its antennas offline. Enter the bunnies and their signal jammers. And then I'd devise some way to measure whether or not I'd succeeded in kicking the system offline. When I knew Echelon was shut down, I'd make my phone call. If I got a warning that Echelon had come back up online, I'd cut off my call fast."

"But in the meantime, I'd have had a window to speak privately without any government agency overhearing me." He added heavily, "From anywhere in North America."

Sam nodded. "If you were a bad guy, what would you want to talk about without Uncle Sam hearing you?"

"I can think of a bunch of things," he replied grimly, "and none of them are legal or good for our country."

She nodded. "I could keep that ability to make unmonitored phone calls all to myself, or if I were an enterprising sort of bad guy, I could sell phone calls to all my bad guy friends and make enough money to support a snazzy compound full of hippies to be my cover."

His stomach sank, a sure sign that his instinct recognized truth in her words. "I do believe you've got it, Sam. We're sitting on the phone company for Bad Guys Are Us. Can you find any proof of it on that computer?"

"I'm going to copy the whole hard drive of this system, too, and sort it out later. I expect we'll find a log of phone calls somewhere on this puppy. I just don't know where to look."

"Fair enough. The NSA's going to have a field day with this."

She copied the contents of the hard drives of both computers onto a flash disk and did something to one of the computers that made her chortle quietly to herself.

"Dare I ask what you're doing?" he murmured.

"I planted a virus in their system. In case we don't make it out of here tonight. In a few days, this thing is going to be so tied in knots they won't know which end is up."

"Where did this virus come from?" he asked, surprised.

"I had a copy of it on that flash drive I just filled up with Proctor's data. Best hackers in the biz created it."

"You're an evil woman, Sammie Jo Jessup."

"And don't you ever forget it," she mumbled in distraction as she shut down the computers.

She had a point. Even he tended to underestimate her. She could definitely take care of herself and wasn't the kind of helpless female he would worry about being taken advantage of when he wasn't around to look out for her. Not like Emily—

No, not like Emily at all.

Shock registered that he'd managed to think of Sam

and Emily in the same breath and not be overwhelmed by guilt. Each in their own way was special and unique, but the two women were so different he would never confuse the two of them.

"Ready to blow this popsicle stand?" Sam asked jauntily.

"Yup. Let's do it."

They piled back into the wheelbarrow-size cart. This time Sam settled into his lap without his having to ask. Optimism oozed from her, and he caught himself soaking it up without thinking.

He was supposed to be depressed, dammit. Shut down emotionally. But darned if she didn't wake him up inside just with her presence. She wasn't saying or doing a blessed thing. Just sitting in his lap. But energy buzzed off her like warmth on a sunny day. She truly was a force of nature.

They reached the end of the tunnel, turned off the lights and hiked back to the barn quickly, confident that the tunnel was clear of traps. He jogged up the first ladder and stood up in the short hole—

Zing. Ping.

He ducked, stunned. Sam bumped into his back and he yanked her down beside him.

"What was that?" she whispered.

"Gunshot."

Chapter 16

Sam didn't waste time on histrionics. She pulled the pieces of the small rifle she'd slipped into her pack just before they left the house and commenced assembling it quickly. Sometimes being able to see in the dark was really, really handy. Like now. When she had to have a weapon fast. It might be small-caliber and short-range, but in her hands, it was accurate and deadly.

"Where's the shooter?" she breathed.

"Didn't see. Outside the barn, I think. Silenced weapon."

"Sound suppressors reduce accuracy," she commented. "And since we're blown, I don't care about quiet." She moved out from behind Gray and approached the edge of the hole.

"What are you planning?" he asked suspiciously.

"I'm gonna pop up, peek at what we've got out there, and take a shot if I've got one."

"Are you insane?" he whispered.

"Have you got a better idea? It's not like there's another way out of the tunnel."

He shuddered at the prospect of being trapped underground. A horrible way to die, to be sure.

Sam continued, "If the tunnel were wider or had some side branches, I'd draw them down there and use my eyesight to pick them off. As it is, we'll have to use my eyesight to pick them off up top."

She wasn't anywhere near as calm as she sounded, but panicking wouldn't do any good at the moment, so she held the terror at bay. She had no intention of dying tonight. Not when Gray was finally thawing out toward her.

Popping up, she looked around fast and ducked down to process the details. "The barn door is wide open. A dozen armed men are arrayed out front. Once I shoot the first one, they'll have to take cover."

"There's not much out there to take cover behind," Gray replied. "They'll have to drive a tractor or some trucks in front of the door and hide behind those."

"Let them. I see better than they do, and I'm a better shot." He looked at her doubtfully, and she added, "Trust me."

To his credit, he nodded. His acceptance of her skill warmed a little spot deep within the cold terror she currently was holding at bay.

"You want to pop up and shoot with me?" she asked. "You won't have to aim. There's a whole line of guys in front of the door."

"Overconfident bastards," he mumbled.

She grinned and breathed, "On three. One. Two. Three."

She stood up, steadied her rifle on the edge of the

hole and shot fast, double-tapping each target in turn. It was like shooting ducks in a gallery. Except these were big, man-size ducks who weren't moving. At least not at first. After she and Gray dropped the first several guys, Proctor's men woke up and dove out of sight. It actually would have been comical if she and Gray weren't trapped, surrounded and seriously outnumbered.

While she reloaded, Gray did a strange thing. He reached into his pocket and pulled out a cell phone.

"News flash, Sparky. There are no cell phone towers to receive your signal."

"Sat phone," he replied, grinning wolfishly.

"God bless the NSA for giving you decent equipment."

"Amen," he muttered as he dialed a number.

He rattled off a series of letters and numbers which she assumed were some sort of identity verification. And then he said, "Send the nearest marines. And tell them to expect a hell of a firefight."

He hung up the phone and reported, "They're on their way. But it's about a twenty-minute drive over here, plus time to gear up. Estimated time of arrival— thirty to forty minutes."

Her heart sank. "We won't be alive that long."

Sam popped up to take another shot and wasn't surprised to see the doorway empty. But she did spot someone standing at the far side of the field, staring in their direction with binoculars. She grinned and took aim. Poor bastard didn't know she could see him a whole lot better than he could see her. She pulled the trigger, and the guy dropped like a rock.

"Who'd you shoot?" Gray asked.

"Spotter. On the far side of the field."

"Have I mentioned lately that I love your eyesight?"

"No, as a matter of fact, you haven't."

"Well, I do."

"Thanks." She smiled over at him. "Any chance I can borrow your phone? Maybe I can get us a faster rescue."

As he held the device out to her, the telltale putt-putting of a diesel tractor became audible. She dialed fast. "Novak, it's Sam. Any chance that Winston field team has arrived in West Virginia yet?"

The Winston Ops controller replied, "As a matter of fact, they have."

"Tell them to get over to the Proctor compound ASAP. Gray and I are pinned down, surrounded and outgunned. We'll be okay until we run out of ammunition, and then we're screwed."

"Got it. I'm on it."

"And get me an ETA."

Novak was off the line for a few seconds, and then said, "Estimated time of arrival, twenty minutes."

They both knew that was a lifetime in a firefight.

"Hang on as long as you can," the controller added. "I'll see what I can do to shave a few minutes off that ETA."

She disconnected without saying any more as a tractor pulled into view.

Gray murmured beside her, "We've got to conserve our ammo. Each bullet has to count."

She nodded grimly. If help didn't get here soon, it wasn't going to matter how careful they were. Still, she wasn't about to give up. "I'll shoot. You reload."

Gray nodded his agreement and handed her his pistol. "I'll save two bullets," he replied grimly.

She scowled over at him. "I'm not planning to die tonight. And you'd better not be, either. You fight to live. You hear me?"

Gray looked startled. "Excuse me?"

"You've got fifteen more days left before you have permission to check out, mister. If you're too big a coward to pull the trigger yourself and decide to go out in a blaze of glory tonight, I'll wring your neck myself if Proctor doesn't manage to kill you. I'm just sayin'."

"Duly noted," he commented wryly. "And where'd you learn about my countdowns?"

"Jeff."

"I'm going to kill him if we make it out of here," Gray commented without any real heat.

"He loves you," she replied. "Don't bust his chops for fighting to save you."

A brief stalemate ensued while Proctor's men drove a heavy truck up beside the tractor. Sam shot a careless ankle she spotted under the belly of the pickup truck, and a shout of pain announced the accuracy of her shot. Gray nodded at her in grim approval.

The quiet didn't last for long, however. Men started popping up and shooting in trios, laying down covering fire for each other and preventing Sam from popping up and shooting back. Every time she poked the rifle barrel above the rim of the hole, a fusillade of bullets pinned her down, unable to return fire.

Gray finally suggested, "You need a diversion. I'll poke up a gun barrel on my side of the hole, and when they shoot at me, you come up on the other side of the hole and do your thing."

Sam nodded. The tactic worked once, and she managed to take out another shooter with what was probably a kill shot to the face. She would feel bad about shooting these guys if they weren't trying to kill her and Gray, and if she wasn't sure that most of them were ex-military and knew the score. But as it was, she didn't have time for guilt. Survival was a slightly higher priority at the moment.

The next time she and Gray tried the decoy gun thing, a shooter spun around the edge of the barn door and she barely ducked in time to avoid having her head blown off. Even though the near miss scared the heck out of her, she popped back up doggedly to fire through the wall at the spot where the guy had just taken cover. A cry announced that she'd gotten lucky.

A short pause ensued. On a hunch, she fired through the thin aluminum barn wall again, at about the spot where she'd just hit the shooter. Another cry rang out. Yup, as she'd expected. Someone had come over to retrieve their hurt buddy. Now Proctor's men had two guys down and exposed. Should she try for a third lucky hit?

She reached over for a freshly loaded weapon, and Gray's hand on her wrist made her look over at him. He shook his head. "Not enough ammo," he breathed.

He was right. They couldn't afford to take foolish shots.

Another pause ensued. She registered vaguely that time was wildly distorted at the moment. Pauses of seconds seemed to drag on for days. From the time the firefight had started till now had been under three minutes.

The pause continued. No doubt Proctor's men were cautiously retrieving the bodies of their downed comrades. While they were busy, Gray whispered, "How 'bout you go blow up the tunnel?"

"How 'bout I stay here and lay down covering fire, and you blow it up," she whispered back.

"I don't want to leave you here—"

She cut him off. "We've been over this before. I can take care of myself."

He gave her one hard look and then nodded. "I'll be back in a minute. If it gets too hot out here, retreat to the tunnel. We've still got your eyes on our side."

Son of a gun. Had the man finally learned to trust her?

"Roger," she replied more jauntily than she felt. He passed her the spare pistol and remaining ammunition. There wasn't a lot left. Their theory when they'd been planning this junket had been that, if it came to a firefight, they were screwed anyway, and it wouldn't matter if they had a ton of ammunition or not. She had about two dozen shots left between both weapons. Time to improvise.

She thought hard about supplies she'd seen scattered around the barn before. It might be possible to blow up the barn with stuff on hand, but that wouldn't do her and Gray a lot of good if they were inside it when it blew. The back side of the barn was maybe a hundred feet from a stretch of forest. If they could make it to the cover of the trees, the two of them would stand a fighting chance.

She went through four more precious bullets firing at shooters probing her defensive perimeter. Surely Proctor's men knew if they were patient enough, she and Gray would run out of ammo.

She felt Gray's presence behind her before she heard him. He put a hand in the middle of her back, and she took a ridiculously huge amount of comfort from his simple touch. "In about ten minutes, the tunnel will be history," he reported quietly. "How are we doing up here?"

"Stalemated. They know we'll run out of ammo, and they're feinting now to draw my fire. I, however, am refusing to fire anymore unless they give me a clear shot."

"They'll rush the building before long," he replied grimly. "It would be a long shot, but maybe we could cut a hole in the back wall of the barn and get out that way. We would have to create some sort of distraction that would buy us time to make for the woods, though."

"How about a trip wire in the doorway that'll blow up the building when they rush it?" she suggested.

"That would do it. We'd just have to be outside before it blew."

"I'll take my chances with tricky timing over no chance at all."

He looked shocked as he breathed, "I actually agree with you."

"Praise the Lord," she replied fervently. If he wanted to live and put his formidable mind to the job, the two of them couldn't help but find a way to survive. Passing the weapons to Gray, she breathed, "Cover me while I grab the stuff we'll need to wire a bomb."

Shock: he didn't argue. Now that they were on the verge of dying, apparently he'd accepted that she could pull her own weight. Better late than never. Now they just had to make it out of here so it meant something.

He took up a firing position and nodded at her. She leaped out of the hole and sprinted across the open space in front of the door to the workbench in the corner. Bullets zinged past her, and one passed so close she felt it lift her hair. So terrified she could hardly think, she dived for cover behind the workbench. She stuck one arm up and grabbed everything she thought she'd need by feel. While she was at it, she randomly grabbed fistfuls of whatever else her hand encountered and stuffed it in her pockets.

Her slacks bulging with gadgets and wires, she crouched in the shadows, waiting, as a shooter popped up from behind a tractor. The guy sent a volley of shots at the hole, and Gray braved the withering fire to pop up and fire a round back. While the two men were occupied, she darted across the barn toward a pair of small propane tanks, the kind used with backyard grills. She prayed they weren't empty. Her whole plan hinged on it.

She hefted the first tank. Oh, yeah. It was heavy. Felt full, in fact. She took a moment to attach the end of a spool of wire to the leg of a table beside her, and then she lifted the propane tanks. Carrying one in each hand, she ran to Gray.

Dirt sprayed up around her feet, and a bullet burned her arm as it creased her. Time stopped as Gray stood up, horror written on his face. All of Proctor's men must have stepped out to have a go at her. She was so dead. She took a running step. Another.

Gray's muzzle flashed and his mouth opened, shouting something she couldn't hear in the deafening barrage. With all her strength, she leaped, diving headfirst for the hole.

She hit the dirt hard, and time lurched into motion as she knocked the breath out of herself. She fetched up hard, barely stopping her momentum before she crashed off the ledge and fell to the lower level. As it was, her legs swung out into empty space. She yanked them back before she overbalanced and fell anyway.

A barrage of weapons fire exploded and she crawled for Gray's side. He passed her a pistol. "You hit?" he bit out.

"No. I'm good."

He nodded, concentrating on the barn door. "They're getting bold. They've figured out we're light on ammo."

"Two minutes," she retorted. "Can you buy me that long?"

"I'll find a way."

She got to work fast. Thankfully, the key components she would need, an actuator and a remote control, were already assembled. She merely had to modify the actuator to create a spark and hook it to the propane tanks. The hole they stood in would work to contain most of the propane gas. She used the tarp she'd covered the computer glow with earlier to cover the open area above the lower level she'd almost fallen into. She used the second tarp to enclose the entire hole above. The pocket she'd created should hold the propane gas until they detonated it remotely.

"Bomb's good to go. Now I just have to connect the other end of this spool of wire to something, and we're ready," she said.

He lifted the rifle into firing position against his shoulder and made eye contact with her over its barrel. And he smiled.

It was just an instant. But it was enough. A promise for if they got out of here alive. Her heart soared.

She held up three fingers. She folded one down. Then another. And then there was just a fist. One last time, she darted out of the hole. Gray shot from behind her as she dove for a pile of spare tires just inside the barn door. Gray shot again. He had to be about out of bullets. But he was managing by popping up and down and moving around within the hole to keep everyone's attention on him. Even if he was taking insane risks with his life.

She rose to her feet as a fusillade of fire wound down and ran for Gray. Somehow, somewhere, in her misspent life, she must have accumulated some good karma because she made it to the hole and dived under the tarp without getting hit.

Now all they had to do was head for the back wall, cut a hole and wait for Proctor's men to charge. When Proctor's men breached the barn, she and Gray would dive outside and let the trip wire blow the building and the men in it sky-high. In the chaos to follow, the two of them would head for the woods.

Easy peasy. Except no plan ever went exactly according to plan. She just hoped their last few bullets would be sufficient to solve any last-minute monkey wrenches.

They each took deep breaths and Gray turned on one of the propane tanks. As the highly flammable gas whooshed out, quickly filling the hole, the two of them eased out of it on their bellies and slithered for the back of the barn. They crawled behind a storage cabinet and Gray went to work on the aluminum wall with heavy shears she'd lifted from the workbench, cutting at it frantically. She pitched in and helped with the wire cutters while keeping a pistol trained on the doorway.

She heard a commotion outside, and Gray swore under his breath. "Are we through?" she whispered.

"Not quite. A few more seconds. What's going on?"

"I don't know. Shouting. And I don't have super-hearing."

Gray worked urgently as she turned fully to face the doorway. A lone figure came out from behind the pickup truck jawing loudly. She stared in shock as Ricki the Rocket came into sight down the barrel of her pistol. What the heck?

"What the hell are you doing, Sam? Come out of there right this minute. I've had enough of your crap. I'll teach you how to act like a proper woman—"

Surely it was no coincidence that her ex had hooked up with Proctor. No way had he just wandered accidentally into the middle of all this. Had Proctor been using

Ricki all along to get to her, to get inside the Winston Operation? Ricki? A spy?

In the millisecond it took those thoughts to flash through her brain, Ricki took a step forward, and time shifted again into slow motion around her.

Her finger started to close around the trigger. Gray whispered frantically from beside her, "I'm not through the wall yet."

Ricki's foot lifted. Moved dangerously close to the trip wire. Her finger pulled through the trigger, and even the deafening explosion of the pistol reverberated in her head in slow motion. Ricki started to pitch forward.

They weren't going to make it. Ricki's body was going to fall across the trip wire, and there was no hole in the wall for them to dive through. They were going to blow up along with the building. Gray wrapped his arms around her and flung her backward violently.

As Ricki toppled over, her shoulder blades crashed into the wall. A bright flash of light blinded her completely as Gray's body weight slammed into her. The aluminum at her back gave way suddenly, buckling under her and Gray's combined weight. As the second, still pressurized propane tank blew, a blast of concussion smashed them the rest of the way through the wall.

A monstrous wave of sound and heat broke over them, crushing them in its path. Were she not plastered flat on the ground with Gray on top of her absorbing most of the impact, she'd have been incinerated. As it was, her lungs felt seared to a crisp, and she couldn't draw a breath.

Oh, God. Gray! Don't be dead. Please, please don't

be dead! She pushed frantically at his prone body on top of hers, rolling him off her with preternatural strength she had no idea she possessed. Finally, she managed to drag a sobbing breath into her lungs. The explosion had flung them maybe thirty feet from the barn, which was now a blazing inferno. And she was blind.

She blinked her eyes frantically, willing her rods and cones to adjust to the bright light flickering all around them.

"Gray!" she cried, shaking him. She made out a shape that might be his face. Was that his eyelids fluttering? She couldn't see past the painful white light in her own eyes. "Wake up! We've got to go!"

He moved his head, turning it side to side sluggishly. "Huh?"

"Come *on*." She pulled as hard as she could on his arm in a futile attempt to drag him toward the woods. He grunted and rolled onto his hands and knees.

"Tunnel," he mumbled. "Gonna blow."

Oh, God. The charges he'd set down there were going to blow any second. And they'd go big. This field was going to be a crater. He staggered to his feet and she jumped up beside him. She put a hand on his back to steady him and felt the tatters of his shirt. It must have been burned away in the blast. But she also felt the familiar bulk of Kevlar. God bless his Boy Scout preparedness.

"Lead on," he mumbled.

Now was probably not a great time to explain to him that she was more blind than not. They'd taken a half dozen steps when a second explosion knocked them to the ground. The earth literally opened up behind them, leaving them lying on the edge of a massive crater. It was as if the entire field had heaved up into the sky. On cue, great clods of dirt began to shower down on their heads.

They climbed painfully to their feet once more and took off in a shambling run toward the woods. It turned out her legs weren't much steadier than his. As they approached the black wall of forest, she panted, "Uhh, small problem. I can't see."

"At all?" he murmured in surprise.

"I'm as blind as a kitten." And it scared her worse than being shot at, worse than being trapped in a barn in a firefight, worse than almost being blown to Kingdom come. Worse, even, than her fear that Gray had sacrificed himself to protect her from the blast.

Thankfully, Gray seemed to be regaining his senses. "This way," he instructed her under his breath. He took her arm and guided her toward the protective cover of the trees. They ducked under the first branches, and he shoved her into a deep shadow. They paused for a moment to catch their breath.

Across the field a barrage of gunfire exploded. She vaguely made out the flashes, and she definitely heard the fire.

"Cavalry's here," Gray breathed. "Those shots are coming from outside the fence."

"Thank God. Maybe we stand a chance after all."

"Grab my belt, Sam, and no matter what happens, don't let go."

With every step, her fear diminished and her disbelief grew that they'd actually made it out of that barn alive. And gradually, something else dawned on her. "You're enjoying this, aren't you?" she grumbled.

"Having you totally dependent on me for a change? You bet."

She scowled as he led her slowly through the woods. His night-vision goggles had been blown off in the blast, and they were stuck with his entirely normal eyeballs. After the flash of the explosion, he probably couldn't see a darned thing out here, either. Of course, the good news was that Proctor's men wouldn't be in much better shape.

She murmured, "If we're lucky, a bunch of Proctor's men were looking at the barn through night-vision gear when it blew. They won't be able to see a thing for hours."

"Speaking of which, how are your eyes?" Gray asked soberly.

"I don't know. I can make out shapes, but that's it. I think I injured my retinas pretty badly in the blast."

They eased through the woods for a while longer in silence. It was Gray who broke the quiet that had settled around them. "I don't care if you're completely blind when this is all said and done. I'll be there to take care of you."

She opened her mouth to give him her usual refrain, but he laid a silencing finger across her lips. "I know, Sam. You can take care of yourself. But I want to be there for you. Will you let me?"

What was he saying? Did he merely mean he'd see her through her injury, or did he mean more? He certainly sounded like he was implying more than a short-term deal. "Do you have any idea how badly I wish I could see you right now?" she groused.

"I told you the day would come when you couldn't rely on your eyes."

She didn't need her eyes to detect the note of humor in his voice. "This isn't funny! I can't see you right now, and I want to know exactly what you mean."

"Listen with your heart, then."

The words froze her in place. She tugged on his belt until he turned to face her fully. "Are you saying what I think you're saying?"

"I don't know," he replied, low. "What do you think I'm saying?"

"Don't you dare play head games with me. Not now."

He backed her up against a tree and followed her with his big, warm, safe body. "Use your other senses for a change, Sam. What does this feel like?"

His head bent toward her and his lips brushed against hers. His hands slipped behind her back and gently pulled her close to him. And it didn't take eagle eyes to feel his heart galloping in his chest.

"What does this feel like to you?" he whispered against her throat.

"Like, uhh, you want sex?"

He laughed quietly. "What else?"

Lord, his mouth was distracting, moving across her skin like that. "Like, umm, you, umm, like me?"

"And?"

"You've lost your mind to be making out with me in the woods when bad guys might be out here trying to kill us?"

"The cavalry has Proctor and his boys handled.

That secondary explosion was the tunnel collapsing, and we've got all the evidence we need on those flash drives of yours to track down whoever's been buying Echelon-free phone calls from Proctor. If anyone survives the gunfight back there, they'll go to jail for a very long time."

For the first time since they'd slipped onto Proctor's property, she actually relaxed. And that was when the shaking set in. Her knees started knocking together first, and before long, her entire body got into the act. Gray wrapped her in his arms and held her tightly in silent understanding.

Finally, she raised her head from his shoulder. Those looked like major branches coming out of the fuzzy blob of a tree trunk. If she wasn't mistaken, she was making out a few more details around her. Abject relief that her eyes would recover—at least partially—from the blast washed over her.

It dawned on her belatedly that Gray wasn't suffering the sort of aftershock that she was. At all. She demanded indignantly, "How come you're not freaking out and shaking like me?"

"I've been through worse."

And she supposed he had. She spoke quietly. "I heard the audio tape of your 9-1-1 call."

He didn't respond. And she supposed he didn't have to. That call spoke for itself.

She changed subjects. "Jeff set you up by luring you to West Virginia, you know. He intentionally threw us together. Tricked us both. He admitted that he told me not to research your past because he knew it would make me run out and do it."

"I figured as much," Gray commented rather more calmly than she'd expected.

"I'm sorry for hurting you, Gray. I shouldn't have pried. And I shouldn't have pushed you to face things you may never be ready to face."

He made a sound that might be ironic laughter or could be just an expression of pain. When *would* she learn to keep her mouth shut and quit hurting him? "Don't apologize, Sam. Not for anything."

"But I keep hurting you—"

"You saved my life."

She went still in his arms, and was startled to realize he was relatively relaxed against her. "Excuse me?"

He sighed. "I needed a swift kick in the pants. You forced me to face events and feelings that it's high time I faced. I can't promise that I've worked through it all yet. I don't know if I ever will. But I'm willing to try… if you'll help me."

Her breath caught in her throat. "Are you sure?" she choked out.

"I've never been more sure of anything in my life. You reminded me what it's like to be alive. I can't go back to being that hollow shell of a human being I was before. I've spent the last few days in that place, and I hated every second of it. I want to laugh and have sex and…" his voice hitched "…and love. Someday, I want a family. Kids. A wife to take care of and to take care of me."

She stared up at him in dawning wonder.

"I don't deserve any of it. And I surely don't deserve you, Sam. But if you're willing to give a relationship with me a try, I'd be honored."

"Grayson Pierce, that is the dumbest thing you've

ever said. Of course you deserve happiness. And I'm the one who doesn't deserve you."

He gave her a lopsided smile. "You'd think I'd have learned by now not to argue with you. I always end up losing. But you still haven't answered my question."

"I wasn't aware you'd asked one," she replied a shade tartly.

"You're going to make me say it, aren't you?"

She could see the chagrin on his face. Yup, her eyes were definitely getting better, thank God. She batted her eyelashes at him coyly. "Why, whatever do you mean?"

He huffed. "Will you give a relationship a go with me, you exasperating female?"

"Are you sure?" she breathed. It was as if the whole world came to a stop. Could it be? Was a dream too marvelous for her to have even imagined about to come true?

"Yes," he answered firmly, "I'm sure. I want it all, and I want it with you. I will warn you, I'm going to keep pestering you until agree with me."

"Well, in that case, I guess I'd better give this thing between us a go."

He stood up slowly, and a huge smile spread across his face. "Are you sure?'"

"Yes, Gray. I'm sure. Even if I were as blind as a bat, I could still see we're meant to be together."

He kissed her gently on each eyelid. "The thing I love best about you is how you see with your heart."

It was a miracle. Somehow, a girl with a screwed-up past and eagle eyes had managed to find a man with a broken heart in desperate need of healing, and together they'd made a little magic. Gray might be ready to kill Jeff Winston for tricking them and throwing them together like this, but she thought she might just lay a big, fat kiss on her employer the next time she saw him.

"I love you, Sparky."

"I love you back, baby."

Yup. A bona fide dream come true.

* * * * *

COMING NEXT MONTH FROM
HARLEQUIN® ROMANTIC SUSPENSE

Available January 22, 2013

#1739 BEYOND VALOR • *Black Jaguar Squadron*
by Lindsay McKenna

Though these two soldiers face death day after day, their greatest risk is taking a chance on each other.

#1740 A RANCHER'S DANGEROUS AFFAIR
Vengeance in Texas • by Jennifer Morey

Eliza's husband has been murdered, and she's in love with his brother. As guilt and love go to battle, Brandon may be the only one who can save her.

#1741 SOLDIER UNDER SIEGE • *The Hunted*
by Elle Kennedy

Special Forces soldier Tate doesn't trust anyone...especially the gorgeous woman who shows up on his doorstep asking him to kill a man.

#1742 THE LIEUTENANT BY HER SIDE
by Jean Thomas

Clare Fuller is forced to steal a mysterious amulet from army ranger Mark Griggs, but falling in love with him isn't in the plan. Nor is the danger that stalks them.

"How *did* you find me, Eva? I'm not exactly listed in any
phone books."

She rested her suddenly shaky hands on her knees. "Someone told me you might be able to help me, so I decided to
track you down. I'm…well, let's just say I'm very skilled when
it comes to computers."

His jaw tensed.

"You're good, too," she added with grudging appreciation.
"You left so many false trails it made me dizzy. But you slipped
up in Costa Rica, and it led me here."

Tate let out a soft whistle. "I'm impressed. Very impressed, actually." He made a tsking sound. "You went to a lot of trouble to find me. Maybe it's time you tell me why."

"I told you—I need your help."

He raised one large hand and rubbed the razor-sharp stubble coating his strong chin.

A tiny thrill shot through her as she watched the oddly seductive gesture and imagined how it would feel to have those calloused fingers stroking her own skin, but that thrill promptly fizzled when she realized her thoughts had drifted off course again. What was it about this man that made her so darn aware of his masculinity?

She shook her head, hoping to clear her foggy brain, and met Tate's expectant expression. "Your help," she repeated.

"Oh really?" he drawled. "My help to do what?"

God, could she do this? How did one even begin to approach something like—

"For Chrissake, sweetheart, spit it out. I don't have all night."

She swallowed. Twice.

He started to push back his chair. "Screw it. I don't have time for—"

"I want you to kill Hector Cruz," she blurted out.

**Will Eva's secret be the ultimate unraveling of their fragile trust? Or will an overwhelming desire do them both in? Find out what happens next in
SOLDIER UNDER SIEGE**

Available February 2013 only from Harlequin Romantic Suspense wherever books are sold.